THE Vagabonds

THE Vagabonds

A NOVEL

NICHOLAS DELBANCO

WARNER BOOKS

NEW YORK   BOSTON

A version of Chapter 1 of this book was published in *Five Points*.
Daniel Mark Epstein's "Letter to Thomas Edison from John Burroughs"—
the last two lines of which are quoted in my epigraph—appeared in *The Book of Fortune*, 1982.

Warner Books

Time Warner Book Group
1271 Avenue of the Americas, New York, NY 10020
Visit our Web site at www.twbookmark.com.

Printed in the United States of America

First Printing: November 2004
10 9 8 7 6 5 4 3 2 1

Library of Congress Cataloging-in-Publication Data
Delbanco, Nicholas.
    The vagabonds / Nicholas Delbanco.
        p. cm.
    ISBN 0-446-53002-6
    1. Inheritance and succession—Fiction. 2. Children of the rich—Fiction.
    3. Brothers and sisters—Fiction. 4. Loss (Psychology)—Fiction.
    5. Mothers—Death—Fiction. 6. Male friendship—Fiction. 7. Saratoga
    (N.Y.)—Fiction. 8. Secrecy—Fiction. I. Title.
    PS3554.E442V34 2004
    813'.54—dc22
                                                            2004006638

To
Larry Kirshbaum and Jamie Raab
In Deepest Gratitude

Author's Note

The four historical figures here named—Thomas Edison, Harvey Firestone, Henry Ford and, from time to time, John Burroughs—did call themselves "the vagabonds" and take road trips together. Three members of that famed quartet took a meal on the porch of "Grandmother's House" some fifteen miles outside of Albany, New York, on August 31, 1916. That day they passed through Saratoga Springs and the lines of verse quoted in Chapter 4 were written by Burroughs himself. Ford did have a Japanese cook named Yukio, and it was the magnate's intention to join the party in Plattsburgh—an intention he had to defer.

Here my accurate reportage ends. No one by the name of Peter Barclay was ever in Firestone's employ, and any resemblance, as they say, of any members of the Dancey family to anyone alive or dead is coincidental. Those who wish a full account of "The Camping Trips of Henry Ford, Thomas Edison, Harvey Firestone, and John Burroughs" should instead consult the authoritative *There to Breathe the Beauty*, by Norman Brauer (Norman Brauer Publications, Dalton, Pa., 1955). Mine is a novel, not a work of nonfiction; a work shaped by fancy, not fact.

Nonetheless I've profited from the expert advice of friends. Harold Skramstad—then president of what was then called Henry Ford Museum and Greenfield Village—first brought "the vagabonds" to my attention in 1988; more than fifteen years thereafter I continue to be in his debt. B. Joseph White—then dean of the University of Michigan Business School—first walked me through the issues of inheritance and, as it were, postmortem trust and control. Thomas Lynch of Lynch & Sons, James Blume of

J.B. Blume, Inc., and Bruce Wallace of Hooper, Hathaway, Price, Beuche & Wallace instructed me in the niceties of undertaking, finance and the law, respectively. They taught me what I did not know and corrected what I got wrong; I could not have fleshed in these bare bones without them, and any errata are mine.

As always I'm grateful to my literary agent, Gail Hochman; she was part of this project from its beginning and kept me at last to the last. My friends and colleagues Andrea Barrett, Andrea Beauchamp, James Landis and Jon Manchip White read the book in nearly finished manuscript. It is the better for their encouragement and close-hauled critiques. I finished *The Vagabonds* in Bellagio, at the Villa Serbelloni, and am grateful to the Rockefeller Foundation in general and Ms. Gianna Celli in particular for providing space and time. That I owe all the rest, and more, to my wife Elena continues happily to be the case. To have such a partner in and witness to the world we share is to beggar language; there's no sufficient way to say it. To my final, closest reader: thanks, thanks, thanks, thanks, thanks.

THE Vagabonds

IX. I hereby give to my said executor full power to sell, lease without limit as to period or terms, and mortgage, pledge, invest, reinvest, exchange, manage, control, and in any way, use, and deal with, any and all property of my estate, without application to any court or authority for leave or confirmation, unless the same shall be expressly required by law and shall be unwaivable even by this provision of my will, and to that end, said executor may sell such property for cash or upon credit, upon such terms as to him may seem sufficient; continue present investments; invest and re-invest any such property or securities in such a manner as he shall deem adequate and safe, free from any limitations imposed by law; borrow on the credit of, exchange, pledge, or mortgage any of such property; deposit any securities with voting trustees or for other purposes; exercise any and all rights which have accrued or may accrue appurtenant to any securities; and use the principal and income of my estate not herein specifically devised or bequeathed as he may deem advisable; and compromise any and all claims in favor of my estate or against it.

From: The Will of Henry Ford, this 3rd day of February A.D. 1936

Come, Thomas, leave your shop while we have time
    And let's take to the open road for the strawberry days!

From: "Letter to Thomas Edison from John Burroughs"
Daniel Mark Epstein

Part One

I

2003

A gull above her circles, pauses in its rising flight and releases what it carries and lets the thing plummet and crack. It is, she knows, a razor clam, or maybe a mussel or oyster; the parking lot has been littered with shells, a white glaze of shattered dropped shellfish, and there are only two cars. Joanna drives past. A brand-new Volvo station wagon, complete with baby seat and snowshoes, waits at the edge of the path to the beach; a fisherman's truck stands idling there also, and the man inside raises his hand. She waves back—it's the thing to do—but parks at the end of the lot. There, smoking, she stares at the bay.

This day it's green and wintry, wind-roiled, with ice in its foam. She rolls her window open and hears the crackling tide. The sound, Joanna tells herself, is like a cocktail shaker's, the salt and sand and wave spume all freezing and mixed in together. No ships are on the water, no line at the horizon's edge beneath a glaucous sky. This is her lunch break and time to be private; holding the smoke, she inhales.

The winter has been long. It is February 10. Ice and snow have settled in, and she feels the way that clam would feel if it knew itself caught in the gull's outstretched beak and ready to be dropped. Last night had been a good one, or as good as she expects to have, with Harry the lodger appreciative and the spaghetti in her homemade garlic and pesto sauce cooked just the way she liked it and both of them, as he put it, lubricated by wine.

"I'm feeling lubricated," he said. "I'm just about feeling no pain."

Joanna had lit candles and the lanterns in the dining room. She was wearing her blue toreador pants and the white Mexican peasant's blouse with the red embroidery, and Harry called her his flag.

"What's that supposed to mean?"

"Red, white and blue," he told her, and they clicked glasses and kissed.

He could be sweet when he wanted, and last night he'd wanted to, so after the salad and ice cream they went upstairs to his room. The whole house is hers, of course, and in the middle of a February cold snap there are no other paying guests, but it excited Joanna to be in his room and not on her own sleigh bed with the cat and bills and unwashed sheets; she took better care of *his* space, since, after all, Harry rented it and expected fresh laundry each week. So they were getting down to business, his mouth a mix of pesto sauce and cigar smoke and that Pinot Noir she'd ordered two cases of for Christmas, and still had three bottles of, his arms about her, leg on leg, when the telephone rang in the hallway and, after two rings, ceased ringing and then began again. This was her signal from Leah and she knew she had to answer because her daughter only called that way on the private number when she needed help, and meant it.

"Oh, lover," breathed Joanna, "wait, I'll be right back."

He could be a bastard when he wanted, and last night he'd wanted to while she got on the phone. It was Leah in trouble, big surprise—who has taken, lately, to calling herself Artemisia, because Artemisia was an artist, a painter in the old days when young women weren't supposed to paint, and who'd been raped for her presumption, or so the story went. And since fifteen-year-old Leah is into nose rings and tattoos this year she likes to think her name is Artemisia, Art for short . . .

"Mom, the car is out of gas," she said. "And I'm up here in Truro and there's no gas stations open and I need you to come up and get us."

"Us?"

"Me and Stacey and a couple guys."

"I'm busy," said Joanna. Because Harry was behind her now, his hand on her ass and his pants off already, and when Leah-Artemisia said, "But Mom, it's *cold* . . . ," he reached over and pulled out the cord from the plug and the phone went dead. And so she was caught in the middle again, the rock that is Harry her lodger and the hard place that's her daughter; by the time she'd wriggled out of it and finished staking out her claim—telling him don't you *ever* do that, don't you *ever* touch this telephone, telling Leah who called a second time that no, she wasn't coming because this is a mess you've made for yourself and the other kids have parents too; whose car were you driving and what were you doing anyhow in Truro? — by the time the argument was over she had been cold sober, the small sweet flare of pleasure gone. Harry lay back with his nose in a book, his stinking feet on the afghan she'd made and had been so proud of, and that was the end of that.

Another gull, rising, drops lunch. In summertime the lot is full, with a line of cars waiting to enter, but now the hard paved surface is a plate for gulls to feast off; no competition on the ground — just her and the truck and the Volvo and none of them looking for shells. She hates self-pity, guards against it, but sometimes — this is one of them — the gray sky and the empty beach and big house near the harbor she tries to make the payments on all seem to be working together and working against her, bringing her down. This morning in the living room there had been birds, a pair of them, terrified and battering at windows and shitting all over the furniture and window wells. Their wings and tails were black with soot, so they must have come through the chimney, and by the time she got them out — removing the screens and opening the windows and ducking under their frenzied rush — by the time she'd finished cleaning up and replacing the screens in the half-frozen frames and shutting the flue in the fireplace chimney she'd been late for work. It made no difference, of course; there were no customers at nine o'clock, and when she told Maisie about the birds — grackles, maybe, or starlings, not crows — Maisie nodded, unsurprised. "It happens."

"Shit happens," said Joanna. "That's what we used to say."

"They gather by the chimney," Maisie explained. "They warm themselves at the furnace updraft and get a little dopey and fall in."

"At your house too?"

"Not since Tom installed a chimney cap. It's good for keeping bats away. And squirrels and raccoons; you ought to get a chimney cap."

"I ought to do a lot of things," she told her boss-friend bitterly. "I ought to sell the goddam house is what I ought to do."

"Who'd buy it?" Maisie asked, and turned to the stock on the shelves.

A light snow falls. Joanna finishes her cigarette and drops it out the door and starts up Trusty-Rusty and, once the engine catches, eases it into reverse. Her lunch break is ending; she needs to get back into town. She helps Maisie out three days a week, and though there've been only two sales this morning—a cardigan, a pair of gloves—it matters to them both that they pretend she's useful and there's a reason to get dressed and drive herself to the store and check the order pads and rearrange the inventory they both know won't sell. In summertime the place is full, young mothers and couples or women alone—on rainy days so many of them you'd think scarves are a necessity, or harem pants, or wide-brimmed hats, which is why the place is called The Bare Necessities. From Memorial through Labor Day, Main Street is busy, hopping, and it's worth your life to find a parking place and what jogs or drives or bicycles past the store is tourists all day long.

But by October the town is half-empty and by February dead. They keep the place open for something to do and to pay the heating bills; they drink coffee and decorate the windows over Christmas and, gossiping together, watch the empty street. It's feast or famine here on the Cape, and lately it's been famine: the plague and seven lean years in which she somehow managed to get fat. Just how, Joanna asks herself, *how* did I get into this and how do I get out of it and where do I go next?

Leah will leave Wellfleet soon enough; she's been practicing departure and trying on identities for size. Last year she was a cheerleader and then a poetry-slam-wannabe and now she's a girl on the dark backseat of a souped-up broke-down car. Her daughter's father Mr. Ex-Right Ex-Husband #1 lives in Chicago now, and every birthday and for holidays he gets in touch and sends Leah fifty dollars and says, Whenever you're ready, there's more. Mr. Ex-Right Ex-Husband #2 preferred Jim Beam and Jack Daniel's and Johnny Walker and George Dickel and even Ezra Brooks to her, Joanna, and by the time he was in detox in Hyannis the preference was mutual; they haven't seen each other since—when was it?—1994. Her mother is dying, her father is dead, her brother David has been doing whatever he does these days in California and paying no attention, and she'd rather not deal with the kind of attention her little sister pays. The house, the lovely ancient house, is an albino elephant, a picturesque wreck like its owner and beyond her to maintain. And Harry is no help at all; her dirty Harry lies there, feet on the afghan and pants on the floor, and expects her to serve him his dinner in bed but won't even take out the trash.

It has been, Joanna thinks, a long slow slide since college and the degree she didn't finish in 1979. It has been a downhill slope and steeper all the way. She is forty-four years old, a woman with an attitude, or so Harry claimed last night while they were fighting; there's only so far you can travel, he said, on a pair of what used to be excellent tits. That's not fair, she said to him, that isn't fair, and he said what does fairness have to do with it, who's talking equity here? You're such a smug son of a bitch, she had said, why don't you try checking the mirror yourself, and he said because it doesn't matter, not to me. She has tried to teach her daughter, do as I say not as I do, don't do the things I did when young, you're worth much more than that.

She closes her eyes an instant while the birds in the living room fly through her head. Those grackles or starlings have nothing on her; there's air outside they're hungry for and once they find the open window there's a slipstream and escape. They're up in the trees now, away. But Joanna herself can't imagine escape; she will remain in her mortgage-strapped house, the staircase off kilter and rooms needing paint, the shingles half-rotten and roof like a sieve—will remain here with her little sign, "B&B, the Bay View Inn," while in the summer couples come to fuck, and off-season fish or sketch, and in the winter no one stays—remain here till there's nothing left and she's the old lady she never imagined she in her turn would become. *My mother is dying*—she says this out loud—and maybe that's why birds appeared and battered at the windows, just the way the old song says they do when a soul escapes this vale of tears: a bird of passage fluttering and gone from dark to dark.

And sure enough, when she returns, walking through the stockroom door and hanging up her parka, feeling the heat of the shop and smelling the sandalwood incense and telling Maisie, *Hey, I'm back,* she knows on the instant that something has changed and not for the better. Her friend has that solemn look on her face that means there's news, and the news is bad, that Maisie is misery's company now and ready and willing to cry . . .

"What's wrong?" she asks, and Maisie holds her hands up, spreading them, her fingernails bright crimson, chipped, and says that Harry called.

"About?"

"Not Leah," she says. "It isn't her."

"When?"

"Fifteen minutes ago, maybe ten. He says they've been calling and calling your line, until finally he picked it up, and it was a lawyer. Oh sweetie I hate to be telling you this. Except your mother's passed."

It's not relief exactly, this shock that floods and fills her chest, but when Joanna, sitting, says, "I knew it, I knew something like this would happen today," she feels a kind of rising release, a sort of confirmation: the gull's maw and desperate grackles and everything bottoming out. "What else," she asks, "what else could go wrong?"

"They want you there," says Maisie. "In Saratoga Springs, I mean. Your sister's flying out from Michigan to deal with the remains."

When the call arrives Claire is making the bed, fluffing up the pillows and folding the duvet; she loves this domesticity, these acts of meticulous habit, and the room is decorated to her satisfaction.

From the Léger print on the south wall where light pours in but cannot reach and therefore fade it to the Calder on the west wall and the pot of freesia blooming; from the wallpaper with its intricate pattern of interlocked grapevines and a trellis to the chandelier and kilim rug; from the yellow shot-silk curtains to the marble-topped oak bookshelf, she has positioned it all: the ottoman, the rocking chair, the cedar blanket chest. The effect she strove for and achieved is one of busy harmony, of clashing motifs that nonetheless match, and everybody admires her eye.

Oh Claire, they say, you should have been a decorator, you *could* have been one anyhow, you have such a feel for design. I do expect, she tells her friends, to live with things I value; it isn't too much to expect, and the world would be a better place if others thought so too.

The whole house is her nest. There are spaces for the girls, of course, and Jim's study on the second floor and his exercise room in the basement, but the master bedroom suite is hers and hers alone. She cherishes the way the color scheme and light and furnishings just *work*. It's hard to put your finger on, hard to explain precisely why, but when her friends say, Claire, you should have been a decorator, she believes they have a point; once the girls go off to music camp at Interlaken this summer she might just give it a try.

She has thought about this lately: branching out. It would be gratifying, wouldn't it, to put your own individual stamp on other people's houses and to unlock the energy and realize the potential of other people's space. She doesn't need the income and wouldn't want to charge her friends, but yesterday at tea, for example, when Julie Cantor said, what's *wrong* with this room—standing in what she insists on describing as her parlor and saying it doesn't feel friendly enough and just doesn't make people welcome—Claire understood in a heartbeat that the problem was the lighting fixtures and how they didn't work at all with that overstuffed couch set and the Queen Anne armoire. The Chinese call it, she knows, feng shui, the art of arrangement and setting, and she supposes she must have an instinct for feng shui. It's the way a room gives out on a hall, or the hallway on the porch beyond; it's a matter of proportion and precise location, really, of knowing where and how to situate your things.

When Claire and Joanna were children they liked to play an address-game: let's go to Manhattan, they would say, in New York City in New York State on the East Coast of the United States in the continent of North America and in the Western Hemisphere and on the earth and in the solar system and then the universe and in God's palm. What's God's palm got to do with it? their mother asked, and Joanna said, oh, Mummy, it's only a mailing address. Don't take His name in vain, their mother said, He's not a mailman, girls.

When the call about her mother comes she is unsurprised. Her mother has been dying now for years. Last month in Saratoga Springs, the last time Claire had visited, she understood they were saying good-bye, or would have done so if her mother understood what they were saying. Alice lay in the upstairs bedroom, the one that gave out on what used to be a meadow and now is Skidmore College, lying back with both eyes closed, white hair fanned across the pillow—the hospice woman in the kitchen saying, *Your mother is expecting you, she's doing fine, just go right up, I gave her a shampoo*—the sheet above her rising, falling with each breath.

"Are you awake, Mom?"

"Who *are* you?"

"Claire. Your daughter Claire."

Her mother opened one eye. "Who? Claire? Claire."

"How *are* you, Mom?"

It is peculiar, isn't it, how something you don't notice becomes all you notice suddenly—how, for example, she had taken air for granted and paid no attention to her mother's labored breathing, and then all of a sudden she noticed the sheet and how it rose and fell. Alice had been sturdy once, not fat or plump so much as sturdy, but now she seemed near-skeletal, the long slow declension from congestive heart disease and the body's collapse near-complete.

"How did you get here, Claire de Lune?"

"No problem. I flew from Detroit."

Alice was lucid now. "When?"

"Do you want anything?" she asked. "Is there anything . . ."

"How was the trip?"

"You're *looking* well," she lied.

The room was hot. The whole house was stifling but this room was worst: the windows shut and sweating from the hot-water humidifier, the space heater turned to high.

"How are the girls?" her mother asked. "How's Jim?"

"Fine, fine. Becky's loving algebra. Everything is sine and cosine and tangent with her lately; I know more about triangles than I ever cared to learn. SOHCAHTOA, for example; it's what you call an acronym. No, a mnemonic device, that's the word. It's something you just can't forget as soon as you remember it, and it's what Becky uses for her test. SOHCAHTOA means sine equals opposite over hypotenuse, cosine means adjacent over hypotenuse, and tangent is opposite over adjacent. Or something like that, anyhow."

She could hear herself babbling, incomprehensible, continuing to chatter about right triangles and similar triangles and isosceles and identical triangles, and how Hannah was finished with geometry and trigonometry and told her younger sister that it didn't matter, she wouldn't ever need to know the word SOHCAHTOA after the test except for, maybe, SATs, which Hannah was preparing for and was a nervous wreck about; she talked on and on about nothing at all (the upright piano they were buying, the amount of snow, the flight from Detroit and how she had rented a Hertz at the Albany airport and it had been no problem, five hours door to door) until her mother's fingers ceased their scrabbling at the bedsheet and she seemed asleep.

Then Alice opened both eyes wide. "How are the girls?"

"They're hunky-dory. You remember that expression, Mom? It's what you used to say."

"How's Jim?"

Claire's husband is the CEO of a string of nursing homes, the Alpha-Beta Corporation. He did not understand why Alice planned to die at home, why she refused the comfort of round-the-clock service and knowing in advance her situation would be monitored, with everything under control. He took it as a personal insult or at least as a kind of rejection that his mother-in-law wouldn't come to Ann Arbor and settle into one of his establishments. When Claire reminded him that Saratoga Springs was home, and Alice had been born and raised in her half-timbered "cottage," he trailed off, cracking his knuckles, saying, "All the same. Round-the-clock care . . ."

"Or she could come and live with *us*."

He studied her. "If that's what you want . . ."

They have sufficient room. The house is an extravagance, but one they can afford—with Jim's new exercise space in the basement, his Nautilus and NordicTrack and rowing machine, his freestanding weights and Jacuzzi. There's a stereo set with headphones and a StairMaster and mirrors all along one wall and indoor-outdoor carpeting and a telephone. "Jim's Gym," the family calls it, and he works very hard to keep fit. He's down there two hours a day.

The truth is Claire worries a little he's growing antisocial and would rather be doing sit-ups with his headset on than in the kitchen with her and the girls, or at the office even, or a football game. He used to be a booster, with season tickets at the fifty-yard line, and every home game Michigan played Jim would be wearing maize and blue and cheering on the Wolverines until he came home hoarse. When they won he'd come back from the game with no voice left from cheering but—it's how he put it—blissed out. He cared about their coaches—first Bo Schembechler and then Gary Moeller, *Bo and Mo*, and now the quiet one, Lloyd Carr. He cared about those football teams more than she thought possible—with his flag attached to the car's aerial on game days and his "Honk If Ufer Michigan" bumper sticker and his high-fiving at an interception or touchdown and his outrage when they lost. It was embarrassing, a little, how he and his buddies rehearsed every play and rehashed what happened over beer and huddled like overage schoolboys outside at the barbecue and made travel arrangements to the Rose or Citrus or the Outback Bowl . . .

Now all of that is finished, or anyhow it seems to be; now Jim stays in his basement-gym and works on his pecs, glutes and abs. That's what he calls them, *pecs, glutes, abs,* and Claire supposes it means something—this new preoccupation—and hopes it doesn't mean that he's depressed. It might just be the time of year: February, football done, and the basketball program so hot-and-cold he doesn't bother with Crisler Arena or the remaining diehards in the stands. When she complained about the blues, the *blahs,* and asked him if he felt them too he said it's just the opposite, you feel much better after exercise, it's an energy booster instead. Then he smiled that closed-mouth smile of his, the one that she knows means he's lying, and turned the volume up and said, *Still got ten miles to go this morning,* and started pumping the Exercycle, working up a sweat.

Her mother coughed. The sound was liquid, sputum-veiled. "Who *are* you?"

"Claire. I'm Claire."

"No, not my little Claire de Lune? My Claire da Loon, remember?"

"Of course I remember," she said.

"I used to make tea for your father. I used to wake up in the morning and turn to his side of the bed—long after he'd abandoned it, long after his side was empty—and say, my goodness, look, I've overslept, I'll just run down to the kitchen and make us tea for two." She smacked her lips. They were colorless, cracked. "How are the children?"

"Fine. Thank you for asking."

"How's Jim?"

Claire fished in her pocket for Kleenex and found one and dabbed at her neck. "He's fine."

"How was the trip?"

And then her mother shut her eyes and truly fell asleep.

So nothing had been accomplished and nothing was resolved. Next morning Claire drove south again, making the flight from Albany and back in Ann Arbor by dark. The girls were at rehearsal for the concert the school orchestra was planning for that

Friday, and she ate leftover chicken and a wilted arugula salad and, since Jim had done the dropping-off, collected them at ten. They asked, "How's Granny? How was your trip?" and she kissed them and sent them to bed.

That night she lay awake. While her husband rumbled beside her, oblivious as always to her night sweats and then sudden chill, she stared at the tasseled canopy fringe and the pattern it cast in the hall light's dim glow and tried to assess what went wrong. It was—she had known this already—the final time she'd visit Alice alive. She could remember feeling both pleased with herself for having made the gesture (the trouble and expense she'd gone to, the obstacles she'd overcome) and cheated of its consequence; there had been no blessing asked for or received. Claire would always want something her mother refused, always be asking for some sort of attention from someone who failed to provide it. She had wondered, bleakly, vaguely, if in her old age the roles would reverse, if she would shut her daughters out and they would feel the same way. In the feng shui of her own house she is well-positioned, central, but in that other household irrelevant as dust.

When the call arrives she is making the bed, and it is the lawyer, Joseph Beakes. He introduces himself, and she says, yes, I know you, yes, you represent my mother. He says our office has been doing so for forty years, your father too when he was alive, and we regret to inform you that Mrs. Saperstone expired last night; we were notified this morning by the Saratoga Hospice. He says you won't remember me, but I remember you—your sister and your brother too—when you were learning how to ride and falling off your ponies and getting on again; like yesterday it seems to me, and now you're all grown up.

When did she die, Claire asks, exactly when, and he assures her the end had been peaceful, your mother did not suffer in her final days. The hospice has been wonderful, continues Mr. Beakes, the management of pain is much much better nowadays and the body has moved—*been* moved—to the funeral home, and are you planning to sit what I think is called shiva and how can I help?

She answers him. Her mother had planned on cremation, the

burial service is standard, and they are nonobservant Jews and will not be sitting shiva and her husband is, as Mr. Beakes might be aware, practically in the business because if you run a string of nursing homes you must be prepared for this sort of procedure; she'll call her sister and locate their brother and fly East in the morning and the others of her family will follow in due time.

"Mrs. Handleman? I hope you'll let me call you Claire. We've been trying to contact your sister and brother—Joanna, David— too. Are they away?" asks Mr. Beakes. "They don't seem to answer, or use a machine."

She swallows. He has tried to reach the others first; she is the third of three.

Then Beakes repeats his personal condolences and they schedule an appointment and the line goes dead.

❧

David has been practicing avoidance; he is getting good at it, and better every day. He can avoid, for example, his own eyes in the mirror while shaving; he can avoid the pavement cracks while walking down a sidewalk and all conversation with strangers and the shrill importunities of headlines or the television news. He can say the word *rhinoceros* and then forget it rapidly; he can choose to imagine and then not imagine a gray mud-spattered charging beast, its pig-eyes and its flesh-clad horns and complicated rolling gait and snout.

Avoidance is a discipline, and it requires work. Avoidance is the hardest task because it seems so easy and you can be tempted to relax your guard. His last lover had complained, "You've been avoiding me, I don't know if you noticed but it's been a week today, it's been since Thursday the last time you called." Then Adrienne had started in with the familiar litany of intimate assertion, the proprietary body language of someone who fears not so much the leaving as being left behind. She had been asking, if not for commitment, for at least a kind of *clarity*, because he simply rang the bell and hadn't bothered to warn or inform her, and what

if she'd been out, or busy maybe, not alone? She had been holding oranges and lemons and steadying a wicker basket on one out-
thrust hip. She was standing in front of the hot tub and jade plant,
the high-breasted willowy arched length of her backlit by sun;
David knew that he must dance away or give it up and stay.

"I'm glad to see you," said Adrienne. "Of course I'm glad to see
you. Except you should have called."

He left. It was a form of avoidance. He left towns and jobs and
people often, and like any other habit it was easier to make than
break; it had been his MO and his SOP for years. "Standard op-
erating procedure," he said. "I'm your dance-away lover, remember? That's me."

"Oh Christ," she said. "That isn't what I'm saying. I'm saying
that I *missed* you, babe."

Adrienne lives near the Rose Garden, on Euclid Street, and on
clear days the view is spectacular; on clear days they lie together
on the cantilevered deck and watch the clouds and islands and the
bridges and the bay. David has been working freelance for an
agency that is abandoning print and focusing on web sites, and
though he understands why web site design is the art of the future
and though he is good at it and makes good money at the job, he
misses the hands-on technique. He has been in Berkeley since
May. This is par for the course, and time to get gone, and so he
drove up to Bolinas and spent the night with Richard and Lucy,
eating soft-shelled crab and smoking what his friends assured him
was their sweetest home grown smoke and listening to the Pacific
down beyond the Mesa; he has been working on a series of pastels about water and the offshore rocks and wondering how best
to sketch a visual equivalent of sound. Not sound waves, David
told them, not a diagram but evocation, an equivalence, so what
you see is what you hear and doubly what you get.

The past, he said to Richard and Lucy, that's *exactly* how it feels
to me: a handheld brush above an empty page. It's like calligraphy,
he said, you practice to make it seem casual, you work to make it
effortless and the stroke no work at all. Or like all those years he
spent at karate and jujitsu, where the price of a black belt, they

say, is ten thousand falls. The thing about pastels, he was saying—
Lucy's head in his lap, her red hair spiked and staticky—is that
they take *forever*, so the trick is to make it seem easy though it's
hard, hard, hard, hard, hard.

Richard has a trust fund and is into hydroponics and he and
Lucy have no children but are planning to adopt. There's a network, they told David, a pipeline straight to China and you get to
go—five couples max—with a pediatrician along on the trip, so he
can check out the babies and help with traveling back. You
wouldn't believe the paperwork, the time it takes to check us out
and have the documents translated and site visits and the rest, you
wouldn't believe what it costs . . .

"Except it's worth it," Lucy declared. "It'll be worth it, I'm
certain."

"Another mouth to feed," said Richard, theatrical, grinning.
"Another candidate for excess to join the favored few."

Then David told them how, that afternoon, he'd stopped, on
impulse, at Muir Woods and walked the trail an hour (past the
sightseers and the instructional signs, the benches with their
carved initials and a pair of men in wheelchairs and a group of
high school students on a field trip with their teacher) to what he
thought of as his sacred grove—well, no more than any other
grove except in the way that it mattered to *him*, this particular
cluster of redwoods where a year before he'd promised himself
that next year would be different, a ring that *counted* on the trunk,
a year to mark a growth spurt since he was turning thirty-five
and that was Dante's fateful year, the middle of the journey in the
middle of this life. *Che la diritta via era smaritta*, that much he could
remember: where the direct way is a muddle and the direction
unclear . . .

"Or remember Yogi Berra," Richard said. "And his immortal
saying. 'When you come to a fork in the road, take it.'"

Lucy laughed. "Well, has it?"

"Has it what?" he asked.

"Been a year that mattered?"

"Not in any good way, no."

And that was when he understood his mother was going to die. That was when he shut his eyes and pictured his sister Joanna, a continent away and staring at the other sea, and sister Claire uneasy in her starter castle—"Oh *excellent*," Lucy was saying, "we give you our premium homegrown and tell you we're going to China and acquiring a baby and you say it doesn't matter"—and then the three of them mourning together, together again for the first time in years, he and Claire and Joanna grown-ups now or all of them anyhow trying to be, *Nel mezzo del cammin*—in the middle of the road, the middle of the journey—and standing in their adult garb beside their mother's corpse . . .

So it is no surprise to him when the lawyer calls. Beakes's voice is fluting, sibilant; David tries to remember the way that he looked.

"Mr. Saperstone? You don't mind if I call you David? It's like yesterday, it seems to me, when you were still in grade school here and we came to the *Nutcracker Suite.*"

Bald, flat-nosed, wearing glasses, that much he can remember, but not if Beakes is short or tall; he has the impression of wideness, a bow tie, a blue shirt . . .

"And I remember how your mother loved to watch you dancing, how she absolutely loved it when you came out on stage. You remember I played piano?"

"No."

There is static on the line. It crackles. The lawyer offers his condolences, and then the rest of it, the request he join his sisters and the prepaid ticket east. "Your mother left instructions. She was very precise about this, Alice was." Beakes coughs. "A trust, you understand, comes with conditions; the provider can establish terms—and that's precisely what your mother did. She wants all three of you to come to Saratoga Springs. It's a proviso of the will."

"All three of us?"

"Of her children, I mean. The grandchildren are welcome too, but it's you three she stipulates."

"Stipulated," David says.

"This proviso that you come to town? It's an interesting codicil."

"Concerning?"

"I have no desire to be secretive. It's not a secret, David, and I'll be happy to disclose the asset as soon as you children assemble together. It's what your mother wanted, it's precisely what she stipulated and therefore what we, before probate, must do."

He agrees. He deploys the techniques of avoidance—formality, politeness—till lawyer Beakes is mollified and says, that's fine then, we'll expect you in the office, see you soon.

David cradles the phone and stares at the window and tries to deal with what he's heard, the size and shape of it, the sudden summons back to what he thought he'd left. Outside a homeless man is picking through recycling bins, gathering bottles and cans. A car siren announces itself down the street and before it shuts back off he listens to the blaring notes, the caterwauling repeated complaint. An ambulance rattles down Ashby, or maybe a police car, and he asks himself in what way an ambulance siren differs from a police cruiser's and how to assess its direction and if you could, listening, tell.

He does his breathing exercise, inhaling for the count of eight and holding for the count of eight and releasing for sixteen. Upstairs, there is gospel music and the muffled roaring of a vacuum cleaner, and a door slams in the entrance hall: two times. He lies on his tatami mat and tries a series of positions and these too fail to calm him; therefore he ceases willed evasion and tries to remember and does:

David is six, maybe seven years old. He's standing with his father at the entrance to the racetrack, so it must have been August in Saratoga, and what he wants is ice cream but his father insists on a Coke. "A Coke won't melt," his father says; "you wouldn't want ice cream all over your shirt." There are horses and trainers and horses and jockeys and he can distinguish between them—the jockeys and the exercise riders—because exercise riders can wear what they want, and he's holding his paper cup carefully, carefully so the soda won't spill when a woman approaches them, smiling, saying, "George?"

His father doffs his hat. He does so with a flourish, bending at the waist and nodding and smiling the way that he does, and sweeping his Panama down past his knees. "May I present my son," he says. Then she says—actually using these words so that David will remember them, because young as he is he can distinguish sincerity from falsity, can recognize when someone means the thing they're saying or is lying through their perfect teeth—"Why, fancy meeting you two here. My, my, what a pleasant surprise!"

It isn't a surprise, of course, it happens every Saturday—a well-dressed woman gliding past and then the soft proprietary touch on his father's arm or shoulder, and then the introduction and the woman's keen, assessing gaze. "He's just like you," she says to his father. "He'll be a heartbreaker, won't he; this apple won't fall very far from the tree."

"I believe the expression is 'acorn,'" says George, and then the three of them stand at the rail and cheer the horses on.

At suppertime his mother asks, "Did you enjoy yourself, darling?" and he answers yes. His sisters don't go to the races; they go to the ballet. He looks around the table where the family sits eating and knows there is constraint among them, a conspiracy of secrets, for he has secrets too. When his father dies in a car crash in the Adirondacks, David is only eight years old, but he knows not to discuss it from how everyone behaves—the way the neighbors focus on the floor or ceiling when they come to call, the way his sisters cease their whispering and Mother will not answer when he asks about the accident . . .

Alice had been protective, hidden and guarded by nature, and now that she was a widow her strict watchfulness increased. His mother would never remarry; her grief became a grievance and codified with time. She was dark and severe and beautiful, and there were doctors and lawyers and college professors who offered consolation, or attempted to, but none of them sufficed. His sisters left. He and his mother remained in the house, and she called him her companion and said, darling, you're my heart's delight, the only man I need. You won't ever leave me the way he did, said Alice—not aloud, of course, never explicitly or in those words, but in the way she waited for him after school or drove him to karate practice or walked with him down

Philo Street to buy a box of pastries, her hand on his shoulder or arm linked with his, the way those women at the racetrack had consorted with his father years before.

And when he went to Williams College—majoring in English, then art history, falling in love with the Clark Art Institute and its Botticelli and the Memling portraits and Renoirs—she came to see him often, driving down for lunch on Saturday or to see his roommate in a play or to help him move in and move out. "You can't imagine," Alice said, *"how happy I am to be useful, how much it means to me to see you growing up this way, it's the only thing I want." This she did say in his hearing, often and out loud. He was proud and then embarrassed and then, finally, impatient;* Get a life, *he wanted to tell her.* Just leave me alone, will you please?

Well, now his mother has done so, and irrevocably. Now David is alone. While he packs he thinks of Adrienne and thinks he could call her and tell her what happened, but knows it would be a mistake. There's the red-eye to Chicago, and then the flight to Albany, and then an hour's drive. He puts his garbage outside in the can, the potted plants in the yard. He is practiced at departure, the one-step two-step dance-away, and he drops the blinds and double-locks the entrance door and leaves.

II

2003

"We're here together. We're all here."

The sisters stand. David embraces them—Joanna first, then Claire. He kisses them both on both cheeks.

"You're *here*..."

"How long has it been?" David asks. In the room the air is stale. "Since the last time the three of us..."

"Two years," says Claire. "Almost three."

"You look terrific." Appraising him, Joanna tilts her head. "You do."

"And *you. You* haven't changed."

"Is that a compliment?"

"Mm-hm. You never change." He drapes his coat over a chair. There are four of them: slat-backed and upright, with plaited rush seats. There are dried flowers and a mixing bowl on the Formica countertop. "How long ago did you two...?"

"An hour maybe, maybe less. Not long."

"*I* came this morning," says Claire.

"No matter how often I do it," he says, "the red-eye still gets me, a little. Gets *to* me, flying cross-country. And this direction is the hard one, this is the one where they don't let you sleep."

"Don Johnson," says Joanna. "Bruce Willis. That's the look."

Above the sink, where moisture rises, the kitchen windows are wet. On the pantry door the February calendar—its first week crossed out with red *X*s—displays a log cabin in snow. Smoke curls from the tin chimney, and there are horses and sleighs and several dogs and roosters and women wearing mufflers and men with whips and hats.

"What I'm trying to say," David says, "is it's amazing to be in this kitchen together. The three of us. Alone, I mean."

"Alone?"

"Without her. Mom," he says.

27

Now there is silence between them. Beyond the window, light flakes fall. The chandelier above the table functions on a rheostat, and David increases the light.

"I've been meaning to ask you"—Claire turns to her sister— "how's Leah?"

"Fine. Becky? Hannah?"

"Thank you for asking. They're fine."

"And Jim?"

"He's fine," says Claire. "He sends his best."

"In Wellfleet," says Joanna, sitting, "we had an ice storm last night. This morning, though, it wasn't bad."

"Oh?"

The drive from the Cape, she continues, was dull, but at least it didn't snow, and there had been no traffic at the bridge. Route 6 was empty as it gets; at Sagamore she'd filled the tank and made it in an hour to the Massachusetts Turnpike. The trip took five hours and ought to take more, but Trusty-Rusty's not the sort of car policemen notice, and anyway she saw only one speed trap and the cop had bagged a Porsche . . .

"In Ann Arbor it was very cold. It was twelve, maybe twenty below . . ."

"You get more snow in the Midwest. We get all that moisture off the Atlantic but you get the lake effect . . ."

"Look," David says. "We made it. We're here together finally, so let's not do weather, OK? Let's talk about what *matters*."

"Such as?"

"Death." He spreads his hands. "She's dead."

They listen to house-noise: the hum of the furnace and tick of the clock.

"I hope she didn't suffer," says Joanna, "in the end."

"I called our lawyer," Claire offers. "Joseph Beakes. He expects us tomorrow morning."

"In his office?"

"Bright and early. Well, nine-thirty. I didn't want to make the meeting—he didn't want to schedule it—until it was certain we all were in town. And this afternoon there's the funeral home, the disposition of the body. We're due there at three." Claire stands. "Mom stipulated we three must be together when he reads the will."

"Tonight"—David watches his sisters—"are we all staying here?"

"*I'm* planning to."

"Are there sheets?" Joanna asks. "Fresh sheets upstairs, I mean. Or should we be making the beds?"

"I haven't looked," says Claire. "Not yet."

"You haven't gone upstairs?"

"You're welcome to Mom's room . . ."

Joanna shuts her eyes. "I'll use the couch. I'll stay down here."

The second floor has three bedrooms: their mother's, David's, the one the girls shared. "Let's check it out," David says.

They climb the stairwell, David in front. The cuff of his left leg is frayed and the lining of his jacket hangs loose beneath the vent. The gray pile of the carpet too has frayed, and the photographs at the top of the stairs hang askew. Claire straightens them. In the hallway stands a wheelchair with a tag affixed to its handle: *Miller's Medical Supply.* The hospital bed has been removed, and their mother's room—the door ajar—seems empty and, since empty, small and airless and bereft.

They continue down the hall and open doors and turn on the ceiling fixtures and peer, room by room, inside. Wallpaper billows unglued. The beds, however, have been made; there are pillows and blankets and quilts. The rooms have been prepared for visitors, with washcloths and towels at the foot of each bed. As though their task has been accomplished, they descend to the first floor again.

"The place looks good," Joanna says.

Claire shakes her head.

"What time did you say they expect us?"

"Three. We have to choose a casket and decide on funeral arrangements, and even though we know she wanted cremation we still have to give them permission. A signature's required; it's the law."

"You know what?" David says. "I could use a drink."

"Me too," Joanna says. "What are you drinking?"

"Do you think Mom still keeps liquor?"

Claire gestures at the pantry. A key ring hangs from a hook on the shelf; she found it there this morning and hasn't had the time, of course, to look at everything—but one of those keys, she supposes, is for the liquor cabinet. David locates the key and opens the sideboard in the dining room and, having examined its contents, asks his sisters what they want and returns with a bottle of J&B scotch and one of Tanqueray gin. He removes a tray of ice from the ice-encrusted freezer and finds a bottle of tonic water on the pantry shelf and selects three thick beveled glasses and measures out two gin and tonics and, for himself, a scotch. "To Mom," he says. "To everything she went through and how well she handled it."

"I'll drink to that," Joanna says.

"To her memory," says Claire.

The three of them click glasses; then they drink. They have been hunting the right tone to take, the right mix of ease and solemnity. They remark on how little there does seem to do: there's no one they know to invite to the house, nobody left from their mother's old bridge club or . . . what was it called, the Friends of Ballet? We are, says Joanna wonderingly, the elder generation now, and I can't get my mind around the way she lived here all alone—well, not *alone;* there had been hospice personnel.

And Gretchen Adams, Claire reminds them, who has been sleeping in the house and doing the cleaning and round-the-clock nursing and letting us know how things go. They agree that Mrs. Adams deserves their gratitude, an extra check, but she'd said that morning when Claire called the three of them would want some space, some privacy, and anyhow she had her own grandchildren to catch up on in New Jersey, and would be back by the weekend, when they could settle up . . .

"It's nearly three," Joanna says, and they collect their coats and walk out of the cottage again. Flourishing his rental car key, David announces he'll drive; Claire locks the kitchen door. The funeral home on North Broadway is simple to find—a dark brick house with white wooden pillars and a portico, a sign saying "Becker & Bushing & Cunliffe" out front, a sign that reads "Deliveries" by the side entrance. A hearse has been stationed there also, and two black panel wagons with the monogram "B&B & C" on the doors. A gunmetal gray Chrysler Imperial and, surprisingly, a trail-bike are parked in the plowed lot.

"Well, here goes nothing," David says.

His sisters do not respond.

❧

Inside, a trim gray-haired man greets them, introducing himself as Bill Becker Jr., and it is less difficult than they'd expected — more comforting, less of a trial; he ushers them into his office, where three chairs have been positioned, and says it's a great shame to see them gathered together for this occasion, but their mother — he glances down at his pad — has passed in the fullness of time. I knew her, he tells them, I won't pretend I knew her well but everybody here admired your mother, in a small town like ours you know who's a lady to reckon with, and if there ever was such a lady it was Alice. He hands them each a pamphlet outlining funeral procedures and says you might want to take a few minutes familiarizing yourself with its contents because, understandably enough — Bill Becker smiles — this isn't a procedure with which most folks are familiar . . .

They do know, Claire tells him, their mother's intentions; she had made it clear she planned to be cremated and did not want a service. I'm cognizant of that, he says, but anyhow there's choices you three need to make. He smells strongly of cologne. What choices? David asks. The funeral director offers up a four-page sheet of "Full Service Selections" and says, please, take your time with this, and when you agree let me know; I do need to be cognizant beforehand, he says, if you want a single urn or possibly — many of our clients feel this way — you want the ash divided into equal containers; whatever you decide amongst yourselves is what we're happy to do.

The wall behind his desk is covered with certificates, diplomas and attestations of excellence; there are framed photographs of children and ponies and children with ponies and an oil portrait of William Becker Sr. smiling down at his successor. It's a family business, Becker explains, and it's important it should stay that way because you get personal service; too many funeral homes in America, if you don't mind me saying so, are run by franchise operations, and if you want or need satisfaction it's pretty much like calling up Colonel Sanders and saying, excuse me, there was a fly in my Kentucky Fried Chicken or calling to complain to someone named Ronald McDonald that the hamburger was raw. There's no one home, is what I mean, there's nobody responsible, and we try to be very different that way; if my sons stay in the business — I myself have two sons, Jimmy and Joe, and they've told me they want to, they *plan* to — it will be the fourth generation of Beckers in Saratoga Springs working at this trade. Becker places his hands on the desktop and studies his manicured nails. Then he hands them a General Price List; the FTC requires this up front, he says, but we'll discuss it all in detail in due course. The best time to discuss these things is now, *beforehand,* now's the time for you to know your options and agree on which to choose . . .

They receive a brochure called "Funeral Facts" and one called "May We Help?" There's a pamphlet titled "Planning the Funeral of Someone You Love" and a pamphlet he gives David titled "Handling Grief as a Man." There are facts they need to know about "Procedures" and "Social Security" and "Insurance" and "Inheritance Tax"; there's a pamphlet titled "Getting Through the First Weeks and Months After the Funeral." They receive an "Authorization for Cremation" form, attesting that they have identified the human remains of the decedent and that the decedent does not possess any pacemakers or radioactive implants, and that they will indemnify, defend and hold harmless the officers and agents of the agency performing the procedure. "We haven't *identified* the — what did you call it? — 'human remains,'" David says.

"I'm cognizant of that," Bill Becker says. "Whenever you're ready, my friends."

Next he distributes three copies of a brochure of "Cremation Choices." They can choose between an "Artistic Collection," a "Hardwood Collection," a "Contemporary Collection" or a "Bronze Collection"; they each are provided with color photographs and descriptions and dimensions. There's a "Memento Series" with "Heirloom Jewelry" and "Personal Expressions" and a description of the two methods of "Personalization"; they can elect engraving of the actual urn or personalization through the use of brass plaques. The two methods allow for different type styles, and the plaques vary in size. They must decide if they prefer the urn or urns to receive a burial or placement in a columbarium urn niche, or if the three of them wish permanent possession of one or more containers of the decedent's remains, or scattering. "I think we've been thinking of scattering," says Joanna, and Claire says, "We have to decide . . ."

Bill Becker clears his throat. State law requires embalming, he says, if burial or cremation fails to take place within forty-eight hours of death. In this case, he continues, we couldn't guarantee a timetable and have proceeded with embalming; the clock starts ticking, understand, from the time of death and you all were traveling to get here. So what we've done is mostly a matter of—well, the word is—prophylaxis, a minimum procedure, I'm telling you more than you may want to know, but if the body has a communicable infectious disease then state law requires embalming. She *didn't* have, she *wouldn't* have, says Claire. Of course not, no, Bill Becker says, I'm simply explaining a legal procedure, and perhaps you'd care to view her now, would you care to accompany me?

They do. They walk through a room full of caskets—wooden and metal and fiberglass caskets, plain and ornate, open and shut—and through a door he holds open for them to where their mother lies. This room is cold. Alice reposes on a table, arms at her side, and with a pink sheet folded underneath her neck.

"I hope you're satisfied," Bill Becker says. "I hope you agree this is how she should look."

On the shelf behind the table sit a box of powder-free latex examination gloves, a box of polyethylene aprons, a box of masks;

there are scissors, knives, razors and needles, there are boxes marked "Dodge Permaglo" and "Dodge Restorative." In silence they inspect the body of their mother where she lies. What they feared would not be bearable is not in fact so hard to bear; she is manifestly *elsewhere,* dead, and David tells himself he's looking at a statuette or photograph of who she was, a dress he doesn't recognize and cheeks and neck improved upon with adult tinting cream. He nods; his sisters nod. Joanna shuts her eyes an instant and Claire shifts her weight on her feet. They have identified the decedent and back in the office of Bill Becker Jr. sign the authorization for cremation. The funeral director points to a line where all three must sign and to the statement *This is a legal document. It contains important provisions concerning cremation. Cremation Is Irreversible and Final—Read This Document Carefully Before Signing* and gives them a worksheet for the General Price List. They promise they will choose among the various options listed and be back in touch in the morning and say that they are grateful and shake his hand and leave.

Ice and plowed slush line the side of the road; the road itself is clear. He has forgotten, David says, how *early* it gets dark back here and how cold a winter afternoon can be. Then he looks at his sister Joanna—the exhaustion in her, the gray face—and ceases his talk about winter and the bitter chill of this part of the East; he turns on the Taurus headlights and maneuvers them past the rows of summer mansions and then the entrance to Skidmore and the less imposing houses—split-level, ramshackle, *lived* in—to where they turn up the driveway again and past the rotten elm . . .

Some things do stay the same. The picket fence still stands. The basketball hoop by the woodshed remains. Inside the kitchen it feels warm, and David checks the thermostat, remembering how often their mother would tell him to turn down the heat, or turn it up, or check downstairs to make certain the furnace was working. They remove their jackets and kick off the snow from their shoes.

"I promised I'd call Leah," Joanna says, and Claire nods and says she has a cell phone and will call home too. David walks into the library—what they used to call the "library" though he can't remember reading there, remembers jigsaw puzzles they would do: a Braque, a Mondrian, a series of haystacks by Monet—and studies the dust on the spines of the books. He pictures his mother upstairs, in her bed, and leafing through a magazine, or drinking tea, or lukewarm soup, and trying to make sense of what the doctors told her and trying to remember which pills she has taken already and which she needs to take. He imagines the hospice volunteer or maybe Gretchen Adams appearing in the bedroom first thing every morning and asking, always, how are we doing this morning, how are we feeling today? His mother always answers, "Fine," and smiles, or tries to, and raises herself on the pillows and commences with the pills.

And then one day when they arrive and ask "How are you feeling?" she cannot answer, does not smile, because that night she died. The lady from the hospice or maybe Gretchen Adams or maybe both together would feel her nonexistent pulse and shut her open, staring eyes; they would notify the doctor or the county medical examiner. Two men with a gurney and perhaps a body bag would come that same afternoon to collect her; they would bring a black van to the house and carry the body downstairs. The job would be an easy one, the stairwell not a problem since one old woman with congestive heart disease makes for a light load. They would deposit her corpse in the van and drive off to Becker & Bushing & Cunliffe, to the doorway marked "Deliveries," and they would have prepared her—how? who drained which vein and filled it with what, who chose the white dress Alice wore?—for the family viewing that afternoon, this thing he and his sisters have done.

⤮

There's a Japanese restaurant out on Route 9 and something Middle Eastern or Indian near the bookstore Lyrical Ballads; they discuss if they should call around and make a reservation or just drive into town. They talk about the kind of meal Saratoga Springs might offer, the kind of place that is open off-season; when we were young, Joanna says, there was only Surf 'n' Turf or—what was that restaurant?—Trade Winds? Let's go cruising, David says, let's see what the town has to offer; I'm not very hungry, says Claire.

Soon enough they find a restaurant on Caroline Street, a parking place, and enter together, David escorting them, holding the door and helping them out of their coats. Joanna wears a dark blue parka and Claire a knee-length camel's hair coat. They are precisely the same height.

A waitress approaches: "Smoking?" she asks them. "No smoking? Three?"

"Three."

For some minutes they study the menu, deciding what to drink and eat and listening to what sounds like Vivaldi on an electric guitar. David orders a bottle of wine. When the waitress takes their order her hip is at his elbow, and she grazes it, swaying on her platform heels; her cheek has metal studs, her nose a pair of nostril rings, and her tongue too has been pierced.

"Heavy metal," he says to her. She smiles. Then, when she has brought their Pinot Grigio and effortfully opened it and determined to her satisfaction the issue of baked potatoes and what salad dressing to serve with which salad, when she has tucked her pen above her ear and told them, "Enjoy!" and departed, he turns to his sisters again. "So what are we going to do?" David asks.

"About what?"

"The cottage. Anybody want it?"

Claire wipes her knife with her napkin. "Is this, what, West Coast directness? Is this what they teach you in California?"

"Right, I forgot," David says. "Here's to never saying what, if anything, is on your mind."

"*What?*"

He lifts his glass. "Here's to Midwestern repression."

"Oh, please," Joanna intervenes. "Tomorrow is when we discuss it. Tomorrow morning he reads us the will."

"I don't want to argue," says Claire. She drinks.

"Remember," asks Joanna, "when we learned about Dad's death? The day he had that accident . . ."

The soup arrives. Their waitress lights a candle.

"So how's Ann Arbor?" David swallows. "How's life in the big little city?"

"You should come visit," says Claire.

"Are you all right?" Joanna asks.

Her brother shakes his head. "I miss her very much."

"It's what children do."

Claire has been trying not to cry. "It's what we're *supposed* to do. Live on."

The music of Vivaldi gives way to Billie Holiday and Billie Holiday to Sting. They eat. The restaurant is nearly empty: a pair of women in the corner, a table of what look like businessmen dividing up the bill. They talk about the funeral home and the cost of the arrangements and how strange it is to buy a container purchased just for burning; they talk about Bill Becker and his signet ring and family of undertakers and the last time they were together in town when everyone went to their high school reunions. Joanna lights a cigarette; she is rationing herself, she says—one every other hour, one per meal. They agree on an oak coffin and three separate urns for their mother's remains. Claire orders tiramisu. "Three spoons," she tells the waitress, and Joanna shakes her head and, pointing to her cigarette, says "Two." David repeats his assertion that this evening ought to matter and this reunion count; the sisters do not contravene him or argue with each other; they have made a warring truce.

<hr />

Once more, a light snow falls. They return to the cottage at nine. As if by unspoken agreement, they walk into the living room; a carpet has been rolled for storage in the corner and the space feels un-lived-in, expectant. There are portraits of Alice and George at their wedding and portraits of grandparents and great-grandparents done in oil; there's a watercolor of the cottage done by some forgotten guest and dated August 1921. Flanking the fireplace, in cabinets, stands the collection of miniature cats.

"I'm tired," Claire announces. "I began this day too early. I was up at dawn—before it—and tomorrow is a busy day and I need to call it quits."

"It's only six o'clock," says David. "California time. Except I didn't sleep last night . . ."

"Wait up with me a little," says Joanna. "Let's build a fire in the living room. Let's sit up together, all right?"

"The fireplace. You think it works?"

"I think so," says Claire. "Check the flue."

He does. It swivels easily, discharging soot, and he lights a piece of paper in order to check on the draft; the chimney is not blocked. From the walkway past the pantry he selects a pile of kindling and old newspaper and an armful of two-foot logs. The dry wood catches readily and flame crackles, rising; he and Joanna sit on the love seat and watch. She misses him, Joanna tells her brother; this man is the man she's lived with the longest, sharing a roof, and now that they are grown-ups they don't seem to visit at all.

The wine has made her garrulous; she talks about living alone all these years and if it's different for a woman and the ways it must be different for a man. Then she talks about Leah and leaving Cape Cod, how once her daughter goes away there won't be any family for her in driving distance. It hasn't happened yet, says Claire; that's true, Joanna says. In *West Side Story*, she tells them, Leah has been cast as Anita, the second most important part for a woman in the musical, and it requires her dancing; the show opens in Orleans on Friday night and she can't wait to get back.

"I might just go with you," says David. "I like that show."

"Oh, Leah would be so happy! Remember when she used to say, 'Bob's your uncle'—whatever that means, and you'd say 'No, it's "Dave." ' It's *'Dave's* your uncle,' darling.' "

He laughs. "Let me think about it."

"Oh *please*," Joanna says. "Don't think about it, or say 'maybe.' Just come."

Claire takes the BarcaLounger and raises her feet from the floor.

"I used to think," says David, "hell, I'm single: white, male, unattached. I could live in Saratoga and be helpful to her — Mom. Why not just move back to this town. I used to ask myself what kept me from calling it home again and if it really *felt* like home and whether she would want me here or not."

"Of course she would have," says Claire.

He pokes at the fire; it flares.

"It couldn't have been easy," says Joanna. "These years. For Mom."

"No."

"What I wonder," she continues, "is how much you understand it when you lose your memory. Your grip on things. If you know, I mean, you're losing it or if it just goes away."

"I can't remember," David says.

"Ha-ha."

"All right. Bad joke," he says.

"So Alzheimer's can be a kind of comfort, maybe, a way of making things bearable. Like going into shock, I mean, when the pain's too extreme for the body to bear. When you're on system overload you faint . . ."

"She didn't have Alzheimer's," says Claire. "Not really."

Joanna stands. "I don't know what else you'd call it. It's like being a little bit, oh, a little bit a virgin. Mom always did seem — what? Forgetful, secretive."

"Secretive?"

"There was a lot," says David, "she didn't want to talk about. Or not to me, at any rate . . ."

"Because you were the baby. You were the one she would try to protect."

"Do you remember that jingle — how does it go?" Now it's Claire's turn to mediate, and she does this gratefully. "'A son is a son till he takes him a wife, a daughter's a daughter the rest of her life.'"

"'Takes him a wife?' Isn't it 'finds him a wife'?" David asks. "Or maybe it's 'brings home . . .' Whatever."

"Will you?"

"Will I what?"

"Bring home a wife," Joanna inquires. "Is there a candidate?"

He shakes his head.

"I'm going up," Claire says. "Beakes will be waiting for us . . ."

"Good night."

"Sleep tight," says Joanna. "Sweet dreams."

"I will"—he turns to her—"I'll go with you. But now I need to try to sleep . . ."

"Good night," says Claire.

"Good night."

III

2003

Sardines, he tells himself, or cat food: the smell in his room is of old canned fish, and he wonders if their mother kept a cat. He does not know. David sits. At nine or ten he had wanted a dog; he read *Lad, a Dog*, and all the Lassie books, and he begged his mother for a collie. He would feed and groom it, he promised, and it would be a watchdog and in case of fire would save everybody's lives.

But Claire was allergic to dog hair, or so Alice said, and by the time she left for college he wanted a pony instead. He had kept hamsters and a canary and goldfish and buried them under the lilac bush when, turn by turn, they died. Now in his bedroom, in the wintry dark, David remembers what it felt like on a school night to be doing homework with his mother at the kitchen sink, her back to him, arranging, rearranging things. There would have been music, the six o'clock news, that parental routine she mustered the years of his childhood. His mother would be occupied chopping or slicing or rinsing or drying until, of a sudden, her hands would go slack, her eyes would go vacant, unfocused, and she would stand immobile for what seemed to him like minutes, facing the wall.

"Are you all right, Mom? *Mom?*" he would ask, and—if he asked it soon or loud enough—break into her reverie. Then she would give a little shake and lift her shoulders visibly and turn to him: "Of course."

At other times the dream or memory or fear or whatever it was that had caused her to pause would seem impenetrable, and she did not hear. Then what were seconds and had felt to him like minutes would be minutes that felt hour-long, and she would neither turn nor smile nor sigh but wait it out, unmoving. "I get preoccupied," she told him. "I get—what would you call it?—lost."

In school they studied outer space and the likelihood of flying saucers, and Mr. D'Amelio, their fifth-grade teacher, said it wasn't likely but couldn't be ruled out. He said the Pentagon and NASA investigate these things. Mr. D'Amelio wore a suit and matching vest and bow tie and had an artificial leg; he walked with a queer rolling gait and had been shot in Korea. So when his mother stood that way David wondered if a flying saucer or a group of extra-terrestrials was visiting, their space stations visible to her but not to him, and he asked if she saw Martians out the window, on the lawn.

"Of course not," Alice told him. "It isn't like that, darling."

"It's what Mr. D'Amelio tells us," he said. "It's what everybody talks about—a bright light out the window and feeling peaceful, not scared."

"You've been watching too much TV. There's no space capsule in Saratoga. Or not on our lawn, anyway. I'm just being quiet, David."

Then, later, when he attended Williams and took a course in ab-normal psychology and learned about manic-depression he thought perhaps that *this* was what his mother suffered from. And when he read of epilepsy and narcolepsy and seizure disorders—petit and grand mal—he thought perhaps she had a case of nar-colepsy or something neurological, some condition a doctor could fix. He wrote a paper about it—not being personal, of course, not naming names but remembering the way his mother would go blank, then shrug herself free like a dog from a dream—and got an A from the teacher and the handwritten comment: "Fine in-sights. Extremely GOOD work!"

This afternoon in the funeral home he'd looked at her glazed stare again—the mortician had discovered it somehow, pasting it back on Alice's face—and it reminded him of absence, how absent her presence had been. Staring unseeing at the sink or floor she went, as she put it, away.

When his sisters came home for Thanksgiving, however, things changed; the house would grow noisy and busy, and the phone would ring. Then Alice made squash and creamed onions and corn and chestnut purée and baked three kinds of pie: apple, pumpkin, mince. There would be cider and wine. She would make yams and mashed potatoes, since Joanna preferred mashed potatoes, and there would be peas and cranberry relish and complicated stuffing and a turkey she had ordered from Pederson's farm at the intersection of Route 372 and 29. The day before Thanksgiving, always, they drove together to the turkey farm, and David can remember standing in the barn mud while his mother chatted gaily with the farmer's wife, not bothering to brush away flies but admiring the fresh-killed bird. Then Mrs. Pederson would weigh the turkey, bag it, and his mother—usually so fastidious, so prim in her pantsuit and heels—would pay and say, "Thanks a million. See you soon," and get into the driver's seat and not buckle up. "She's a beaut," Mrs. Pederson said.

It was his job to carve. David would whet the knife edge carefully, then remove the legs and second joints, and then slice white meat and dark. This was his business, said Alice, because it's a job for the man of the house; always put white meat on *this* platter, darling, and the dark meat and wings and the giblets on this. His sisters were part of the cooking team too, and everyone helped in the kitchen, but he had been responsible for knives and proud of how he sharpened them; he tested the edge of the knife blade along his wrist and thumb. That was the way to do it, and he had learned by watching: you whet the knife on the sharpening stone and turn your wrist just so . . .

By the time he had turned nine years old, he was the man of the house; both his father and his grandfather were dead. Dimly he remembers his grandfather Aaron, sitting in the easy chair and saying, yes, that's right, and talking about Roosevelt and the Washington Baths and the war in Vietnam. Aaron died at ninety-two, almost entirely deaf and blind in his right eye; he was proud of his eyesight, however, and liked to supervise.

"I'm only halfway blind," he declared. "My doctor tells me I could get a driver's license. If I wanted to."

He wore horn-rimmed glasses and squinted and talked but did not listen; he liked to say the proof of God—not the white-haired white-bearded old man they talk about in Sunday school, but a principle of divinity, the idea that makes me pious—is how the willow and the chestnut tree can live together, side by side, and never once in nature will you find a chestnut on a willow tree. That's the kind of pattern only God Himself could have created, the divine presence everywhere, boy.

His mother's father, Aaron Freedman, lived two streets away. He had been much older than her mother, and when Alice married he was in his seventies, a widower, and it was time for a change. The cottage had belonged to him, but he gave it to his daughter as a wedding present and moved into an apartment complex and then a retirement home. You and George take the cottage, he said, and I myself will live around the corner and go to Florida in wintertime and not have to worry anymore about the gutters or the furnace or the lawn . . .

In the beginning, David understood, his grandfather did go to Sarasota, spending winters down in Florida and coming back to Saratoga Springs in April. From Sarasota to Saratoga, he would say, the best of both possible worlds. But then his grandfather had had a stroke and lost the use of his right arm and after he turned eighty could no longer travel south. Then Aaron moved into a managed facility—a half-timbered summerhouse that had been renovated for the purpose and divided into single rooms, with a glassed-in wraparound porch. Every morning Alice telephoned and went to take him shopping, or Aaron came to visit, wheeling up the driveway, or in fine weather in the spring and summer walking with his cane.

Betty Livingston, who worked at the home, would call him always, only, Mr. Freedman; if he was tired she would wheel him to the cottage in the wheelchair, and stop and take a cup of tea, and tell Alice how her father had been doing fine, he was such a good-humored person and not one to complain. Not like some of the others, I tell you, she said; he's got a twinkle in his eye, Mr. Freedman does, and enjoys his chocolate bars. I only hope I'll be in anything like that good shape when *I'm* ninety-two, I only hope I can be *halfway* as hopeful by then. His grandfather's shape did not look good to David, however, all bent over and hunched and slow and with teeth he kept adjusting. When Aaron said I'd like another piece of chocolate and perhaps a glass of wine to keep you company, Betty Livingston complied. Then he would sit and rock and hum and speculate upon the nature of the universe, that cloud formation there, he'd say, that color red in the westering sky. This pattern is not accidental; it makes me feel pious, he said.

Many years later, when Aaron was dead, he had asked his mother what her father had been like to live with when she herself was a child. There was a time, said Alice, when piety was not his thing and he would rage and rage and had a terrible temper. The stroke fixed that, she said, it gentled him, it made him seem, well, not a different person entirely, but calmer, it drained all the bitterness off. What bitterness, David had asked her, what did he have to feel bitter about, but his mother did not answer and went, as she put it, away.

⚮

In bed Claire tries to sleep. Sleep will not come to her, however, or at least not easily; she lies on her back and stares at the ceiling, then turns to her left side. She hears her brother in the room beside her, breathing. Her sister stays downstairs. She has been watching their old interplay with—what? she asks herself—disapproval? envy? the sense that all Joanna needs in order to be happy is some male someone in the room . . .

Claire rubs at her back with her fist. Then she rolls to her right side instead. She considers the next morning's schedule, the things she has accomplished and what she has not yet accomplished; she walks, in her mind's eye, through each of the rooms of the cottage—from storm cellar to the attic eaves—and divides up the linens, the wedding china and pictures and the cutlery and rugs. There's little she chooses to choose. She does want the picture of Heidi on a hillside, sitting with her dog and sheep—but only for its sentimental value, only because it has been here since her childhood and she'd stared at it for years.

It hangs above her bed. There are snow-covered mountains,

and clouds. A waterfall spews from a rock. The picture is not black but brown, and Claire wonders if it always was intended to be brown or if the canvas yellowed over time. She counts the sheep: five, six. The gilt of the frame has worn thin. This home that once contained them all seems, tenantless, much smaller now, and she cannot fail to notice how shabby the curtains and furniture look, how her mother's collection of porcelain cats has lost its childhood sheen. There are wooden cats also, and glass and ceramic and metal cats no bigger than Claire's thumbnail, and two brightly colored papier-mâché cats perched life-size by the fireplace. Idly now she wonders if she should carry a pair of statuettes back on the plane for Becky and Hannah, and what to wrap them in . . .

She can remember how, when young, she'd spent long after-noons absorbed in setting out these animals, arranging, rearrang-ing them so that the Siamese and tortoiseshell and black and long-haired cats belonged together in cat-families and perched or sat or lay down together on separate shelves, how she made par-ties and dances of cats and gave them each separate names. A memory assails her of Joanna knocking down a shelf: careless Joanna with her ribbon-wrapped baton. She'd been practicing cheerleader routines and twirling and doing the split and dropping and catching the aluminum stick until she knocked over the shelf. Claire still can see her sister, jumping and prancing and shouting, "Go, *Go!*" and still can hear the breakage, the clattering wreck of the porcelain cats and how the glass shattered. "Oh shit," said Joanna, "shit, shit."

It has been this way, always: the china shop that she herself built carefully, so conscientiously, and then her sister-bull. They have been in opposition from the start. If one of them would nod the other one would shake her head; if one of them said *yes* the other would say *no*. When one of them chose white the other wanted black; when one of them could eat no fat the other ate no lean. You two, their mother used to say, you lick the platter clean . . .

Claire yawns. She has spent the day arranging things, making telephone calls and to-do lists, confirming the appointment for to-morrow at the lawyer's office and calling the 800 number for the *New York Times* to complain about last Sunday's paper in its blue wrapper in the bushes and to make certain delivery has been can-celed and calling home to say she's fine and calling the insurance agency and bank and post office and the *Washington County Post* and the *Daily Saratogian* to place obituary notices and writing a check to the hospice and one for Gretchen Adams and starting a log of expenses incurred and what the others owe. By lunchtime she had been hungry and took a piece of moldy cheddar from the fruit bin and toasted a piece of frozen bread and boiled a can of chicken noodle soup. She began an inventory of the household ob-jects, room by room, but after an hour gave it up as hopeless or at least as something she could wait for her brother and sister to help with when finally they came. At least they arrived for the funeral home, at least she didn't have to deal with *that* alone and identify the body by herself and smile at that awful Bill Becker. She will ask for the picture of Heidi and sheep, then let the others take a turn, and they will go from room to room and draw straws and divide . . .

Now, counting sheep above her on the hillside in the painting, she recollects a joke about a king who calls a mathematician to court and asks, how many sheep are grazing in that pasture there, and the man takes a quick look and says, Your Highness, two hun-dred forty-three. That's remarkable, the king avers (having or-dered a head count previously); how ever did you know? It's easy, the wizard answers; I count the legs and divide them by four.

Once she had a boyfriend called Tommy—this was at Colgate, before she met Jim—who dreamed of doing what he called "stand-up." That had been one of his jokes. He practiced in front of the mirror and then in front of Claire, making her watch. "Be my audience," he liked to say. "Pretend you're two hundred peo-ple, OK?"

"It's not a joke," she said, "it's a funny story, maybe," and Tommy said, "People laugh. *'I count the legs and divide them by four.'*"

He had been—she knew this even at the time—completely

without talent; his voice was high-pitched, his delivery too broad, and his gestures and timing were off. Nonetheless Claire laughed, or tried to, at his repertoire of sheep-jokes: the one about the shepherd who preferred his ewe to the ladies in town, the one about how dumb sheep were and how they believed they were goats. Now, lying in her single bed, Claire calms herself by counting sheep, remembering Little Bo Peep. But what she remembers instead is the way Tommy stood practicing a monologue about his devotion to his mother; he had admired Woody Allen and wanted to do Woody Allen routines.

Their courtship had been brief. She had liked his curly hair, the way he cared for her opinion and wanted her to laugh with him and worked hard at making her laugh. They slept together for six weeks, from Homecoming Game to Christmas break, and he told her jokes. When she failed to laugh he stood in front of her, naked, or in his Mickey Mouse boxers, waving his hands in the air and doing the routine about Minnie Mouse fucking Goofy. The lawyer says, "Hey, Mickey, here in California insanity's not grounds for a divorce." "I didn't say she was crazy," says Mickey Mouse. "I said she was fucking Goofy!"

These are one-liners, Claire told him, not jokes, and they certainly won't be routines. They simply aren't funny, she said. In January of junior year Tommy left college and spent a season in L.A. working as a waiter and trying to break into movies; he called her daily and then weekly and then not at all. The last she heard of him he had a job on a cruise ship as backup comic to the crooner and the dancing girls . . .

She will not think about it. She thinks about her daughters: which pictures they might choose or what furniture select. She does not know. She wishes she could be at home, in her own kitchen, with a wedge of cheese on table water crackers and those cured black calamata olives you can buy at Hiller's Market, with Jim downstairs on the exercycle and Becky and Hannah—one or the other or, less likely, the two of them saying, "Mom, what's for dinner, when's dinner ready, I'm *starving*!"

There had been a time, of course, when she had known just

what to cook or buy for them—known all their habits, their hearts' desires—and they would smile and shriek with glee and clap their hands at what she bought and wrapped. Birthdays and holidays were a bonanza, an overflowing cup. In December, she had driven to the farmers' market in order to purchase a Christmas bayberry wreath. As always she took Division Street and turned left on Ann, and there were a group of men huddled waiting for soup at St. Andrew's, shivering but orderly: the home-less and the wretched of this earth. She had offered up ten dollars to a toothless black man on the corner; it had been sleeting, Claire remembers, and the streets were slick . . .

But now she cannot imagine what matters to her daughters: which cats she should take from the shelf. Therefore little by lit-tle, imperceptibly, with her hand on the small of her back and her mind on the counting of sheep and the telling of jokes, then the waters of the Caribbean, green and warm and lapping at the bright white beaches—Caneel and Cruse and Montego Bay and Negril and others she had traveled to that second winter with Jim—with her mind awash and drifting to the little pink drink with salt on the rim and an umbrella and a cherry and a slice of lime awaiting him, awaiting them, Claire knows she is falling asleep. And when she stands in that black scoop-necked bathing suit he liked so much, wearing her sun hat and sandals and touch-ing the rim of her glass to his glass, SOHCAHTOA, when she laughs and laughs at the flock of four-footed sheep on Division Street she knows she has been dreaming, has fallen asleep in the furnace-generated warmth and sees her mother's powdered face, the lipsticked mouth, her past, their past, the past.

⌘

Her brother and sister have changed. David has thickened and Claire has lost weight, but when Joanna pictures them she sees the way they used to look when young. Her brother is a handsome man, with that air of aloofness about him arrival from a distant place confers. She had watched the waitress shift her hips when tending to their table, the way she came back needlessly to ask if everything had been OK, if anyone wanted anything else. Her nose ring looked like Leah's, and Joanna hopes that, years from now, Leah will not wear a nose ring and not be waitressing; she lights a cigarette.

When she told her daughter, "Granny died," the girl had been sweetness itself. That's one of the things about Leah-Artemisia: you never can be certain which card will come out of the deck. Joanna had been waiting, and as soon as school was over, while her daughter shrugged out of her backpack, said: "It happened. Granny died." In a heartbeat the girl became Li-li again, the hard abrasive shell of her sliced open and shucked free. She said, "Oh, *Mom*," and flung both arms wide and they hugged each other and didn't stop hugging; then they drank tea and honey in the kitchen and sat together, knee to knee, staring at the wallpaper and discussing how long Joanna would need to be away. Li-li offered to skip school and go to Saratoga too, but they were doing *West Side Story* and she was playing Anita and opening night was this Friday and it would be hard.

"I'm sorry, Mom. It's, like, the pits."

"Don't even *think* about coming along."

"I'll stay with Stacey, OK?"

"OK." The wallpaper was trellised grapes, and Joanna had been noticing where the trellis matched and where it failed to and where the pattern was curling and would have to be reglued.

"It's tech rehearsal, and then dress. Will you be back by Friday?"

"Yes."

"Promise?"

"Promise. Cross my heart and hope—" She stopped herself. "Claire and David will be there."

Her enormous-eyed daughter was crying, a little, and she herself was trying not to; snow drifted past the pane. She would leave for Saratoga in the morning, said Joanna, and spend a night there, maybe two, then return by curtain time. "We'll make Harry hold the fort."

Leah did a little stutter-step and twitched her hips. "*A boy like that . . .*"

Joanna stood. The thought of Harry alone with her daughter was not one she wanted to have while away.

"*Stick to your own kind,*" the girl was singing, doing her Anita-accent. Then her face grew grave again and she kissed her mother on both cheeks. "I'm sorry. *Désolée.*"

"Maisie knows. Both Maisie and Tom know where I'm going, and you call them if you need to, right?"

Leah collected the teacups, nodding. She turned on hot water and washed out the cups, rinsing twice and settling the white porcelain into the dish drain carefully. "Don't worry, Mom, we'll be fine . . ."

"I love you. Break a leg."

Now she finishes her cigarette and drops the stub in the fire-place ash. Above her head Joanna hears her sister and her brother moving, settling in their rooms to sleep, but she herself will stay here and watch the fire die. She can remember Claire when young, defiant in a party dress, refusing to come to the party. "You can't *make* me do it, you can't," Claire would say, then throw herself back on the bed. Why can't we just be friends, Joanna wonders, why should it be so difficult? She herself has always had the gift of friendship, an easy back-and-forth with strangers at her B&B. But Claire resists her, adamant; Claire is having none of it and drinking ice water, not wine . . .

The fire is red embers now; Joanna shuts her eyes. She tries to remember this living room full, the noise and bustle of guests when she was five or six years old and wanting to serve canapés or, later, drinks. She would go from visitor to visitor and do her lit-tle curtsy or simply stand there waiting till they looked down and noticed and she'd ask, "Would you like another canapé? Can I freshen up your drink?"

This was the expression her father taught her for parties, and it always got a smile. If a guest said, "Thanks, I'm fine," there would be nothing else to do, but if the guest said, "Thank you, yes" then Joanna had to ask what kind of drink was in the glass and remember which was which. "She's the life of the party," they said to her parents. "A real little charmer, that one. I bet you two are proud."

They were, they said, they both were proud, and Joanna can remember her parents in the living room, standing together and greeting the guests and making people welcome turn by turn. Then she would play her waitress-game and try to be a charmer, a real little firecracker, that one, and then be sent upstairs. If she couldn't fall asleep she'd creep to the heat register, and with her ear against the grate would listen to laughter, the chattering adults and din of the party beneath. Or, later, on the top stair of the stairwell, wearing the nightgown with the red cherry pattern and trying to determine from the noise below whose voice belonged to whom . . .

On the screen of her shut eyelids, now, she sees her father lounging in the doorway, resplendent in his white jacket and bow tie and straw hat. He has just returned from—or perhaps is just about to leave for; in the instant of this memory Joanna cannot tell—the track. She catches the faint whiff of gin. She does not recognize it yet, will only learn years later that the high sweet acid odor of his breath is the tang of gin and bitters, or gin with just a splash of vermouth or gin straight up with a twist. She cannot remember him falling-down drunk or anything other than courtly, ever, but always with a flask or cocktail shaker near to hand. "The juniper berry," he tells her, "it's the gift God gave to men. That, and the apple," he says. "Nothing like them for sweetness," he says.

He smells of lilac vegetal and talcum powder and, if he is returning, sweat; he bends down toward her and holds out his arms and scoops her up while she wriggles and giggles and kisses her smack on the cheek. "How's my precious J-J girl?" he asks her. "How's my little firecracker? Have you been behaving yourself?" If he's leaving she says, always, "Daddy, take me with you," and if he's returning she asks, always, "Daddy, how much did you win?"

"Enough for an ice cream, J-J," he says. "Later." Then he pats her on the bottom and deposits her on the floor again although she

keeps her arms, or tries to, locked around his neck. On summertime Saturday mornings he takes her for an ice cream to the Dairy
Queen, or the Saratoga Dairy Bar, walking down Broadway and
holding her hand and, if she is very tired, hoisting her up on his
shoulders and telling her hold tight now, hold tight as you can to
the reins.

Then Claire was born, and David, and then the four of them
would walk down Broadway, her brother riding pickaback, so she
would walk in front. For all the years of her childhood and, later,
growing up and growing away from her parents—their constant
squabble, their drawn lines—Joanna took his side of things, ador-
ing his swagger and laughter, his gallantry and ease. Her father
was a charming man and she loved him very much and all their
guests did also, but her mother was unmoved. "For better or for
worse, in sickness and in health. That's what we agreed to when
we married," said Alice, "and nowadays everything's worse . . ."

She had tried to take her mother's side, trying to see the car
crash as the last in a series of insults, the final reproof and slap in
the face—but all Joanna felt was sorrow and all she was was
bereft. When she tasted her own first dry martini in a bar on East
69th Street she understood on the instant that *this* was what her
father drank, and the boy who had been plying her with gin was
rewarded when he took her to his room not with compliance but
tearfulness, not with sex but rage. You cannot be angry at dead
men, she knows, you should save anger for the living; you cannot
hate a corpse. "I don't," her mother answered when she asked, "I
don't really hate him. It's only there's a kind of peace in knowing
it's all over now, and it can't happen again."

It could; it did; it would happen again. For years she could not
enter a car without an image of her father and some stranger with
her skirt hiked up, the two of them driving away from a party with
a thermos of martinis and smashed into a tree. When he died she
had been seventeen and old enough to know how long her parents
had been angry at each other, unhappy in the life they shared yet
unwilling to divorce. Theirs had been a tight-lipped silence or the
noise of argument and, on her father's part, evasion and, on her

mother's, disdain. When Joanna asked, years later, while her own first marriage was falling apart, if she herself ever thought of divorce, her mother said, "Of course not, no, there were many things I thought about but divorce wasn't one of them. Maybe revenge. It wasn't the way we behaved back then, or at least not the way *I* behaved. So not divorce, no, that was never in the cards."

"Why not?" she'd persisted. "If you were—incompatible."

"David," Alice said.

"David?"

"You were old enough. Claire too. But David wasn't old enough," she said.

Part Two

IV

1916

The Vagabonds' progress has been unimpeded: thirty-five miles since they broke camp at breakfast and nothing untoward. They have been under way, now, four days. That this region of the country should have well-paved arteries was no revelation to Edison, or less a revelation than a confirmation of his long-held faith in the all-leveling impulse toward advancement in and of the populace: *take that tree, that hillside, that mountain stream and cut and level and ford it.* He laughed. He must remember to tell Henry of the happy nature of such wordplay, the accident of nomenclature that caused them to ford the ford in a Ford, though regrettably not as yet with.

Nor would it be affordable for most. Their caravan, if neither ostentatious nor excessive, was—it must be admitted—not small. Those who journeyed to America while it was yet a newfound land took what comfort they might find in numbers, the solidarity of fellowship: not for the Pilgrims isolation except insofar as enforced. And, later, with the pioneers, those wagon trains that flourished did so at least in part because of size: the more the merrier. *My wheel has broken, brother; might I pattern a new one on yours? My jerky and biscuit have furnished a saltwater banquet for rats; might I sit at table with you, o dear companion, instead?*

So they traveled in some style. Not wasteful or inordinate, he told Minna when she queried him and he was taking his husbandly leave; we do not shave at breakfast time when breaking camp, nor dress for dinner routinely. We're roughing it, old girl. Next year perhaps you'll join us and we'll smooth the rough-hewn edge of what behavior might offend you: the tall tales and the stories and the old men being jocular and sleeping on the ground. John Burroughs in particular enjoys a salty story and we trade them turn by turn; do you know the one, I asked him, about the farmer's son who pushed the outhouse off the cliff? Burroughs had not heard the tale, or claimed not to remember, and so I gave him the rest of the jest, the way the farmer asks his son, *Now answer me and tell the truth, did you push that outhouse off the cliff?* The boy admits it: *Yes sir, I did, I cannot tell a lie.* So the farmer wales away with strap and stick and when finally the beating is done the tearful young fellow protests: *But Father, you instructed me always to be truthful, to behave as did George Washington and confess all error, as when he felled the cherry tree.* Then the father says, *That's true enough, but George Washington's dear papa wasn't in the tree!*

Again, Thomas Edison laughed. The day had been fine, the end of it tapering down now to dusk and this the thirty-first of August: still seasonably warm but not intolerably so. A small breeze kept the flies at bay, and yonder was the appetizing prospect of their evening meal, the dining tents readied already by Peter Barclay and efficient Yukio and Sam. The cookstoves were unloaded and the fires being built. Here, concluded Edison—the self-declared Magellan of their journey, the map reader and route planner— they would pass the night.

What vagabonding have they not between them undertaken; what pleasures remain still in store! They have planned to reconnoiter with their fellow tramp at Plattsburgh, where Henry Ford will join them, or so he promises. Drawing daybook out of pocket and the pen he carried constantly, Edison perused a passage entered there: *We must consider volume as an aspect of preparedness. At what point in a caravan does size itself prove counterproductive, a liability, not asset? The very dinosaurs outsized themselves, requiring more by way of sustenance than their great bulk could forage for; the bending reed outlasts the hurricane that fells a mighty oak.*

For lunch he'd taken toast and milk, for breakfast much the same. A man should eat sparingly, sparingly, and all the more so if inclined to bulk, as Edison inclined. Old Burroughs required no such caution, a bundle of sticks in a waistcoat: mere gristle and sinew and bone. But whether this was lifelong habit or a function of increasing age, John Burroughs matched him, slice for meager slice, whereas Firestone mocked their abstemiousness and slathered butter on. A pup, a whelp, a rich man's boy—but good company nevertheless.

Young William Dancey approached. The boy was whispering something; Edison cupped his right ear. "Say what?"

"Have you been to Saratoga previously, sir, have your travels brought you here?"

He shook his head.

"Let me commend it. A pleasant town. Most pleasing. My uncle keeps a cottage hereabouts."

"And do you wish to see him?"

"The news of our arrival, sir, precedes us."

"As everywhere," said Edison. Did not the birds send out a notice of their caravan's approach and then fall silent up above; did not the ground-based creatures scurry and scuttle away? The wilderness, he had observed, is a conduit for gossip unequaled by the telegraph . . .

Young Dancey proffered inaudible answer.

"So everywhere," continued Edison, "we have these journalists. Photographers. And why not your uncle, my boy?"

The driver smiled. "He does hope to make your acquaintance."

" 'Together with his sisters and his cousins and his aunts,' " said Edison. He was feeling jocular. He liked the young man's countenance. "We'll give the sisters and cousins to Firestone, the aunts to Burroughs, eh?"

"I'll set additional place at your table then. Thank you kindly, sir."

They had sported in this fashion last year equally and would again, again. The proposition that they should explore the Adirondacks had been Ford's; he had been primum mobile, although not of the party tonight—rather the way, mused Edison, that those who hold a patent for invention need not supervise an installation or fine-tune each engine itself. When he and Henry traveled first in California, from San Francisco down to San Diego—by private railroad car and then automobile, with Luther Burbank and the potentates, with name-days in their honor and prearranged festivity and the wearisome attentiveness of those who think proximity to power is itself a form of achievement— when they had had enough of speechifying, sanctimony and affairs of state, the friends together had declared a preference for roughing it, for the simplicity of bygone days and a return to nature's cradle. No railroad cars hereafter, no fawning hoteliers!

He shrugged himself out of his coat. Hard to remember now and bootless to debate which of them first proposed a caravan, who added the idea of wandering for its own sake and not with an end view or target in mind—but only the pleasures of camping together, of friendship unalloyed by staff or the importunities of business. And these pleasures proved (no better word for it!) keen. Keen the enjoyment that Edison took in his naps in his clothing and hammock; keen the enjoyment of cutting down trees and pitting himself against stopwatch and comrade; keen their shared pleasure in the close examination of waterfall and sluice-way and mill-site, and keen the enjoyment of flower and rock . . .

He had to admit it: old Burroughs knew much. Give the man a net and hammer and he returned from his forays replete. Give the man a double-bladed axe and, hey presto, down the tree! Approach a hollow log with bees and John the naturalist, the expert on behavior, would discourse at such fervent length that Edison found himself grateful to be, for all practical purposes, deaf. A nod, a knowing wink sufficed by way of answer, since any half-formed query would occasion such a lecture that the others of the party would despair of its completion and, when the bee-lover turned his back to point to some particularly salient feature of the apiary—a honeycomb, a drove of drones—those who had to hear him out would shrug and roll their eyes.

The occasion of their friendship was itself a form of fun. Old man Burroughs, with his prophet's beard, his memories of Whitman and his tracts against the modern age, his vigorous espousal of the virtues of simplicity, his jeremiads as to engines and the American landscape despoiled, his eloquent inveighing at the very *idea* of internal combustion—this voice in the wilderness trumpeting was one Ford determined to silence or at least to sway. Clever Henry sent Burroughs a car. My Model T, he said, is at your service, sir; please know your enemy's nature before you are certain it cannot prove friend. I respect your writings far too much to try to contravene them but would respect your opinion even more if experience-based; drive Tin Lizzie till you warrant if she be real or fool's gold.

And Burroughs was enthralled. No city swell or society boy could have been more elated than John-of-the-hills, no young spark more afire with the pleasures of the wheel. Later, they would joke of it: Saul on the road to Tarsus, King Constantine before the cross—no convert more committed to this latter-day true Grail. So it was wholly natural they should motor up from Orange and collect old Burroughs at his farm and then motor on. *"How are you, John?" "How are you, Tom?"* and the briefest of pauses for loading and then hail and away . . .

Young Harvey Firestone by contrast embraced his creature comforts. Last night in Albany, for instance, he was unable to withstand the offer of a hotel room and shower, and this morning appeared fresh-shaved and glistening, his moustache trim, the sheen of his boots newly bright. When Edison reminded him that the hallmarks of the vagabond were stubble and dullness, he laughed. And then, as so often surprising them with his memory's acuity, he offered up a tercet from Burroughs himself:

> *To the woods and fields or to the hills*
> *There to breathe their beauty like the very air*
> *To be not a spectator of, but a participator in it all!*

"Not bad," said Burroughs placidly. "I meant it then, I mean it now."

"Accordingly," said Firestone, "I shaved."

"And why?"

"To be, as you put it, 'a participator in it all!' and not a mere spectator."

"You refer to your beauty, I take it?"

"With a face like mine," said Firestone—disarming them, as was his wont, with modesty—"a moustache to cover it helps."

So Edison, clean-shaven, and Burroughs aping Father Time and Firestone with his pruned facial hair made a sampler for their supper guests: an empty plate, a half-filled one, a full. It had been several decades since John Burroughs viewed his own ungirdled chin; the eldest of their party would celebrate eighty next year. He was ten years Tom Edison's senior, and more than thirty Firestone's, and they accorded him due deference though in truth he was their equal if not better in the woods. When the guests arrived—William Dancey's uncle, and his wife and daughter—they saluted Burroughs first. Mr. Dancey and his wife, Elise, were jovial, both, and furnished with affable chatter, and they commended the three vagabonds on their cuisine and equipage and inquired after Henry Ford—"We're to meet at Plattsburgh," Burroughs said—and spoke in detail of Gentleman Johnny Burgoyne and the way the colonials planned their campaign (Mr. Dancey had been in the army, and he drew a map in the campground dust of how and where the British had been snookered after Schuylerville) and of the healthful waters that natives call the Springs.

It was hard not to notice the girl. Whereas the father had grown portly and his consort overflowed her stays, the Dancey daughter was lissome: bright, light. Her gaze, though modest, was direct, her eyes a clear gray-green. The ringlets of her hair were brown and her cheeks were petal-strewn, a hint of rose on porcelain; the lips suggested ardor though as yet they had not practiced it; she was, she owned, sixteen. Old Edison felt stirred by sweet remembrance of his vanished youth, old Burroughs much the same. Young Firestone pulled up his chair.

They were sitting under tamaracks. The tamarack tree, so Edison knew—for Burroughs was extensive, not to say exhaustive in instruction, and for twenty minutes he discoursed upon the salient characteristics of deciduous and nondeciduous trees—is the sole member of the family of pine that sheds its leaves in autumn; the English call it larch. This gives a special poignancy, said Burroughs, to its foliage; all else endures the wintry blast but tamarack needles will yellow and soften and fall. There be tamarack swamps to the north. Just so—the Sage of Slabsides knelt and sifted the thick humus at their feet—will we in turn be carpeting for what must follow after; our children's children, Tom, will prosper where we rot. That girl there, for example—and Burroughs bent his wild white head, then ceased to speak, or ceased to say what Edison could hear. *That girl there....*

As a signal of his good intentions and soon-to-follow arrival, Ford had sent his man ahead: the Japanese cook Yukio, with hatchet and honed knives. It was delightful and informative to watch the fellow work. Since carrot and beef shank and onion cannot be rendered uniform—retaining in their very nature that irregularity which some say is the spice of life—he cut and chopped and trimmed. Variety of size and shape, although intrinsic to the provender, did not deter the cook; the rate at which he diced those irregular foodstuffs before him proved more rapid and less wasteful than would have been a machine. Last trip Henry had proposed a wager; he'd said, take these fifty-weight potatoes and divide them equally and give my half to Yukio and yours to this shaped cutting box. Then let's see which peels and slices them with greater yield.

Why not five hundred, Edison had countered, or, come to that, five thousand? Because, said Ford—the sponsor of interchangeable parts and a massed assembly line—we are not feeding multitudes. Our party this night numbers thirty, or at the most thirty-five. What's good for the goose is good for the gander, Edison had teased him, but Henry shook his head. No, no, it's mere indulgence; I think of Yukio as expert in the culinary arts and not as a factory worker; there is only one of him here.

And yet he did seem multiple, so rapid with cleaver and chop-block that his hands were but a blur. His shaved head gleamed, his hairless forearms too where he rolled back his sleeves. There were assistants to help him (fetching water from the nearby spring, straining it through cheesecloth and thereafter boiling it, and a sous-chef for the sauces and another for the pastry) but the fellow gave no vocal instruction, or no orders that proved audible—a nod of the head here, a shake of it there—assembling the repast alone. He mounded fruit and legumes and the dressed birds on the serving trays with lightninglike celerity, seeming never once to need to buttress what in other hands might, wobbling, topple or from other platters fall. Such expertise, thought Edison, is worthy of you, Ford . . .

The vagabonds gathered to table and settled themselves to the meal. Having said a heartfelt grace, the men raised their tumblers and drank. These excursions were intended to remind those who conjoined in them of simple pleasures, early times, and that one need not be archaic to reside in Arcady. John Burroughs in particular said his old bones required motion or they'd seize up and grow immobile as though calcified by dew; the exercise I take, he said, is more necessity than choice. But it has been my habit now for decades and I could no sooner cease such bodily exertion than cease breathing altogether; indeed, the two are one.

"We have a home nearby," the elder Dancey announced to his hosts. "A farmhouse you'd be welcome to, should you prefer its rustic comfort to the fields."

"How so?" inquired Firestone.

"We keep it furnished now for guests. It is my mother-in-law's."

"And how near do you mean by 'nearby'?"

"It *was* my mother's," said the lady. "But she has grown infirm and lives in our house nowadays and will not relinquish the farm."

"How so?" asked Firestone again. "And where?"

"It is abandoned of necessity," Mrs. Dancey explained. "She cannot climb the stairs."

Beyond the tent flap darkness fell, and as it descended so too did the level of grog in the glass, the lowering soft-lidded glance of the girl.

"A farm"—the elder Dancey embroidered the theme—"that serves us now for grazing just behind that stand of split-leaf maple. And fields we keep planted for sentiment's sake. The skies are good to Saratoga," he concluded. "They look down on us benignly, do they not?"

His remark, as it was intended to, furnished a new topic for discussion. It is rather *we* who view *them* benignly, said Thomas Edison; the skies do not "look down," as you would have it, sir, so much as we look up. I hold man to be the measure of all things—

or, more particularly, to be he who does the measuring; our Creator's elsewhere occupied and need not be bothered with plumb line and rule. He does not bring a yardstick to the task.

Mrs. Dancey appeared—or strove to appear—not to notice, since the irreverence of the great man's observation, while not a blasphemer's precisely, might nonetheless have been construed provocative and as a challenge to complacence in his guests. He liked to do this, the inventor, and was forever stirring up the hornet's nest of piety to discover what might fly out. "God created man in his own image," Edison was wont to say. "And man, being a gentleman, returned the compliment."

The others were well used to this and continued unperturbed. Such a nighttime view, said Burroughs, is not possible in cities, nor will it long adorn the countryside, which too must prove contaminate by coal soot and the detritus of modernity: rust, dust. Or so I fear, the old man said, or so I sometimes think. That clarity of evening light which we thought to be a standard is a standard that our children's children will not know. The steady hum of engines and—I do not exempt you, Tom—the wire and the wireless will soon enough make silence be but a thing remembered; no true wilderness nor quiet anymore.

"Or anywhere?" asked Harvey Firestone.

"Or anywhere," said Burroughs.

Now there was silence in the tent. Young Dancey stood before them, his fiddle in one hand, his bow in the other. "Suggestions, gentlemen? Ladies? A particular tune that you'd like us to play?"

"'Skip to My Lou,'" said Edison. And then 'Green Grow the Rushes, Ho!' I want something lively, not mournful."

"I want something *lovely*," Firestone said, and sighed, and shut his eyes. "A song, Peter? What would you sing?"

Peter Barclay was Firestone's man. He had been in the employ of the family since aught-six, a decade since, and traveled everywhere with Firestone—whom he called equally master and friend. The former did the latter service: arranging his clothing and schedule, setting out his refreshments and correspondence, presenting his own person as a kind of shield or buffer between the wealthy Firestone and an importunate world. In consequence he had free access to society, the hurly-burly of companionable encounter, and may better be described as secretary than valet. His was the second opinion his employer sought and valued in matters of horseflesh and commerce and waistcoats and wine. Whether from his naturally gregarious and all-embracing nature, that characteristic wide-ranging American enthusiasm, or whether from the civilizing nurture of his benefactor's fortune, Barclay combined the oil and water of the well-bred swell and common man, and did so with an effortless insouciance that those without it call "charm."

He was well-favored, well-proportioned, a great favorite with the weaker sex,whom he in turn would favor with a democratic inclusiveness, embracing them not so much collectively as turn by turn. There were Mary and Susan and Jane. There were Lisa and Margaret and Kate. There were others whose eyes he remembered, or their teeth and scent and limber limbs, but of whose present whereabouts he had to admit to ignorance, and though he could recall down to the nicest detail the details of their dalliance he was not in full possession of their names. He was, in short, a rake. And that wandering eye of his, once fixed, would gleam with bright persuasiveness and fairly illumine the object it lit on—in this instance, it goes without saying, the Dancey girl, whose glass he filled twice, thrice.

"A song?" repeated Firestone. "Will you oblige us, friend?"

"I will," said Peter. "Yes."

Such entertainment, however, although requested, was postponed. There would be no music forthcoming just yet, for Dancey and his uncle had engaged in politics. Young William was martial, or wished to become so, and he yearned to fight in the Great War and show those European namby-pambies how to stand and fight. Woodrow Wilson is my man, he said, he'll get us over there.

But once you've been a soldier, said his uncle, you relish the bloodletting less. Trust me, Bill, we're well out of it here. Then he turned to Peter Barclay and inquired, What think you of our cider? It comes from my own orchards, and the Saratoga apple is the sweetest one for pressing, is it not? I have not pressed it yet, said Barclay, therefore am ignorant of its delights. Drink deep, the uncle said, let's hoist a glass to the health of my daughter. Standing, he suited the action to word. They drank.

Becomingly, the maiden blushed and said, her handkerchief in her right hand, "It's nothing, nothing at all to concern you, but I must get some air."

And then she stepped away.

Now Edison and Burroughs resumed their badinage. This too was habitual, frequent between them; they liked to tell stories and jokes. Encouraged perhaps by the view of the girl, her white back small and fading in the ardent, all-embracing night, the inventor asked the naturalist, "Do you know the definition, John, of 'virgin forest'?"

"I do," said the self-styled old rascal—whose store of wit seemed somehow to be new-replenished daily, and whom in any case the carrot soup had fortified. "It's a place where, so to speak, the hand of man has not set foot."

They laughed. Next Peter Barclay gave a spirited rendition of "Coming Through the Rye" and the mournful "Barbry Allen." His voice was sweet, untutored, yet in intonation correct. There was laughter and applause, and then the talk resumed. The men began a discussion of warfare and its current state in Europe. "As to the Jews," said Thomas Edison, "I share Henry's opinion, as you know, and believe them to be profiting—shamelessly, shamefully—from honest people's need."

"Wartime is profit-time," Firestone said.

"*Prophet*-time," said Burroughs. "And not a happy prospect for the wilderness, for wildness . . ."

"By the waters of Hudson I sat down and wept." Firestone smiled at his own jest and thought to point out the affinity of "Babylon" and "babble on," but then he thought the better of it and did not. "You cannot blame the mercantiles entirely. They also choose 'To be not a spectator of, but a participator in it all!' To visit Saratoga and enjoy—as we do—country air."

"Country matters," Burroughs said.

Unbuttoning his waistcoat, the elder Dancey opined that this part of the nation was second to none in its actual yield as well as in the prospect of fertility. There be a future here, he said, and while he delivered himself of a speech as to the splendors of the planted grass and, with specific reference to horses, husbandry, the chance—were one to take it—of speculation's profit, the good companions noticed Barclay—not furtive but deliberate—push back his chair at table and rise and leave the ring of light and vanish in the outer dark to which the girl had gone.

V

1916

Of what transpired in the humid night Peter Barclay spoke no word. He kept his own counsel throughout. Although voluble by nature and by contrast in this instance the more noticeably reticent, he made no answer when asked; neither direct nor offhand inquiry elicited response. "A gentleman," he'd say, and, falling silent, shake his head. "No gentleman . . ." and then again withdraw. Day after day he remained—on this one topic—mute.

Yet Firestone who knew him well could not fail not to notice how the fellow's gaze would wander and smile arrive unbidden. Pressing fingernail tips to his shut eyes, he pursed his lips and beamed. As though memory had fixed on some most pleasing inward spectacle on which he looked with evident and repeated satisfaction, he rubbed at his cheeks with his palms. Too, the sonority of his heaved sighs made speech itself irrelevant; here was a pup in love.

Or so, at any rate, said Edison to Burroughs and then Henry Ford, when at last he joined them in the town of Plattsburgh. You call him a whelped pup, said Burroughs; was not the bitch in heat? Speak civilly, said Ford, himself the most civil of speakers, or I will not hear you out; what went on between them, friends, and what do you make of it now?

Peter Barclay was busy with baggage; the travelers sat in the shade. They occupied their camp chairs, drawn close to facilitate conference and render it inaudible to those who wished to pry. Although vigorous and sturdy yet, they could not keep from consciousness of the season's turning; it was September 5. Tomorrow the four would go south through Vermont—through the towns of Burlington, Shelburne, Middlebury, Rutland, Wallingford, East Dorset, Manchester—and make their camp near Arlington. The year's vagabonding was soon to be done, and though they talked of and were planning a renewal in the year to come, the plans were but provisional and would in fact be canceled: their own well-being and that of the world seemed more than ever at risk. No fool like an old fool, the old saying goes, and yet the sojourners were provident men: such a reckoning had to be settled and such bills marked *Paid*.

Again Ford asked, what happened, and what do you make of it now? Tom Edison cupped his good ear. John Burroughs repeated the question, but shouting, and Edison nodded and smiled. I cannot be precise, responded the inventor, and this as you know is vexatious to me; we must attempt precision even if conjectural, even when we speak of matters of the heart. The heart, said Burroughs, or the glands; which think you, Tom, proved operational here?

Where, *where?* said Ford again; I was not with you, remember, and need to be informed. The particulars, gentlemen, please.

So Firestone and Edison and Burroughs spoke about the dinner party, the farm in Saratoga and the girl with whom—or so the companions deduced—Barclay whiled away the hours of that night. Next morning his cot showed forth unrumpled and his tent pristine. At ten o'clock when he appeared he was wearing what he'd worn to eat at their previous shared repast, though considerably disarrayed and in more than one spot stained. Through the long day's sport he yawned, taking little part in their festivities and pleading a headache when chaffed; you must excuse him, observed Edison, winking, he didn't sleep a wink.

Of William Dancey's family—the garrulous uncle and plump silent aunt—there was no further trace. And of the girl herself—whose given name they could not now recall—there remained only the lingering scent of a languorous presence at table, her beauty untainted by commerce or age. You will forgive me, said John Burroughs, but I understand what bewitched him, and had I been our Peter I'd not have been more careful; it's a thousand pities, Henry, you were not there to see. He shaped the air with his long fingers into an hourglass, then smacked his wizened lips. He made the joke he'd made before, the one about flint on a stone starting fire, and fire in the stony heart of their fellow-traveler's man . . .

Of the Vagabonds Ford was briskest by far, the least suscepti-
ble. Too, he'd been absent from the scene as such and had no fond
remembrance thereof; we are the more inclined to sanction lewd
behavior in which earlier we joined. Therefore, clapping his hands
on his knee-knobs, he stood; inserting his hands in his pockets, he
walked. The men took a turn down the siding where railroad cars
awaited them, and while they were inspecting track Ford mused
aloud, well, possibly, well, yes. But did he take precautions; was
he careful, do you think? Such practicality—not to say matter-of-
factness—was characteristic of the man; he was, his fellows knew,
chary of soft sentiment and cautious to a fault.

Yet caution and Barclay, Firestone claimed, would be far
stranger bedfellows than a young man and a beautiful girl; he
threw it to the winds. "Threw what," John Burroughs asked, and
Firestone said "Caution" and, again, he smiled.

Be that as it may, said Henry Ford, the question is what need
we do if anything, what's expected of us now?

Expected, said Edison, tapping finger to ear to signify that perhaps he had not heard correctly what perhaps the other said, we
don't know as there's anything expected, do we, John? And re-
volved his great bald head toward the white-maned dome of his
companion, and in unison they nodded and then in unison shook.

"You find the situation funny?" Ford asked. "You find it a
source of amusement?"

"Don't be so rigid, Henry."

"Stiff," said Edison. "I stand at attention. *Stiff!*"

"As the Bishop said to the Actress," said Burroughs, and the
two men clapped each other on their upright backs.

To such bait Ford would not rise. Although he could well have
spoken at length, this afternoon he elected restraint. Were he of
Burroughs's antic disposition or Tom Edison's blunt suggestive-
ness, he might have pointed out that limp behavior would indeed
have been much preferable to rigid: the wandering eye is a prelude
to trespass and must not be blinked.

Firestone sighed. From his right boot, with a rag for the purpose, he removed a mud smear and wiped bright leather clean. He

discoursed briefly on temptation and the duty to resist it, the self-policing requisite to men of position and wealth. We are prone to error since the fall; we embrace unoriginal sin. Yet where unbridled license reigns and where the man in power exercises it without restraint, then how to say democracy is better than the despot's realm and who to call it less licentious than the Frenchified *droit du seigneur*? Our revolution was fought against just such ascendancy; is not each citizen equal to all others and in theory (as well as in factory practice) both master and acknowledged mistress of the empire of self?

He and Ford and Burroughs had engaged beforehand in this argument, yet Burroughs disagreed with them and said all nature consists of dependency, subordination, rank. We pretend to pure equivalence but it is unnatural. Similarity, yes, similarity I grant you, and that root and trunk and leaf and branch belong to the one tree. But the arrangement, Harvey, is hierarchical and you yourself cannot deny it; the man who oversees the overseer of the factory is godlike in ascendancy over the third worker from the corner. It is a ladder, not line.

Yet if that worker shirk, Ford interrupted, if he be corrupt or she prove careless the edifice comes crashing down; the least is indispensable to the largest component thereof. When we speak of a linked system we are no stronger finally than is the weakest link. And *that's* why I embrace what you scoff at as mere prudence—a good behavior, a decent comportment—and that's why I insist there be no rutting here. The wormy apple will destroy the peck if left long enough in the barrel to rot; let looseness continue undeterred and everything is lost.

October 30, 1916

   Dear Harvey Firestone, Esq.,

   You may not remember me, and I beg pardon in advance for troubling your business hours with business that's not properly yours but I don't know how else to proceed with the matter or whom else to address. You did us the great honor two months since of visiting, of coming to our campsite outside of Saratoga Springs and spending the night with several companions whom you called the Vagabonds, and a member of that party—the one who sang—whose name I never caught is someone I would willingly contact if you could assist me in this business, please.

My nephew William commended our campsite and would no doubt be privy to the information but he is gone to train to fight abroad and cannot be contacted, so I am told, for weeks. Nor would I wish to involve you except insofar as necessary to procure the information. It is a matter of some delicacy, having to do with my daughter, and I don't wish to trouble you with the particulars thereof. Some urgency also, it seems. But Elizabeth herself is ignorant—a willful girl, resolutely discreet—and either unable or unwilling to furnish the gentleman's name. He was five foot ten or thereabouts, brown-haired and well-proportioned, and since it is with him I'd speak I'll trouble you no further but await your prompt response.

In the hope that you and yours will soon return to this region where many who remember you await with eagerness the prospect of reunion I am, sir, yours sincerely

William Dancey
163 North Broadway
Saratoga Springs
New York

November 30, 1916
Harvey Firestone, Esq.,
Last month I asked a question of you, at the office address furnished by your vintner here, and now am resolved to do so again. I have not had an answer; perhaps you are away. No doubt you are busy with pressing affairs, both public and private, of commerce and state—but it is not polite, not gentlemanly to ignore the letter of someone who not three months ago served as your host and who requires assistance.

I am a blunt man, sir, as you no doubt remember, and I will be blunt with you: our daughter is with child. Please write me at your earliest convenience the name of the man at your side. He sang for us;

*I plan to make him do so again and in the meantime remain yours
truly*

William Dancey
163 North Broadway
Saratoga Springs
New York

Time passed. Ford hoped that it might pass according to the
workweek and the sequence of the balance sheet (more profitable
with each succeeding quarter), and not that inner calendar whose
completion requires nine months. Elsewhere there was loud alarm
and much business to tend to: a conspiracy of financiers, those bee-
tle browed moneylenders and mercantile grubbers on Wall Street
and those Jews he so disdained who filled their fleece-lined pockets at the trough of America's banks. The "Wall Street Tories" and
"armor-plate patriots" hoped for war at any price, whereas his
peace ship, *Oscar II*, ran fruitlessly aground. These matters
weighed on him—he was considering, for instance, an entry into
politics—yet always in Ford's busy mind there proceeded the bill
of particulars and of payment due.

It was winter now. The autumn leaves had gone. Aware of what
might well eventuate a season thereafter as issue, the millionaire
collected himself and bade Firestone approach.

Blithely, politely, his associate did so; blithely, politely, he pulled
at his pants leg and smoothed out the crease from the cuff. Of late
in the office at Dearborn he had been occupied with rubber, preoccupied with how best to produce it in guaranteed abundance
and deliver the product with ease. The great thing is, he was convinced, to know beforehand how the supply may be made sys-
tematic, and Ford approved of this and urged his younger
colleague to apply the selfsame rationale to matters of the single
body as opposed to the collective; why should we not behave, he
asked, as though the outcome of what seems like chance encounter may be prearranged? The River Rouge assembly, as he
was fond of saying, is a whole made of component parts, a ran-

dom-seeming sequence in the service of rigidity: predestined, preordained.

"Ordination?" Firestone asked. "Would you have me a subscriber to such indolence in action, such self-limiting progress as *ordination*? I had thought your every action militated, mili*tates* against such casual construction. It has been preplanned, admittedly, but you are the sole author of the planning and the system."

"Oh?"

"To your worker in the factory the assembled result may well be inconceivable; to your foreman dimly apprehensible . . ."

"Correct," said Ford.

"But surely you yourself can see it steadily and whole!"

This flattering diversion failed; Ford smiled and let it pass. Supervision in such matters enables strict morality; it is an adult's duty to watch children at their play. What some might label prurience in the engineer was instead, or so he told himself, precision; insatiable for knowledge, he could not bear not to know. The playful scene by now was distant both in time and place, and it might have been permissible to let the watcher blink: out of sight is out of mind. Yet rumored sport at the encampment worried Ford persistently and nipped at his heels, refusing to obey—as though rumor itself were an ill-trained dog—his repeated injunction: "Down, down!"

Harvey his "pup" was wearing tweeds and reading glasses, every inch the courtly gentleman and only by association guilty of a dalliance; Barclay remained on the payroll and had not been dismissed. Meantime, Firestone bruited a business plan. He had notebook and fountain pen in hand; he was organizing information on the rubber plant and speculating bravely on what it might entail to harvest the material and where to establish plantations. To organize the supply, they agreed, would be to confirm the demand, and Firestone intended—though the outline of his project was at this stage but sketchy—to institute a system of production and delivery that might benefit the commonweal: a public husbandry. So natives would be nourished by the very plant they planted and—happy accident of opposition!—enlarged by what they cropped. When the young visionary took, as it were, the rhetorical bit between teeth he could speak and speak without pause for breath, expanding phrase to paragraph and paragraph to page with a facility for utterance that swept doubt before it like dust.

Yet on the matter of indulgence he proved silent still. In private interview the orator proved scarcely more forthcoming on his man's behalf than earlier had been the case in Plattsburgh and September. Though he chatted willingly of natives and their rubber plants, of the fertility in Ecuador and tropical heat of Brazil — though he continued in this vein till lunch he mined no other quarry and tilled no other field. When Ford at length and interview's end positioned the "Plantation" file in its wooden cabinet and inquired of the girl again, again he met with opposition, the same pursed moustachioed lips.

"He has done nothing," Firestone said, "to which I am privy or would not in the presence of ladies repeat."

"Then why not speak of it?"

"Because there's so little to say!"

"Say on . . ."

"I *did* receive a letter. Two."

"From?"

"From the girl in question's father. But he was uncivil, and what he wrote me failed to signify . . ."

"Might I look at the letters?"

"Unhappily, no. They struck me as presumptuous, and I tossed the things aside."

"Presumptuous?"

"Requesting information to which he was not entitled" — Firestone stood, capping his pen, collecting his briefcase — "and of which he had no need. With a whiff of the blackmailer also . . ."

"Sit one more minute, will you?" Ford rallied and moved to retain him. "Let us call your Barclay in to join this conference. He waits outside?"

"He does."

"Invite him, if you please."

And so Peter Barclay came in. His shirt was pressed, his suit new-brushed, his brown shoes polished to the point of gleaming.

Yet the man's posture was visibly strained, and he stood at shaken attention till his employer pointed to an empty chair. Silent, the libertine sat.

Henry Ford regarded the ceiling. Then he remonstrated with the air, reminding it (or so it seemed, his eyes half-closed, his expression speculative) how their reputations—not to mention that of the nameless she who had occasioned this interview—must remain unsullied. Or else, he said, we cannot have free access to the countryside, to such continued vagabonding as has made our party welcome wherever we elect to travel; next year, for example, we hope to go south, and southern gentry are notorious for umbrage in the issue of honor assaulted, and all the more so, it goes without saying, if the honor assaulted is that of their issue as such. Having said that it goes without saying, however, the elder repeated himself: they keep daughters safe.

"Agreed," said Firestone. "I am wholly in agreement with your admirable caution, sir." This emphasis on "sir" was lost on neither of the two, for in casual colloquy they used each other's names.

"Is there something you wish to report?" Ford asked of Peter Barclay. "Something you might better tell us?"

The deponent shook his head. As though sight itself were a duster, the engineer stared at the spot on his sleeve; there was nothing to do but accept, at face value, their young employee's word. All further questions seemed predictable, beside the point or at least too far after the fact to alter the fact of the matter, and he was weary, wanting tea, and made short work of this amorous business; he proposed to Firestone that they provide a gift.

"A gift?" said Harvey. "I'm not sure I follow." And Ford said, "Contrariwise, my friend, it's appropriate you lead."

"How so?"

"A cottage?" Ford inquired. "Was there not a cottage?" Taking silence and the fellow's flush on cheek as blushing acquiescence, he said to Firestone, "Very good. Let's buy it. Let's give it to the girl."

Peter Barclay demurred. "It's already in the family. 'Grandmother's place,' they call it."

"Oh?"

"It's her grandmother's house."

Of a sudden he appeared to see how this piece of privy infor-mation argued, if not intimacy, at least a degree of familiarity hith-erto unadmitted; that he should possess such knowledge suggested the possession of other knowledge also. "What else do you know?" Ford inquired, and if he were John Burroughs would have asked not what but whom, and this in the biblical sense.

"Excuse me, sir?"

"Answer him," Firestone warned.

"Oh, nothing special." Blushing full-bloom, Barclay smoothed his moustache. "Nothing very much."

"But?"

"Only that they spoke of Granny as unwilling to relinquish it, and Mr. Dancey offered up the use of the place."

"The use?" repeated Ford.

"If Mr. Edison or Mr. Burroughs wished to lie in comfort . . ."

"Scarcely their purpose."

"No, sir."

"But yours?"

Once more the man went mute. What happened in the cottage was not a matter of which he would speak, and grudgingly his interlocutors credited this reticence and determined to probe it no further. Instead Ford sent him from the room to tarry in the outer office, intending that he cool his heels and enjoining him to wait.

Alone together yet again, but in substantial agreement, the two men conferred. Now when Firestone recalled the letters sent by William Dancey, their contents seemed persuasive; once the girl became a mother—so the Vagabonds concluded—her child should be provided for in time and times to come. "A sum of money, possibly," the elder said, "sufficient to have purchased the cottage if it *had* been for sale. What think you, Harvey?"

Harvey thought. "Deposited to which account?"

"Not—what did you call him?—Dancey's. To hers, of course," said Ford.

"We could establish a fund," mused Firestone, "not for the girl herself to squander, not as a reward for *her...*"

"No. But for the child, if any..."

"Yes!"

"That her child and her child's children might be well provided for. Educated, clothed and fed..."

"Precisely so. An act of kindness, Henry..."

Thus in ten minutes it was done—a period of time, the magnate reflected, that might well have equaled that of the action itself. The engendering spurt of existence, he knew, requires at most a split second of contact; bright manhood's stream is but a droplet in that dark lake, the womb. And there are some who pay and pay, who spend a lifetime ministering to what a precipitate moment has precipitated: life. But he and Firestone were managers, both; the decision, once arrived at, was rapidly achieved.

"Agreed?" asked Ford.

"Agreed."

That night at dinner they conferred with Edison as to their shared intention. The Sage of Menlo Park was visiting his friends in Dearborn, and he concurred with their purpose and soon enough proposed a means whereby to implement the plan. The mood of the three men was one of easy conviviality, not to say collective relief, for there was self-interest also entailed; there had been music once again, schoolchildren playing violins, and Yukio the cook did honor to the fowl. At a given moment over cheese the eldest of the three averred that General Electric might prove a useful *vehicle*—at which word he winked at Ford—since we do not want our names too broadly bruited here. But General Electric is now a public company and anyone can buy; what I propose, he told them, is a gift of stock.

As his companions knew yet might not on the instant remember, the enterprise itself had been established thirty-eight long years before. It had been known at first as Edison Electric Light and then, in 1892, created from the merger of Edison General Electric Company and a chief competitor, the Thomson-Houston Electric Company. For 855 dollars apiece, said Edison—who did the calculation without benefit of pad or pen—we may purchase five shares each and consign them to the girl. The sum is not extravagant but neither is it negligible, an investment in the future and a cap tipped to the past. It will set her on her feet who on that starlit night so heedlessly had lifted them, and though Barclay must not know of or be party to philanthropy, it would, would it not, help their child?

And so it was transacted and so this little history came to its rapid close. Peter Barclay would remain in Firestone's employment but no longer as close confidant or in the role of valet; he was sent abroad. The checks were drawn and an account established by Henry Ford and Thomas Edison and Harvey Firestone in equal parts subscribed. John Burroughs they kept out of it, since he had few disposable funds and might not approve such settlement but consider it a bribe. In December 1916, fifteen prime shares of the company called General Electric were transferred to the central office of Adirondacks Savings Bank, for the benefit and use of Miss Elizabeth Dancey's heirs in trust. She herself was not to know of the transaction or be informed of its existence until two full years had elapsed, and it was stipulated that not Miss Dancey but solely her child and her child's children be the beneficiaries of this gift of stock.

The sum would grow.

Part Three

VI

2003

The snow stays unimportant, a white dusting only, and it brightens the slush at the side of the road and the roofs of the buildings in town. At nine o'clock the sun is up, and icicles are melting, and there is a good deal of traffic; delivery trucks clog the streets. The lawyer's office occupies the front-facing portion of the second floor of a three-story brick building overlooking Congress Park. The hallway lights are dim. They climb the wooden stairs.

Outside the smoked glass door of the offices of Beakes, Chilton, O'Dwyer & Rosenbaum stands a fig tree in a basket, its plastic leaves curled and shredding and its trunk built of interlaced vines. Gum wrappers and a half-smoked cigarette festoon what looks like Spanish moss in the tree's wicker container, and the whole effect is so dispiriting that Beakes's clients pause. One of the arms of the coat rack has sprung, and two umbrellas stand in the umbrella stand. Turn by turn they wipe their boots on the welcome mat; then David opens the door and the three of them walk in.

Inside there is a single desk and upholstered chairs and a series of sepia-toned photographs of Saratoga in the past. Men in top hats drink the healthful waters; men with wagons are ferrying ice. There are photos of horses and scenes of the spa and a poster of Lillian Russell; there is, however, no one at the desk. Irresolute, they wait; then David rings the bell again and Claire and Joanna sit down. A toilet flushes, and out of a door at their left a receptionist appears. Wearing a pink woolen suit, she sits, smooths freshly hennaed hair; she peers at them in silence while Claire says they have an appointment at nine-thirty with Joseph Beakes; is he in?

She nods.

"We're the Saperstone children," says David. "Alice Saperstone's . . ."

"We've got an appointment," Joanna repeats.

91

Again the woman lifts and drops her chin, then selects a "to-do" pad from the blotter and writes "*Laryngitis*" and points at her throat.

David smiles at her. "I'm sorry," he says, "you don't need to talk, but is Mr. Beakes in the office?"

"I am," the lawyer says.

He has appeared from the door on the right; he shakes their hands in sequence: David, Joanna and Claire. Then he pilots them into his office — a jumble of papers, a desk and four chairs — and says, "Sit down, sit down! I'm delighted you could make it, though not of course delighted by the reason we're all here." He too sits, then stands again: "Can I get you anything? A glass of water? Coffee? Tea?"

They thank him and decline. He is in fact a man they remember, a person they did know in childhood, and he is much older now but someone they still recognize: the one with the Polaroid camera at the dance recital, the one who would stand on the cottage front stoop wassailing on Christmas Eve. You're looking very well, he says, you've grown up, haven't you, and repeats how long it's been since they were all in the same town together.

Beakes's office occupies a corner, its windows facing east and south, and sunlight illumines the bookshelves: fat leather-bound volumes of judicial opinions and case histories, books of New York State statutes and the annual proceedings of the New York State Appellate Court. There are colored lithographs of horses wearing colors, and large framed photographs of the Saratoga Track. On the paneling behind his desk hang a series of diplomas and a mounted set of miniature silver snowshoes from the Lake Placid Winter Olympics Committee, with *Joseph Beakes: In Gratitude* incised along the base.

The lawyer's voice is high, mellifluous, and he takes pleasure in the sound of it. He inquires as to their journeys, their experience of travel yesterday and, in the case of those who flew, the promptness of their flights. Are they comfortable, he wants to know, and certain that they don't want tea, and then he leans back in his chair and folds his hands together and regards the three of them.

"Your mother Alice," he observes, "was one of my favorite people, one of my very favorites: a *lady*. Not, I'm afraid, a word we
can apply to many women nowadays." Inclining his head at
Joanna and Claire, he says, "I mean no disrespect, of course. But
as I don't need to tell you, my dears, I'm an old dog who can't be
taught new tricks; I've been in the habit of speaking my mind for
so long by now it isn't a habit I know how to break. She was a
lady, your mother, and though her death is no surprise I did want
to offer condolences and before we begin these proceedings say
how very sorry I am."

Beakes coughs. It is a dry cough, nonproductive, and he produces a handkerchief and wipes his cheeks, then mouth.
Meticulously, he adjusts his horn-rimmed glasses where they balance on his nose. "Proceedings," he repeats. His desk lamp functions on a swivel, and this too he adjusts. His every action, Claire
decides, has been rehearsed and repeated, as though years before
he had watched *Perry Mason* and patterned his behavior on a television lawyer: not the sleek impatient ones they feature now on
Law and Order or *The Practice* but the old-fashioned grandfatherly
lawyer, the one with the hair fringe and watch on a chain and
speculative manner of questioning a witness or examining the ceiling with his one good eye.

He produces three sets of documents on legal-size paper, their
cover sheets blue, and offers one to each of them and says, "With
your permission I'll read this to you—the salient passages anyhow,
the principal provisions. It's a simple will, straightforward enough,
and she was entirely clear about her intentions; you'll remember
that, I warrant, her *clarity*, her—how to put it?—*decisiveness* once she
had made up her mind. The world would be a better place if more of
us were like your mother, and her last will and testament is a model
of precision and simple enough to enact. The document is dated, as
you will observe, some seven years ago—10 January, 1996—and
though she was in failing health there's no question of her competence. With your permission, ladies, David?"

He clears his throat. He takes a swallow from the mug of coffee on his desk. He reads:

I, ALICE FREEDMAN SAPERSTONE of Saratoga Springs, County of Saratoga, State of New York, being of sound and disposing mind, memory and understanding, do make, publish and declare the following as my Last Will and Testament.

1. *I hereby revoke any and all former wills made by me.*

2. *I direct that all my just debts, taxes and funeral expenses be paid as soon after my decease as conveniently can be done. All federal, state and other taxes and all administration expenses shall be paid out of my estate and be charged against or deducted from the respective bequests and devises herein provided for proportionately as nearly as may be.*

3. *I give and bequeath to my three children, Claire Handleman, Joanna Saperstone, and David Saperstone, as tenants in common, the land and premises where I have resided at 47 Meadow Street, Saratoga Springs, New York, and the contents of the residence except as otherwise provided herein.*

4. *I specifically give and bequeath to Claire Handleman my entire collection of cats—porcelain and wooden, metal and clay, etc.—as the same exists within my home.*

5. *I specifically give and bequeath to Joanna Saperstone all of my silver—cutlery and serving implements—as the same exists within my home.*

6. *I specifically give and bequeath to David Saperstone the contents of the library and the oil portrait of my father Aaron Freedman as the same exists within my home.*

Here the lawyer pauses, adjusts the reading light and looks up from the document and across his desk. "There are individual bequests to local citizens and charities; we will proceed to administer articles seven through twelve according to your mother's wishes—but these need not concern you; they are, relatively speaking, few, and relatively small. You understand, of course," he says, "that most of what remains will be disposable by you in private and by agreed-on choice. If one of you, for example, wants a specific piece of furniture you may lay a claim to it and indemnify the others; this happens all the time. If you decide to keep the cottage as a collec-

tive asset then you may do so by the terms provided; if you choose
to sell instead you divide the profit in thirds. If one of you wishes
to buy out the others, then the usual procedure is to have two—
three, if there's a wide discrepancy—assessments made by local
Realtors, and thereby establish an averaged value and purchase the
remaining two-thirds of the whole. Do you follow—am I being
clear on this?"

They nod. The sun is high, and there are dust motes thickly
clustered at the window; telephones are ringing in the outer office.
Beakes resumes:

13. *All the rest, residue and remainder of my estate, real, personal or mixed, wheresoever situated, or to which I may be in
any manner entitled, or in which at the time of my death I
may be interested, and not otherwise by this will be disposed
of, I give, devise and bequeath, to my executor within named,
or successor or successors, to divide and distribute the same
among my three children, if living, or their issue, if any, in
equal proportion; my executor having full power to sell, lease,
operate, use or need of such property, as division or distribution thereof, or any part thereof, shall have taken place.*

14. *I appoint my lawyer Joseph Beakes as the executor of this my
will and testament. I direct and request that such executor be
allowed to serve without giving any bond or security whatso-
ever. I authorize my executor, if and whenever in the settlement of my estate, to execute and deliver all deeds,
instruments, transfers and other writings necessary to pass a
proper title thereto.*

Their mother's signature is bold—black ink, unwavering—and
familiar to the three of them; they have been reading as the lawyer
reads, and now they close their folders and look at each other, un-
smiling. There has been nothing remarkable here, and though none
of the children has done this before the procedure feels routine. A
clock chimes the hour: ten times. The lawyer takes another sip of
the liquid in his Starbucks mug, explaining that he next must read

a letter, and this is why he called them here, and needs them here; he lifts a piece of paper from its white manila folder: "I direct, authorize and empower my executor Joseph Beakes to notify my children of my passing, to request their personal presence at the reading of this will and to disclose to each of them in person the existence of that certain trust created for my benefit and the benefit of my issue, the proceeds of which I declined to accept, which shall now be distributed to them in equal proportion."

The wall beneath the window has a radiator, painted gray, and water rattles and clanks in it loudly; David tries to establish the rhythm of the knocking—three beats, four?—and cannot; he shifts in his seat. Joanna crosses, uncrosses her legs. Claire, watching the two of them, coughs.

"There is another issue," Joseph Beakes resumes. "An issue we need to discuss. That 'certain trust' is a matter of considerable interest," he says, "and I may as well say at the outset that it violates the rule against perpetuities. This is a rule we learned about in law school"—he spreads his hands—"in my case very long ago, and it's been around since, oh, the twelfth or thirteenth century in common law." He looks at the ceiling, the rug on the floor. "But I don't believe it need concern us; we have the assets in hand, do we not, and ready for distribution? In other words, although there may have been some question at the time of the *creation* of the trust— the rule against perpetuities stipulates that the trust must vest not later than twenty-one years after some life or lives in being at the time the trust is created—it was not your mother's fault, of course, and we honor here the spirit if not letter of the law. What I mean is, what I want to make clear, is that *now's* the time to deal with this, and without contestation. All right? All right. That's fine."

He has removed his glasses; he peers across the desk at them; he is not, Claire understands, as vague as he pretends or without a lawyer's cunning; he has waited till this moment to tell them what's at stake.

"The Saratoga Savings and Trust Bank has delegated me to inform you. I do a good deal of work for them—*with* them—and the issue is simple enough, but it may possibly take you—as it took *me*—by surprise. I'm not even certain you *knew* of the Saratoga Savings and Trust Bank, which is what they call themselves nowadays, or its role in our little drama, for Alice never seemed to pay attention to the question of her parentage. She was an excellent daughter, of course. As responsible a daughter as her own father could have wished and as you two have no doubt been in turn. Her values were—how does one put it?—traditional, and she valued family above all else." Beakes clears his throat. "But there were certain aspects of her history, her *mother's* history, I mean to say, which she refused to dwell upon and entrusted to others instead. Which is why she insisted you all must be here."

The sisters glance at each other. They cannot decide if the lawyer is commending or reproving them, if he means this as insult or praise. But the engine of his eloquence has warmed by now, kicked into gear, and he shows no sign of stopping. "I myself," he says, "recollect your grandmother a little, but I was of course too young to *know* her as an adult; I might have been introduced once or twice and I surely remember her carriage—by which I don't describe, although it would have been appropriate, a horse-drawn carriage but the way she walked, the positively *regal* fashion in which she conducted herself. And that she was kind to little children—which is, I always say, a mark of breeding; to be kind to the children and the animals among us is a sure sign of good manners, don't you think?"

David rubs the armrest of his chair. All this may be leading them somewhere but he has no idea where. Beakes ceases for a moment and consults the file. "I'm sorry," he says. "I do want to make myself clear. I do apologize. You will be speculating rather more on the contents of this folder than upon my theory as to mannerly behavior with other persons' pets. Are you"—he puts his finger on the page and returns his reading glasses to the bridge of his broad nose—"familiar with the term *per stirpes*?"

Joanna shakes her head. Claire has, however, heard of it and wants to pass what seems like a test, and nods her head repeatedly. The lawyer ignores them; his question is, again, rhetorical, and he persists. "It means, in effect, 'equal parts,' as opposed to, say, 'per capita.' Let's imagine there's a sum of money to be distributed equally to you and your descendents. Well, unless I'm much mistaken you, Claire, have two children; you, Joanna, have a daughter; and you, David, at present have no child. So the sum could be divisible by three or, alternatively"—he counts this out on his fingers—"six. If we're talking *per stirpes* it's equal parts, if we're talking 'per capita' Claire would receive three times as much as David, and Joanna would get twice as much, correct? Well, in this instance the sum is *per stirpes* and that's quite simply that. No question about it at *all.*"

Beakes leans back in his swivel chair to gauge the effects of his speech. He makes a tent of his fingers and examines the ten cuticles and nails. "Excuse me," Joanna admits, "I'm not sure I follow . . ."

"No, my dear. Why should you? We were not appointed the trustees of this particular account, and therefore I share what will no doubt be your own astonishment as to its size. The size of the bequest, I mean, the trust of which you three are sole and equal beneficiaries. I feel rather like that fellow Regis Philbin or, let's say, a fairy godfather"—amused, he titters—"when all I am, of course, is a mere messenger. With very—I might even say astonishingly—good news."

And then he does explain it. In 1916 their grandmother, a young woman whose birth, Beakes reminds them, was coeval with the century, came into entitlement of some shares of stock—fifteen, to be precise—of the General Electric Company. She was herself to have no access to the sum, since it was held in trust for her own child, and that's where the rule against perpetuities comes in; the child was yet unborn. But that needn't concern us, Beakes repeats, it's milk spilled very long ago and water far under the bridge. The bank has sent him figures, and he's happy to disclose amounts and will do so in a moment, but he wants to make certain beforehand they understand the situation here. I mean by this that, given the relatively modest circumstances of your mother's life, the size of the estate to which she in fact had access would have come as a surprise. And even, perhaps, as a shock.

At any given moment, Beakes continues, your mother could have sold the shares, but for whatever reason Alice did not choose to; she left the trust untouched and simply let it grow. And *that* was a wise fiscal move. General Electric, as you no doubt know, has had some problems recently, and there's been quite a drop-off from the historic high. Still and all you could have done far worse and couldn't do much better; there are few, if any, companies whose stock has multiplied so often, who have been listed on the New York Stock Exchange for so many years, and the fifteen shares I spoke of—he consults the sheet in front of him—now represent, you'll be I think amazed to hear, 69,120 shares. *Sixty-nine thousand*, Beakes repeats, from fifteen shares in 1916; it's what I think they mean by standing pat and sitting pretty, isn't it, it's doing very well indeed by leaving things alone . . .

Again, he consults the spreadsheet he holds; he runs his fingers down a column and reads out the stock's history; there were splits of *four* for one, he tells them, in 1926 and again in 1930, of *three* for one in 1954 and again at the millennium, in the year 2000. In addition there were splits of *two* for one in 1971, 1982, 1987, 1994 and 1997; put them all together they spell *jackpot*, ladies, David; sixty-nine thousand, one hundred twenty shares from an investment of fifteen . . .

Wonderingly, he tents his fingers and remarks about modernity, the exponential way things grow and grow and grow. Your mother must have known, he says, she must have had an inkling—but Alice did not spend a cent, not a red cent, and these last years, as you remember, she lived in straitened circumstances. I overstate the point, says Beakes, in order to establish it; she did not live in "straitened" circumstances—at least not by comparison with most of our neighbors in Saratoga County—but certainly in more modest ones than would have been the case had she elected access to those funds.

"So what does this amount to?" asks Claire.

"Today," Joanna says.

"Or as soon as we can liquidate," Beakes cautions them. "A tidy sum, a goodly sum, I can't be exact to the penny because it changes every day, but if we were to sell right now we're gaining on two million dollars. Which, after the estate exemption of a million now and even when the tax is paid—as per proviso two of the will—should net you in the neighborhood of half a million each. At yesterday's share price of General Electric and at current market value"—he picks up a calculator and punches in the numbers—"it's, to be more precise, one million, seven hundred and sixty-two thousand, five hundred and sixty dollars—not what it was last year, of course, but still a tidy sum!"

In the silence that follows he empties his mug. Then he smiles at them, avuncular, and says, "It's funny, isn't it, my secretary Harriet Robison is at her desk and unable to speak, she has a world-class case of laryngitis, whereas *I'm* doing nothing but talking. You must forgive me, children—and forgive me for calling you children, but it seems like only yesterday I watched you on your ponies or in school assembly, and it warms an old man's heart to see you here again . . .

"Which leads me to my final point and then I'll let you go. There's one additional aspect of your mother's letter"—he holds up the sheet for inspection—"that concerns everyone here; it doesn't have the force of law, it's not an obligation, but it was her hope that one of you might choose to remain in the cottage. David."

"Excuse me?"

"We did discuss this," Beakes continues. "We talked about it at length. It was your mother's conviction that her daughters had households already and you—she called you her 'rolling stone,' David—would profit from such residence. An address which she hoped you'd make your own again. She was, I think it's fair to say, *concerned* about impermanence, quite worried that you'd fail to find a resting place, and though she did not give the house to *you* alone, and though by law you can't of course be forced to make your permanent abode in Saratoga, it was her fondest wish you'd think of the cottage as home."

"We all do," Claire declares.

Joanna nods her head.

"I cannot speak" the lawyer says, "to the nature of her decision with reference to which of you might settle most readily back in the house; I can, however, report on her intention in nontestamentary terms. This is clearly not an asset divisible by three until and unless it is sold, and Alice was explicit in the hope the house on Meadow Street might stay in the family. And I think she thought that David—"

"It feels like preferential treatment," Claire interrupts. "To me." And then, inquiringly, she turns to Joanna and asks, "To us?"

"To us," Joanna says.

But the truth is she feels nothing, feels only the size of the change in her life, the shape of the future diverging, divergent already from present and past: how much all this money will mean. "I look forward," says Joanna, "to looking back on this."

Beakes laughs. "Just so," he says. "Just so."

"It isn't amusing," Claire persists. "We were equal parties, all of us, and everything was meant to be divided equally, correct?"

"Correct."

"Except for the cottage," says David.

"I hope I'm being clear; I want to be quite clear about this," Beakes says again. He is, Joanna sees suddenly, old; he is tired and has done his job and wants this interview over. "What your mother has expressed here is a desire, only a *wish*; she could, of course, have deeded the cottage to David alone and made compensatory arrangements for you two"—he nods at the sisters, the daughters—"but did not choose to do so. Let me remind you of the third provision in the will: 'I give and bequeath to my *three* children, as tenants in common, the land and premises where I have resided . . .'

"It would have been simpler, no doubt, if she had directed the house to be sold. But she did hope that one of you would call it, in the future, home, and *that's* why I explained the matter of assessment—two local Realtors, fair current market value and so on— because it may well come to pass that *that's* how you choose to proceed. And I think you'll also be surprised at what's happened to real estate hereabouts, the positive *boom* in the market! But this is something for the three of you to work out together, a discussion you don't need me for. Or *want* me to be part of, I imagine."

Beakes removes his reading glasses and folds them into a worn leather case, then snaps it shut. With his thumb and middle finger, he presses the sides of his nose. "So if we're finished, ladies? David?"

He stands. "One final *final* thing," says Beakes, "and though you'll find it in the paperwork I myself don't mind admitting it did bring me up short. Those shares of General Electric, those fifteen prime shares in 1916 your grandmother received? I've kept you long enough and won't take any more of your time, but it will astonish you to learn which men conferred them. Thomas Edison himself, and Harvey Firestone and Henry Ford were the ones who established the trust. They *knew* her, it develops, way back when in this part of the world, and it's clear they must have thought very highly of her, and I hope and trust you'll take this" — he smiles — "*trust* as the compliment they would have intended to your lineage, your family. It's no small pedigree to claim, and your grandmother must have been proud . . ."

They stand. They shake the lawyer's hand and gather up their copies of the last will and testament of Alice Freedman Saperstone and file out of the office. Mrs. Robison is smiling, pointing at her throat and nodding her head ruefully. Then she holds out her memo pad, with the word *Laryngitis*, and points with her red ballpoint pen to where beneath it she has printed, in red block capital letters: HAVE A PLEASANT DAY.

VII

2003

In the cottage once again they gather in the kitchen; they have stopped at Mrs. London's and acquired coffee cake and a baguette with cheddar cheese and Genoa salami and lettuce and mustard and *pain au chocolat* and a pot of loganberry jam. On china from the breakfront in the dining room they lay out the fresh-baked provender and sit down to eat. There is a sense of ceremony and a shocked constraint between them; they speak about the bakery: how it used to be on a side street but now seems much more visible in its new location, and does anyone remember when Mrs. London's moved? The Adelphi Hotel has a fresh coat of paint, new balcony trim, and does anyone remember if it's the same shade of brown? Today is Lincoln's Birthday, February twelfth; and they talk about St. Valentine's and how, before they leave again, they should buy something special for Valentine's Day to take back to their separate homes: a set of marzipan hearts or *milles feuilles* or that chocolate roulade on display . . .

Sun illumines the dirt on the floor. The linoleum has cracked. Joanna says, I need to be in Wellfleet by Friday, I promised Leah I'd be home in time for *West Side Story*. But it will be so excellent to bring back cake from Mrs. London's; nothing on the Cape is half as good. Or half as expensive, she adds. When are *you* leaving, Claire inquires, and David says I don't really know, I haven't yet decided. Remember, says Joanna, you said you might drive out with me, you wanted to see Leah's performance, and he looks up but does not answer and cuts the baguette in thirds.

"Not for me," says Claire. "I'll have a piece of *pain au chocolat*."

"Do we sell right now?" Joanna asks. "Is that what we're supposed to do?"

"You mean, GE?"

She nods. Joanna has been saving this to think about, to talk

105

about, and now the time has come. There will be money arriving—
enough to pay off the mortgage or shut up shop and cut and run to
Mexico: enough to do whatever she pleases, and for Li-li too. It will
be five hundred thousand at least, and maybe more, and that's half a
million better than her bank account; it's a lottery ticket and
Publishers Clearing House prize and trifecta all rolled into one. It
might not matter to her brother and might not change her sister's life,
but it matters to her very much, and she cannot believe her good
luck. This is more money than she has imagined, more than she had
ever *dreamed*; good news, great news, and Joanna lights a cigarette
and smiles at her siblings and stubs out the match.

"We need advice," Claire ventures. "It might be smart to wait a
little." She spoons herself a portion of loganberry jam.

"How long?"

"Not very long," says David. "She means, until the price
goes up . . ."

"And if it doesn't?"

Claire does not say, *Don't smoke, at least not here inside the house,
I'm sick of your smoking, I hate how it smells*. Instead she says, "You've
got a point. What happens if GE continues to drop?"

"We ought to sell. It's what he told us," says Joanna. "Beakes,
I mean. What did he call it, the law against perpetuities? The 'rule'
against it, anyhow?"

"Agreed. I think we ought to cut and run," says David.

The jam is tart—both sweet and sour, syrupy, and with a bitter
aftertaste. "That's *always* what you think," Claire says.

"It's the procedure our lawyer advised. And I don't know about
the two of you but *I* could use the cash." Exhaling, Joanna curls
her lip; smoke billows by the hanging lamp above the sink.

"We all could," David says.

"Right. But some are more equal than others . . ."

They smile at each other. They eat their baguettes. Half a million is not nothing, Claire reminds herself; half a million is much
more than she'd expected, flying East, and she decides upon a college fund. Five hundred thousand ought to cover it—Jim will say,
"Whoee, what a relief!"—and when they sell the cottage there'll

be more. It will yield twenty thousand per annum at least, even with the market down and these catastrophic interest rates, and will go a good long way to covering tuition. She has not been worried, really, about the cost of college, but this will make a difference, this will make it simple in the years to come . . .

"I think he had a crush on her," says David.

"Who?"

"The lawyer. Beakes. I think he was one of her, her admirers way back when . . ."

"You're not serious," Joanna says.

"Not really, no."

"Gentlemen callers," says Claire. "It's what she called them, remember?"

"Is he married? Did he ever marry?"

"You know, what I've been thinking about"—Joanna shakes her head—"is it's hard to believe how *young* Mom was, no older than *I* am when Daddy died. I don't mean I feel young, of course, and lord knows I don't look that way but she seemed such a *grownup* in, when was it, '76? You were, what . . . ?"

"Eight," says David.

"Think about it. All those years, those *decades* of living here all by herself, and with all those gentlemen callers. The doctors, the lawyers, the Indian chiefs . . ."

"The college professors," says Claire.

"Joke," says Joanna. "I was joking. I *do* know she didn't date Indian chiefs."

"I don't think Beakes did marry," David concludes. "There weren't any photographs, were there, of the wife and kids?"

They shrug. They drink their tea. Claire says, "Imagine, just imagine showing up for work and answering the telephones and not having any voice. But being Mrs. Robison and writing *laryngitis* all day long."

While his sisters discuss laryngitis, David assesses the kitchen: its cabinets, the snow on the pine trees outside. He asks himself if he should stay in Saratoga Springs and buy two-thirds of the house from his sisters and what it would feel like to live here again. Lawyer Beakes as much as said to him, *She wants you back, she wanted you here. Unto the third and the fourth generation she hoped you would stay in the cottage.* He is the youngest of the family, the one without a mortgage or roof, and he wonders how his mother's will will change his life.

"But our grandmother?" Joanna asks. "Elizabeth. Doesn't it just . . ."

"Just what?" Claire finishes her pastry.

"Oh, I don't know—just blow your mind? To think of her entertaining them. To think that Thomas Edison . . ."

"And Harvey Firestone. And Henry Ford," says David. "I wonder if he ever knew she married somebody Jewish, a Jew? That world-class anti-Semite, that major league son of a bitch . . ."

"We don't really know what *did* happen back then. All we know is that they gave her stock. In General Electric, which was Edison Electric . . ."

"Let's sell it tomorrow," Joanna declares. "Let's just get rid of it, OK?"

"GE," says Claire. "'It brings good things to life.'" And then she pauses, quizzical. "Or is it 'light'? 'Good things to light'?"

"Whatever," David says.

❧

They clean up the kitchen. They wrap the coffee cake and close the jar of loganberry jam and wash their plates and cups. The water from the kitchen tap is a thin trickle, but hot. Claire checks the to-do list she taped by the telephone yesterday and calls Bill Becker Jr., informing him of their decision as to coffin type and funerary urns. He is polite, attentive, and she gives him the several addresses to which their mother's ashes should be sent. For purposes of dotting the *i* and crossing the *t*, Bill Becker says, he'll read the three addresses back. He does.

Then David takes the receiver and says, Don't send my urn to Berkeley, please, I don't really know when I'll be there again; can you store it in your office for me—keep it, I mean, on hold?

We have, the funeral director says, a closet of memories, yes.

Claire has been trying not to mind that David was given the portrait of Aaron; she has never liked it anyway: too stern, too brown, his hands inexact. She might lodge a claim for the portraits of great-grandfather William Dancey and Elise his wife; they make a matched pair—primitives, but well enough framed—and should not be split up. Where will we hang them, she wonders, and shuts her eyes an instant and *sees* them in the living room: above the Biedermeier desk and by the standing lamp. She has been trying not to think about the way their mother faded in and faded out, so you never knew for certain if she was remembering or misremembering or flat-out inventing things. At least their mother understood that *she* was the one who liked porcelain cats; the collection has been willed to her, and she will pack it up. "We'll have to have a grab," she says.

"A grab?"

"Where we go through the house with stickers—a color code for each of us—and take turns in a room, saying *this* is the object or painting I want. In the kitchen, say, I'd be the one who makes the first choice, then David goes second, Joanna third, and in the living room it's Joanna who goes first, and in the dining room David, and we do this room by room until we've tagged it all. Let's say I get red and David blue; Joanna, you'd be white. And then we can trade if we want to, and if nobody lays claim to a chair, say, or a mixing bowl then we sell it or give it away."

"Have you done this before?" he asks. "You've got it all worked out."

"Of course not, no. It's standard procedure," Claire says.

"But first," asserts Joanna, "we need to get rid of the obvious junk. Stuff no one could possibly want . . ."

They walk through the cottage together. The rooms have nothing new in them, nothing from the recent past, but the prospect of dismantling their shared childhood home is nonetheless a daunting one. The sisters check the mudroom off the pantry; there are gloves and scarves and umbrellas and a Dustbuster and brooms and a lightweight snow shovel and, improbably, a volleyball.

There are dried-flower arrangements and dead plants still in pots. David carries down the wheelchair from the upstairs hallway; he calls the telephone number on the tag and the woman from Miller's Medical Supply says they'll pick it up tomorrow afternoon; just leave it by the kitchen entryway if you won't be around.

The three of them examine the dining room and living room and library. There is accumulated clutter everywhere, cabinets and shelves and closets stuffed with their mother's leavings. There are skirts and hats and shoes and cardigans and many winter coats; there are throw rugs for the Goodwill store and quantities of blankets and boxes of old photographs and canceled checks and letters from the three of them and keys and key rings in triplicate and carefully saved clippings from the *Daily Saratogian* and the *New York Times*. The clippings do not signify: old wedding announcements, obituary notices, old letters to the editor about an election long since decided or a local referendum voted up or down. There are articles about the Adirondacks and fishing expeditions and their high school and college yearbooks and ancient AAA TripTiks and worn, much-folded maps. There is a bookcase full of wallpaper paste and cans of paint and an unopened gallon can of turpentine and brushes and rollers and Spackle and wood stain and oil.

Thick glass carafes—quarter-liter, half-liter, full-liter carafes— occupy a basement shelf; so do an assortment of teapots and drip coffeemakers and espresso pots. There are chipped plates and cups and plastic glasses they might have used on picnics, once; there are chafing dishes and electric can openers and a fondue set and shish kebab skewers, their long thin blades spotted with rust. They sort through cookie tins and Pyrex dishes and lamp shades and frying pans and salad tongs and kerosene and propane lanterns and a set of candleholders with wickless burned-out candles—the detritus of decades of hoarding and possessions set aside.

I never thought of her, Joanna says, as so surrounded by objects; she wasn't a pack rat or anything like it; she just never threw stuff away. And some of it probably comes from Mom's *own* childhood, David says; this was Aaron's house beforehand, and her grandparents' house before that. Yes, says Claire, it's been in the family since way back when, and David says there were *Cultivator* magazines stuffed in the attic floorboards from 1830, remember; remember when she had insulation blown in and they discovered those old newspapers from when the house was built?

I remember, says Joanna, but these shish kebab skewers are recent enough, and she never threw anything out. What's that disease about newspaper-piling, old people who can't bear to get rid of newspapers, it has a medical name, and Claire says, Don't be silly, this isn't *anything* like that, it's not a disease, she was just plain forgetful and didn't throw objects away.

"Well, somebody has to." David shrugs. "We need a Dumpster, looks like . . ."

"There has to be some sort of service. A company that cleans stuff out."

"Or an estate sale," says Joanna. "We could advertise a tag sale. If we set up an auction here, they'd come from miles around."

Claire looks in the telephone book under "Auctioneer" and then under "Estate Sales"; indeed, there are listings to call. She selects three possibilities and writes their numbers down. Meanwhile her brother is talking; he has always been a talker and is giving them a speech about retrieval, how there's a system for old objects where nothing is ever lost. We think of ourselves as a consumer society, an economy built around planned obsolescence, but that's wrong, says David, that really isn't the case: *everything's* in second-hand shops, everything's an antique now and what our parents or grandparents threw away is a *collectible;* there are whole barns and shopping malls devoted to this—forgive me, but it *is* the word for it—junk. You can find everything anybody ever threw away, whole shops are devoted to what's been recycled; there's a collector out there somewhere for every single thing on every basement shelf.

Are you serious, asks Claire, do you really want an auction, and he says, remember, I said what we need is a Dumpster. There's a lot I *do* want to preserve, David says, but it isn't Pyrex dishes and teapots with a canary motif and carafes with all those cute little pieces of lead to show that the Italian government officially approves of them; it didn't matter much to Mom and doesn't matter to me . . .

"I need some air," Joanna says. "I need to get out of the house."

⌘

The wooden shingles of the roof are glistening with snowmelt; the cedar stand droops, burdened with old snow. How strange, she thinks, to think of this as "home"; she hasn't lived in Saratoga Springs for years and visits only rarely. Joanna walks along the driveway, and there's a tune in her head: *I'm going away, for to stay, a little while—but I'm coming back, if I go ten thousand miles.*

Last night's snow is dry light powder on the hood of Trusty-Rusty, and pine needles have collected where the windshield wipers lie. She brushes them off with her hand. The idea of her mother alone in the house makes her too sad to think about, and she shakes her head to clear it but the song stays in her head. *I'm going away, for to stay, a little while.* She walks the yard's perimeter, breathing, inhaling, remembering Alice at forty and how she'd seemed so old already, staid, set in her adult ways, and how her own daughter must think this way also; returning, she will talk to Li-li and say we don't mean to be difficult, darling, it's just what mothers do. It's what we're *supposed* to do, and someday you'll find yourself also explaining to a teenager why there's a midnight curfew and why not to smoke dope . . .

She lights a cigarette. Ten thousand miles used to mean something; it used to mean a world away, but now ten thousand miles is less than you drive in the course of a year; it means you come back home. Therefore, approaching the door again (seeing a deer at the edge of the woods, seeing a birch tree uprooted) Joanna is half-unsurprised to find the light on in the kitchen and her brother at the sink, his back toward her, gesturing, and a figure at the table who because of the red flowered curtain fails to see her on the path but has her chin on her hand and her elbow on the white

Formica tabletop in an attitude of waiting, of patience, abnega-
tion, fury, as familiar to her now as then only it's not their mother
but Claire.

"Say hey," says David. "Welcome back."

"Did you have fun?" Claire asks. "Did you enjoy yourself?"

Joanna shrugs out of her coat.

"Did you have your Garbo moment? Your *vant to be alone*?"

"What's wrong? Has something happened here?"

"Nothing. Nothing worth discussing." David smiles at her.
"Your sister's just being a bitch."

"And your brother's being"—Claire bobs her head—"the perfect
gentleman, of course. The completely decent and courteous man."

"Whoa, both of you; what *happened*?"

"It doesn't concern you," says Claire. "It isn't your business,
really."

"Of course it is. Of course it does."

"He thinks he's being patronized."

"Not *thinks*," says David. "Knows."

Joanna sits. "By you? By us? About what?"

"My 'lifestyle,' as she calls it. My lack of commitment, my
catch-as-catch—"

"No, not at all," Claire interrupts. "It isn't that. It's just I don't
think David's up to maintaining this place by himself. To taking
care of it, I mean; I don't think he should call it home unless he
means to, really *wants* to, and I really don't think he has any *idea*
how much hard work it will be. Housekeeping."

He shrugs.

"Don't you *dare* pretend I'm being Martha Stewart and talking
about casseroles or vacuuming the floor. I'm talking *responsibility*,
about being here on a daily basis and being a caretaker.
Caretaking." She turns to him, both hands upraised. "Just let me
finish, will you, just please let me finish just once! I'd rather we
sell the house lock, stock and barrel than watch it fall apart."

"What you mean is," David says, "you'd rather we get rid of it.
If Mom didn't leave the place to *you*, you don't want it belonging
to anyone else."

"Oh please," Joanna says. "Are we arguing already? Beakes reads us the will just this morning and we're at each other's throats?"

"So when did you get so grown-up about it? So big-sisterish all of a sudden?"

"I *told* you it doesn't concern you," says Claire. "I *know* you know how hard it is. Housekeeping."

"So I'll *hire* someone," David says. "There are people everywhere in Saratoga who make a living out of other people's houses, out of—what did you call it?—caretaking. The house has stood two hundred years and it can stand some more. Just because Mom stayed here all alone doesn't make the place a prison; it's been in the family since, Christ knows, the early nineteenth century, and I'm free, white and thirty-five and able to take care of it . . ."

"Don't turn this into Tara. Or some ancestral seat, a *manse*. It's a gussied-up, broken-down farmhouse," says Claire. "It's a cottage on what used to be a meadow and now's a side street going nowhere in a nowhere part of town. It's dime-a-dozen real estate and nothing to write home about . . ."

"Except it's home," he says.

⟐

And this is true. I'm thirty-five years old, he thinks, and not a baby anymore; before I leave I'll find a caretaker—the lawyer will know one, I'm certain, or maybe Mom had one already—to keep an eye out for the place. David pictures himself with an easel, a skylight, a smock and a canvas and model or bowl filled with fruit. What I want to do is paint, he thinks, I want to stop pretending I want to do anything else. He imagines himself with a palette knife, oil paint, a sunset emerging or maybe the contours of somebody's leg, a brown leg draped over a chair . . .

Then David admits it: he dabbles, he's indulged himself for years and is doing so again. He's indulging himself in a daydream of art, a vision of steadfast production, but he has been a dilettante and is being that way still. His mother had known this about him; she'd understood he was playing at permanence, only pretending to call Berkeley home and working on web sites and, before that, advertising and a TV pilot that was in development and optioned twice and dropped . . .

"Is this about money?" asks Joanna.

"No, why?" Claire kicks off her shoes.

"Because I'm the one who suggested we sell. The shares in General Electric, I mean. And I need the money most."

"All right," says Claire. "You need it most."

Joanna sits. She extracts her pack of cigarettes, then returns it to her handbag.

"GE's a major government contractor. Or at least it used to be," says David. "And if the trouble in Iraq goes on for years then maybe stock will rise again. But I think everything's about to tank, and what we'd get for it today is more than we'll get later . . ."

"So you do agree with me? You think we ought to sell?"

"It isn't about the *money* at all. And it isn't about *you*, Joanna," Claire says. "It's about, oh, continuity and knowing when to say good-bye to what you've left behind."

"All right."

"Are you accusing me," asks David, "of having done that or *not* having done that? I need to be clear . . ."

"I'm not accusing you of *anything*." Claire rubs her hands against her hips. "Can't we agree to disagree?"

"We've been doing so for years, for *decades* . . ."

"Stop it, stop it both of you," Joanna says.

"Yes, Mom."

"See what I mean? It's like there's some sort of poison," says Claire, "some kind of rage he can't control. All I did was say maybe we should think about it, think what it means to *maintain* this house and he's treating me like some sort of absentee landlord or real estate agent who's planning to evict—"

"Well, aren't you?"

"Enough," Joanna says. "That's enough from both of you. I go away for twenty minutes and the two of you are fighting."

"You said that already," says David.

"'Blessed are the meek,'" says Claire. "Or is it 'poor'—I can't remember. 'Blessed are the poor, for they shall inherit the earth.'"

And then they do control themselves; they have come to the edge of a genuine rupture, and they all pull back. They agree that they should get some air, should sleep on it, should let the dust settle a little. They understand these are clichés and what they've each been feeling in the aftermath of grief is a predictable set of reactions; what they ought to do is keep their options open. They will sell the stock and not the house and David will decide in time if he does or doesn't want to buy his sisters out . . .

They call their homes in Wellfleet and Ann Arbor and leave messages on the machines. David puts his mother's wheelchair outside the kitchen door, where Miller's Medical Supply will pick it up, and while the afternoon darkens to dusk and then night they deal with their mother's used useless possessions. There is no disagreement now, or at least no argument; they fill old suitcases and boxes and paper bags with bric-a-brac and clothing they know none of them will claim. They fill ten basement shelves. At seven o'clock he says, OK, enough, let's call it quits this evening and go out to eat.

❧

Again they take the rented Taurus and drive into town and choose a restaurant, not last night's with the waitress and overcooked food but—at Claire's suggestion, for, they have insisted, they want her to choose—a wine bar with young men who come up to them smiling. The place is called Toulouse, and there are several reproductions of posters by Toulouse-Lautrec: the entertainer Jane Avril lifts her thin leg enticingly above the bar, and La Goulue purses her lips. There are oversized posters of Aristide Bruant in costume, in profile, presenting the viewer with his broad back: the cabaret singer wears a black jacket and boots, red scarf and his signature black hat.

The meal takes a long time arriving. They make conversation, or try to, discussing terrorism, the prospect of war and El Niño or is it La Niña, and how old-fashioned this winter has been, how cold and hard the snow. They talk about the lawyer, and how they remember him watching them ride, and they try to remember the name of the stable where the girls had kept their ponies—Bliss and Checkers, says Joanna; at least I remember the names of the *ponies*—and whatever happened to that fat friend of yours—Chuck, Chucky?—who became a policeman and then the police chief in town. I don't think he stayed here, says David, I don't think they let you *be* police chief in the town you're born in any longer; too many traffic tickets and DWIs to fix. Too many favors for people to call in . . .

They announce their travel plans. Claire's on the afternoon flight tomorrow but it's a quick trip from Metro, so anytime anyone needs her she'll be back again. I'll go with you, David offers, I *will* drive out to Wellfleet but I'll keep the rental car so I can drive myself back; oh good, says Joanna, wonderful. They agree the grab, as Claire has called it—and she protests it isn't her word—can wait a while, and should. The cottage and its contents will be fine. They will hire someone to keep an eye out for the furnace, to be a caretaker, and when they can they'll meet again and schedule a formal division; I'm going to drive the silver home, Joanna says, and Claire says I'll fly back a couple of cats.

It's weird, Joanna says, to think we got here yesterday and think how much has changed. I never thought, she says, I never imagined, and smiles and lights a cigarette; my hour's up, she says. Claire says, do give my love to Leah, and they promise they will do so, and she says, on Friday, please tell her break a leg. Give *my* love to Becky and Hannah, says David; and *Jim*, Joanna says. Friday is Valentine's Day, they remind each other, and talk about old autocratic Henry Ford and why he and his cronies gave those shares to their young grandmother; was it a tip, they wonder, an act of generosity or some sort of payment for services rendered, and what would the service have been?

Their waiter hovers; he refills their water glasses and empties the bottle of wine. "Another, sir?" he asks. David nods. Claire says—as soon as the waiter has minced off, the bottle dangling from his wrist—you've made another conquest, brother, you're our big strong protector and he'll stick you with the bill. The privilege of manhood, David says. We'll split it, says Joanna, we'll divide the bill in three. At meal's end in fact they do so, and with a sense of completion, although little is settled between them and they are ready to leave. They think about their grandmother and who she was and how she lived her life.

Part Four

VIII

1940

Elizabeth turned forty. Bone-weary on her birthday, she felt as though she turned sixty instead; she sent Alice off to school and cleaned the living room and baked herself a sponge cake and set the table for two. She spent the day alone. When Aaron came home after work and took off his overcoat and hung his hat in the closet, it was all she could manage to rise from the sofa and walk to the door and welcome him. "Hello, dear," she offered, and gave him her cheek. "How are you feeling?" he asked her, and she said, "Better, thanks." "So you're feeling all right?" he inquired, and she answered—lying—"Fine."

Her husband was wearing galoshes, and when he bent to remove them he reeked of his time at the office, the smell of tobacco and sweat. His hair bore the line of his hat brim, his breath was stale, and she noted this not because it upset her but because of the way she must look to him also: worn out, wan and old. He was twenty years her senior; *he* was the one who was sixty, but Aaron produced a gift-wrapped pink sweater and a bottle of perfume and said, "Happy birthday. Many happy returns." Opening the packages, she found herself touched by his gesture, though the sweater did not fit her and the perfume was offensive: sharp and oversweet. He said, "Why don't I take the birthday girl to dinner," and she said no, she'd cooked it already and wanted to stay home. They sat together on the sofa and she said, "You must be tired," and he admitted it, "Yes."

Elizabeth felt tired every morning and each afternoon and night. It was as though the house had enlarged, as though the distance from the pantry to the stairwell and the bathroom to the bedroom had been extending, expanding. The shelves in the kitchen were too high to reach, the ceiling fixture lightbulbs impossible to change. The noises of the household—the radiators and the gramophone, the clanking water pipes and sound of the toilet when somebody flushed it—all these afflicted her. She lay on the living room sofa with a washcloth spread across her eyes and listened to the squirrels scampering along the roof, their chittering, the wind. You ought to see a doctor, Mom, said Alice, why not let him fix what's wrong . . .

Because they fix nothing, she wanted to say, because calling a doctor is useless and they come too late. They always come too late. Alice was having a sleepover date; it was good for her to be away when Elizabeth felt indisposed or, as Aaron put it, blue. It was blue she saw when she opened her eyes and black when she closed them again; it was pain beyond the reach of pills or the syrup she took for digestion, and she did not tell her family how far beyond a doctor's help she knew she had traveled already. We'll celebrate this weekend, she promised her daughter, you go from school to Janey's house and spend the night with Janey and sleep just as late as you can. We'll bake a cake tomorrow; don't worry, I'll be fine . . .

In the course of time, of course, Alice would lose her bright-eyed hopefulness; her body would begin to change, and that part of the body called mind would change—but not just yet, not now. Now she was eight years old and ignorant and blissful because ignorance is bliss. Elizabeth wished to protect her. The recipe for sponge-cake, for example, is not something a person keeps hidden, and she would share it willingly, but how she felt on her own fortieth birthday was a different kind of secret and difficult to tell . . .

When she herself was bright-eyed and young and living in her parents' house, she contracted influenza. She had been seventeen, unmarried and alone. Except she hadn't minded, did not mind; there were widows everywhere and girls who loved soldiers and raised children by themselves, and Elizabeth was grateful and proud to be a mother; she admired Harold's perfect hands, his feet, his bright enormous eyes and how he laughed and clapped and burbled all day long. Her pregnancy was painless, the delivery painless also, and for the first year of her baby's life and last of the Great War she reveled in his company and was untroubled, fancy-free. In the light of the bedroom window she lay with Harold, her sunshine child, and then the pandemic came and claimed him and took him away.

"You opened the window, and influenza"—that was a chant of the time. It was as simple as that. It had seemed complicated but was simple, really: she had been deluded, seduced into believing the world could be a happy place when all was pain and loss.

For that first year, however, she had been deluded: the war would be over and all would be well and she and her beautiful baby would live together forever. She gave him a bath every morning and loved the way he loved his bath, the way he splashed and cackled and the scrubbed pink folds of baby fat at Harold's wrists and knees. She made plans for him, great plans; she would take him to Paris, she promised, and take him to London to visit the queen, and she read him fairy tales and nursery rhymes until he fell asleep. She loved the way he fell asleep, the way he heaved and tumbled out of wakefulness—just shutting his eyes with a great noiseless crash and putting his thumb in his mouth. Elizabeth was optimistic that whole year. Then, when the war was over and they declared an armistice and there was dancing in the streets and a new day dawning, what came to her instead of happiness was influenza—a headache, a cough, nothing serious really—and then it did get serious and the world went dark.

To begin with she tried to ignore it. At first she believed it was only a cold, only an indisposition, and even at its worst, her worst, it wasn't all that terrible; she was young and strong and hopeful and she nursed Harold all week. He had seemed well enough—impatient a little, querulous even—but she blamed herself for disappointing him, for making him stay in the house all day long because she couldn't walk. She would get better soon. "You opened the window, and influenza," and then you closed the window and kept your child inside.

And sure enough, after two or three days and three or four nights—she wasn't certain, she stopped counting—she did indeed improve. The fever went away. She had been foolish, a little, believing herself back in Barclay's arms and believing herself his companion aboard some oceangoing yacht or in a grand hotel with marble floors and staircases, dancing her way down the deck or the stairs. She imagined in her foolishness that he cared for her and was concerned and she wanted to tell him to not be concerned, she and Harold would be fine. Then the fever broke and she knew she had been only dreaming and then she understood that Harold too was sick, had caught it, and it was a nightmare, not dream.

Those days were the worst of her life. Those nights were unthinkable nights. Upstairs, in the bed they shared, the narrow single bed beneath the sloping west-facing eaves, she held her child and kissed and rocked and soothed him and dried his dear face when he sweated and wept and wet it with a washcloth when he shivered, needing water. She had wanted to die for him, die in his place, but that would have been too easy, and the world was hard. While she had been enraptured, dancing with her partner down broad marble stairs, her son—their son—was dying, and she could do nothing to help. She tried everything to succor him, to make a difference and be of some use, but everything amounted to nothing and there had been nothing to do.

The doctor came. He arrived too late, of course, and of course was helpless and in any case exhausted, but what he said—first gently and then not so gently and then finally impatient and summoning her parents—was that Harold was past saving, dead, and had been dead for hours and she had to give him up. "He isn't breathing, Lizzie," said her mother, "he can't be alive if he isn't breathing," and the doctor collected her beautiful baby and took him from her, away.

❧

Then everything went dark again, and what they called the Roaring Twenties passed her by. "You're young," they said, "you've your whole life to live," except that was the problem; she had nothing left to live for and didn't want to try. The seasons succeeded each other, the years succeeded each other, and she helped her parents with the farm and, when they stopped farming, the chores. "You should take some pride in your appearance," said her mother, and so Elizabeth took pride in her appearance, and when she was twenty-eight their neighbor Aaron Freedman noticed and asked her to go walking and riding and then he proposed.

She wanted to refuse. Aaron was cautious to a fault, respectable down to his wing tips, and he said he did not know or care what had happened to her earlier; he was twenty years her senior and had considered the matter. She was a beautiful woman, he said, and as far as Aaron was concerned he would be the luckiest man in Saratoga if she would consent to be his wife. He took her hand and requested a kiss and gave her two weeks to decide; he hoped she would view his proposal in a favorable light. He believed it was his duty to confess his failings to her: he had, he confessed, a terrible temper, but for her sake would govern it; he had, from time to time, been envious, but he would envy no one if she became his spouse.

In this fashion their courtship proceeded. He worked as a bank teller, and he was Jewish, practical and frugal and an atheist; on their second promenade together he announced that, although he did not entirely accept the *Communist Manifesto*, it had some valuable insights and religion was, he informed her, the people's opiate.

"You're not a socialist, are you?" she asked.

"No, not at all. A freethinking person is how I describe myself. A person who thinks for himself."

In truth she liked it that Aaron was Jewish; it made her imagine him some sort of renegade, not living on rich bottomland and farming it by birthright. Her family, the Danceys, had been bottomland farmers since time out of mind and soldiers for generations, and all was for the best in this best of all possible worlds. That was what the Frenchman said, Monsieur Voltaire, and her father shared the opinion, but Aaron said No, not a bit, he wrote it tongue-in-cheek. Her father recited a Robert Browning poem, declaring all's right with the world. But all was not right; God was not in his heaven, and she wasn't Pippa passing by in that poem by Robert Browning. When she accepted his engagement ring,

Elizabeth made certain Aaron understood her history; she told him she had had a son and that her son was dead.

He knew all about it, he said, and wasn't shocked. In Saratoga Springs you hear about your neighbors, and the boy she had married went off to fight and died a hero in the Battle of Belleau Wood—so he had heard—and he was proud to think he had proposed to the widow of a hero and that a decade afterward she would allow herself to be by him consoled. He did not think her spoiled, he said, not soiled and—though you believe you are damaged—not damaged goods at all.

This amused her. At some point her parents had made up a story and spread it around and this seemed amusing to Elizabeth; she left the lie alone. If her new husband wanted to think she'd been married before, and needed to think she was somebody's widow, well, why not, she asked herself, what possible harm could there be? There had been a passionate encounter, a single night with Barclay, and as though she was a character in a bad romantic novel strict retribution followed: disorder, early sorrow, a love child come to grief. She had not felt that way to begin with; there had been no damage and nothing to regret; there was neither grief nor harm. The harm came in 1918. That was when the world went dark; that was when the great joke of existence came clear, the celebration that was not a celebration and armistice that brought with it no peace. Once her baby expired beside her, in the narrow single bed they shared, it was a matter of indifference—a joke, a bad joke, a burlesque—if people lied or told the truth, and the tale her parents told was just another piece of foolishness about a wartime hero dead in a ditch in France. When she and Aaron married, Elizabeth wore black.

They were married by a justice of the peace. Because she was not Jewish they could not be married by a rabbi, and in any case it would have been unseemly to wear white and have bridesmaids and throw a bouquet. The service was a quiet one: upstairs, in an office where they signed documents. The JP who married them was sparse-haired and incompetent; he kept losing his place in the service, and he explained to her parents that he'd lost his spectacles and needed spectacles to read the text, which, although he knew it off by heart, he wanted to make certain he got right. He got it wrong. He said, for example, "worthly goods," when he meant "worldly goods," and when he said, "You may kiss the bride" he did so, first, himself. "In sickness or in health," he said, "in poverty or wealth."

On their wedding night Aaron took off his jacket and shoes and placed them in the hotel closet and when he touched her touched her as though she were ready to break. This too was a source of amusement. She satisfied him, it appeared, and he was appreciative and grateful and soon fell asleep. For their first wedding anniversary he took her to the cottage where she'd been romanced when sixteen years old and said, guess what, you'll never guess, I bought this from your parents and it will be our new house. It was your grandmother's, wasn't it, once? You've always loved it, haven't you—and now it's yours, it's ours!

Her husband seemed to think she would be happy in the gabled house: it held—or so he seemed to think—glad memories of childhood and the innocent frolics of youth. He had no idea at all, she knew, of how she'd been with Barclay, how animal her appetite before the world went dark. Aaron showed her the cottage room by room, with a proprietary air, as though she had not been there nakedly and rutting on the very bed he said would be their bed. Elizabeth was shocked, was speechless, and her husband took that as a compliment until finally she taught herself to think of this as funny also, a joke played by the vengeful God that neither of them believed in, and rearranged the furniture and called the cottage home.

Years before, the year she turned eighteen, a man had called her to the bank and said, Miss Elizabeth Dancey, there's something you should know. He talked about a gift of stock allocated to her child, and that a period of waiting—two calendar years—had elapsed and therefore he was now at liberty to inform her of the trust account. He ushered her into his office with a great show of courtesy, and made a point of pulling out her chair. When she told him Harold died, the man offered his condolences and said the trust will nonetheless accrue. He smiled at her. She had been wearing her blue dress, the one with white lace piping, and she tried to tell him while he failed to listen—nodding, smiling, tapping his pencil against his front teeth—that none of this mattered, nothing mattered; in a world without her son it made no difference to her if there was or wasn't money, and she didn't care about the shares of General Electric and he was welcome to watch them—what was the word?—accrue. What Edison and Ford and Firestone had done for her was by Harold's death undone; there had been an epidemic, a pandemic of increase and plenty, and none of it mattered at all. It isn't so simple, he said, it's never that simple, you might well have another child, and Elizabeth said thank you, sir, and left the bank and never spoke to the trust officer again.

⊂≈⊃

Her parents died. Aaron's parents too had died, though in New Jersey and an old people's home; they had been dying for years. Aaron continued to work at the bank and was promoted and did well and then, in 1931, he lost his job. On that day he came home early, saying the bank had closed its doors, saying it would surely reopen for business at some point in the future but until that time times would be hard. Elizabeth said she also had a piece of news and had been planning to announce it at dinnertime—there was a casserole, chicken and carrots—and hoped he would be pleased. She hadn't expected it, hadn't been paying attention, but she was two months pregnant and hoped he wouldn't mind.

The truth was she was terrified and could not let him know. She herself was thirty-one years old and alone in the world and everything went dark once more; it made her hate this body that was loved by men and made to thicken, quicken with life in the presence of death, that dominion of ashes and dust. She was afraid to bear another child and did not want to gain what she feared again to lose. All through the pregnancy Elizabeth lay terrified in the back bedroom of the cottage or downstairs on the sofa or, for the final weeks and days, in the rocking chair on their screened porch; fresh air will do you good, said Aaron, and she heard the echo whisper: *air, share, despair, there, where . . .*

The doctor came. But he arrived too late, of course, because by now she was in labor, and the great fist of her body held and squeezed and wrung her dry. Her contractions were impossible; it was impossible to govern them, and she bit her hand and bit the washcloth Aaron offered, first hot and then cold like the wash-cloth with Harold, bucking in the sweat-wet sheets the way she had with Barclay and screaming shamelessly until the doctor told her husband to step outside and take a walk and try to enjoy the spring air. *Air, there, despair,* she was shouting, but nobody was lis-tening, and she danced down marble stairs to an orchestra no one could hear. By the time her second child was born—a daughter this time, Alice—she was begging for deliverance, an end to all her suffering and asking the doctor to please let her die.

"What nonsense, child," Dr. Jacobsen said. "You're fine. She's fine. She's a beautiful baby. You two will be just fine."

And Aaron was elated and called himself the most fortunate man and, later, when Lou Gehrig called himself, in his farewell speech at Yankee Stadium, "the luckiest man on the face of the earth," Aaron folded the newspaper with satisfaction and said, "The second luckiest, he means."

He was devoted to his wife and daughter, telling Elizabeth they would inherit what he had so carefully put aside, keeping them sol-vent throughout the Depression, though barely, and making do with what they had and scrimping and saving on clothes. He would not scrimp on Alice, however, would not hear of corner- or cost-cutting, since nothing but the best was good enough for his little darling, his princess. No toy was too expensive, no item of clothing too fine. He took odd jobs all over the county, doing bookkeeping or accounting for whatever payment was offered, and often he did so gratis. He worked hard and uncomplainingly and was gentle with her, always, and did not lose his temper. Through the worst of it he stayed, he said, an optimist, and Elizabeth respected this and tried to share his good humor, his boundless optimism.

Things improved. Aaron believed in Franklin Roosevelt and when the bank did open again he returned to his office and was promoted to the Department of Trusts and Bequests. When the Gideon Putnam opened its doors he took her there to celebrate and, in the ballroom, to an orchestra, they danced. For her thirty-fifth birthday he bought his wife an automobile and taught her how to drive it, and they motored up and down the lanes of Saratoga County—feeling prosperous and fortunate, with Alice bundled between them in her bonnet and red scarf.

And now she was forty and Alice was eight and Elizabeth was weary unto death. The wolf was at the door. It was not the wolf of want or need but the beast of desolation she tried to keep at bay. It was a pack of jackals snarling at her there beyond the window and keeping her from sleep. All day she had attempted sleep; all day she had failed to achieve it and dreamed of not having her wolf-haunted dreams. When the birthday meal was finished, and while they were doing the dishes—she with a towel for drying and her husband with his sleeves rolled up, the soapsuds on his forearms where the dark hair clustered—Alice telephoned to wish her happy birthday. She and Janey were going to sleep. "I'll see you in the morning, Mummy," Alice said, and Elizabeth promised to bake a sponge cake, and wished her daughter sweet dreams. They had opened a bottle of wine, and she was unused to it, yet Aaron insisted they finish the wine and drank it off by himself. He was distracted, she could tell, and there was something troubling him, but he would not answer when she asked and said, "Later. After dinner. After we wash up."

"Let *me* do the dishes."

"We'll do them together," he said.

She dropped a wineglass. It shattered. There were glass splinters at her feet, a clustering glitter of small shards of crystal, and Elizabeth retrieved the broom and dustpan and wet a rag for fragments the broom would fail to find. "You'll never guess," Aaron was saying, "what I uncovered at the bank today." She made no answer, and he said, "Well, aren't you curious, don't you want to know what I found in the listing of Trusts and Bequests?" Wordlessly she shook her head and he said, "A trust fund, Elizabeth Dancey. And not one endowed by your parents, but in your maiden name."

"Oh?"

"Oh."

Aaron was no fool, she knew, and knew she had to answer him, but there was nothing to say. It's very curious, he continued, the donors dictated the terms of the gift, and all this time I thought you had a soldier boy for husband and we were poor and I needed to work and you were laughing every day while I went to work at the bank. You had *protectors*, didn't you, you had Mr. Thomas Edison and Mr. Henry Ford and Mr. Harvey Firestone who were paying for that child of yours; *hush money* is the word! And all this time I thought I knew my wife but you were keeping secrets, keeping a trust fund of stock market shares; why, *why?*

A splinter of glass lodged in her palm, and she felt it prick her and a drop of blood emerged. She dropped the dustpan, then the rag, and fell to her knees on the floor. When she began to cry he said, "Don't give me that, don't play your dainty tricks on me, I know I've been stupid and turned a blind eye. But not any longer, missy."

"Blind eye?"

"These fingers"—Aaron held them out—"I worked them to the bone. I worked and *slaved* for you, the two of you, and all the while you'd been somebody's mistress and at the bank they were laughing . . ."

"What tricks," she asked, "what dainty tricks?" but knew he could not hear her and knew she could not tell him that she had to see a doctor. "Get up from there," he said. "Get up off the floor, bitch, goddamn it to hell"—this from a man who never once in her presence before had sworn, or spoken in anger, and now was calling her a bitch, a slut, a whore. He had a terrible temper, but never before had he turned it on her, and so she gathered herself to her feet and he slapped her twice. When she stared at him through the storm in her eye the face she saw was Barclay's, redly, and behind him their son Harold, whom she reached for to embrace, could not, and when she fell again she heard herself saying, "Don't, darling, please. Please don't die."

IX

1952

Alice was twenty and going to Skidmore and finishing school by the skin of her teeth. It was boring, boring, boring, and she *hated* her professor and how he was making them study *The Origin of Species* and how dull it was, dull, dull. The better word was *blame*. He was to blame for making them read it, for what he called the tangled bank of Darwin and Frazer and Karl Marx and Freud. Her professor, Mr. Atkinson, was small and bald and nervous; he fingered his watch chain all during the lecture, and when he sat at his desk he jiggled his leg and polished his glasses and sneezed. He was famously in love with Darwin, Frazer, Marx and Freud and taught the same class every year. She herself wanted to sleep. Charles Darwin should have stayed at home or drowned in a storm off the *Beagle* or killed himself like Captain Fitzroy instead of producing her reading assignment and making her write about the Galápagos Islands and the yellow finch and turtle, five pages due for Monday's class and make sure you footnote, please. It was boring, it was dumb and dull, and what she really wanted was a cigarette outside.

Outside the sun was shining and there was spring growth on the trees; she could see the wind in Congress Park and how it lifted the leaves. Today was her roommate's turn to take notes, and she watched Alison bending and writing—*Alice and Alison, Alison, Alice* was the joke they made of it—so Alice could pay less attention in class; she stared out the window instead. Clouds scudded through the sky. Last Friday night at a mixer she'd met a boy called George from Williams, and they did the lindy and Charleston together, and the boy could dance. At the end of the evening, which was a fox-trot, he asked if he could call her, maybe drive over this next weekend, and Alice told him yes. He was tall and gray-eyed, with a straight nose and a gap-toothed grin, and she thought she might like him a lot.

"Charles Darwin," Mr. Atkinson was saying, "struggled all his life with headaches—migraines, probably, or something he picked up in the tropics that the doctors couldn't cure. Against tremendous odds, ladies—overwhelming odds, in fact—he completed his life's work and transformed our understanding of the species. Which is to say, you and me. He worked out how we got here and what we're doing on this earth and what our ancestry consists of in the evolutionary chain. So it isn't too much to ask that you should complete a five-page assignment—even if you have spring fever or are suffering from senioritis. Questions?" He sat, jiggled, sneezed.

Mr. Atkinson was forty and lived on East Street with his mother, in a brown-shingled house with red trim. His mother knew Alice's father and they played bridge together on Thursdays, and it embarrassed Alice that their parents should be the same age. Her father had retired and was always getting casseroles from widows like Harriet Atkinson, but he had grown forgetful and sat all day in his pajamas, reading the paper, drinking cold tea, so she never could drop by with friends or come home unannounced. "I'd like to, Daddy," she told him, "but it's really really hard to introduce you to a person when you're wearing pajamas and still haven't shaved."

"I'll shave," said Aaron. "You tell me you're coming, I'll shave."

On the streets of Saratoga Springs she was always meeting someone who had grown up with her mother and who remarked how much she looked like Elizabeth; it was too small a town for her to pass the post office or drugstore or even to walk past the entrance to the Adelphi Hotel without meeting someone she knew. This was a comfort, mostly, a way of feeling recognized, but it didn't help that Mr. Atkinson was saying, "Alice, are you with us? Are you suffering from senioritis?"

The bell rang in the hall. He was smiling at her, not unkindly, and so she waved *The Origin of Species* at him and dropped it in her bag of books and gathered her notebook and stood.

"What was that about?" asked Alison, and Alice said, "Oh, nothing. He just wants to show us he's cool."

"Cool?"

"Right. Really a hepcat," she said.

She could remember her mother, of course, but who she remembered was somebody else, not a woman she resembled or was the spitting image of, the way Mrs. Hildebrand said. This had happened yesterday, downtown. She had been riding her bicycle home to get a record she wanted, and her yellow full-length skirt, and on the sidewalk in front of the Adelphi a woman stopped her, saying, "Alice? Aren't you Alice?"

"Yes."

"I'm Dorothy Hildebrand, dear. And I could recognize you in a heartbeat; you look just like your mother, just exactly how she used to, you're her spitting image, dear."

"What's a spitting image?" she asked her father afterward, and Aaron said, "It's spit *and* image, you spit on the mirror and shine it and then you get to see."

"Do I look like her?" she dared to ask, and Aaron said, "A bit."

"Am I *like* her, Daddy?" she asked him, and he turned away.

The high clouds were cumulus clouds. There were cirrus and nimbus clouds also, and she could tell them apart. What matters is the difference in similar things, said Mr. Franks in art history class; that morning he had lectured on *resemblance, imitation,* and he showed slides of examples and she had copied them down. Mr. Franks said we have to distinguish between paintings—apprentice copies, tip-of-the-cap compositions—that at first glance seem the same. What George from Williams saw in her was not the way her mother looked, or how much they resembled each other; he liked it that she knew the lindy and could sing and dance. He told her she looked like Elizabeth Taylor, the girl in *National Velvet,* and she said flattery will get you nowhere, and he said he was telling the truth.

George came from New York City and was a senior too. He wanted, he told Alice, to be an architect or airplane pilot or accountant; she said those seemed a strange choice of careers, and he explained he hadn't even gotten to the Bs—*banker, bandleader, baseball manager,* you name it, I'll try it, *comedian, count, clown.* Then she understood he was joking, unserious, and when he pressed her to him in the fox-trot she could feel the power in his arms and legs. "I'm coming back on Saturday," he said. "I'm taking you out for a spin."

"A spin?"

"Let's call it a spin," he said. "A picnic. The movies. Whatever you want." His smile was knowing and playful and she couldn't wait for Saturday and whatever it was she would want. In the meantime there was art history class and a spot quiz on Frans Hals and Peter Paul Rubens and Rembrandt and how they represented a different way of portraying the world than did Van Dyck or Vermeer; there were five pages due for Mr. Atkinson on the turtle and the yellow finch and how they both were crucial to *The Origin of Species.* So Alice tried to concentrate except it wasn't easy and she'd wear her yellow skirt.

❧

When he arrived that Saturday she was in fact dressed for an outing, with her skirt and wide tin-studded cinch belt and scoop-necked light blue blouse. He himself wore white flannel trousers and a straw boater with a crimson ribbon, and white bucks. The rest of his clothing was a surprise. Over an old flannel shirt, George wore a rumpled seersucker jacket, and his tie was string. "I couldn't decide," he told her, "if you were a Tom Dewey or Harry Truman kind of girl. So I thought I'd take no chances and be a bit of both."

"Which one is which?" Alice asked.

"You guess."

"The President's a haberdasher . . ."

"Right. Except that he's a Democrat, and this is my Democrat shirt."

They were flirting; she was flirting with him. "Which one did you vote for?"

"I couldn't, I'm not twenty-one. I don't get to vote in elections."

"Which one *would* you have voted for?"

"Truman, of course."

"Oh, good. That's a relief."

"What, you never date Republicans?"

She smiled and shook her head.

"So what's your idea of a good time today? Where would you like us to go?"

Sigmund Freud, said Mr. Atkinson, had a friend who was a princess, a woman called Marie Bonaparte, and he had asked her famously, *"Marie, was willst die Weib?"* This is German for, "Marie, what do women want?" and Freud—who also suffered constant pain, although the doctors understood what *he* was suffering from, inoperable cancer—completed his life's work in agony and is an example for us all. If Charles Darwin transformed our understanding of the species then Sigmund Freud continued the work, as did, of course, in their separate ways, both James Frazer and Karl Marx. In Freud's case, however, the exploration was inward, ladies, focusing on the unconscious, the subconscious, and he was particularly interested in what the poet Goethe called *ewige Weibliche,* eternal womanhood. His question was quite serious; the issue of *volition* is a question for us all.

George had packed a picnic bag with a blanket and two towels and, for some reason, radishes; he had pretzels and a chocolate bar and what she later learned was a flask of brandy and several bottles of beer. His car was a midnight blue Oldsmobile, a 76 with black seats; she signed herself out at eleven o'clock on the parietal sheet. Alice had written "Lake George" as destination, and "Family Visit" as reason; they were used to her departures, since she went home so often, and the woman tending the switchboard smiled and said, "Have fun."

It was a beautiful morning—bright, warm—and when he turned on the car radio the first song was "Oh, What a Beautiful Mornin'" from *Oklahoma.* This seemed like an omen, a sign. She knew the words and knew the tune and the two of them joined in the chorus, and then there was "Surrey with the Fringe on Top" and Alice asked him what isinglass curtains might be, the ones that you could roll right down, and he said, "Haven't the foggiest,

my dear," and they laughed and laughed. She was twenty and
giddy and daring and happy to be out with him; Alison called him
a "dreamboat" and that morning had made their old joke. "Be
careful, OK? And if you can't be careful then name it after me!"

They smoked cigarettes and sang. George was a fast driver, and
they made their way through Fort Edward and Hudson Falls and
Glens Falls and up to Huletts Landing on the lake she teased him
he was named for; she wasn't hungry yet, she told him when he
asked, but anyhow he bought her a hot dog with the fixings and
helped himself to a bottle of beer. He asked if she felt like a spin
on the lake, a little excursion in a canoe, and she said yes, why not.
His politeness pleased her, and his formality—as though he was
practicing being an adult and expecting she would too. They
rented a birch bark canoe at the Huletts Landing slip—two dollars for the afternoon, with a five-dollar deposit in case of loss or
damage—and George held the gunwale for her and, balancing,
shoved off.

The water was deep blue and cold, and they were alone on the
lake. He told her to take off her sandals; she complied. He had removed his shoes and socks and rolled his flannels up to the knee
and knew what he was doing with the paddles and canoe. He told
her ever since he was ten his family had sent him to summer camp
in Maine, a place called Camp Androscoggin, and before he went
to college he had been a lifeguard there. He talked about what it
felt like to be a junior counselor, with eight kids sleeping together
in a bunk at night. He liked to sail and fish but most of all he liked
canoes; he feathered his paddle and smiled at her and asked if she
wanted a turn? She shook her head. Because his parents were di-
vorcing they sent him out of Manhattan, and the divorce took forever; each year he went to camp his mother and father had trial
separations and then trial reconciliations; he was an only child.
She was an only child also, she said, and George said he knew, he
could tell.

"How did you know?"

"We have that in common, don't we? It takes one to recognize one."

He kept them close to shore, and she watched the pine trees and the maples jostling, shaking, and the shuttered cabins they passed. The wind increased. Two white-tailed deer, startled, ran off. She pointed at them, turning to see if he had also seen the deer, and he smiled and nodded yes. There was a campsite and a large flat rock and she was turning back again when suddenly the canoe tipped, tilted, and Alice fell overboard. She was not so much frightened as gulping the cold water, shocked, embarrassed, trying to laugh, and he was shouting "Are you all right? God, God, hold on, OK?" Then he was close beside her in the upright canoe and holding out a paddle, saying, "Easy, easy." Her teeth were chattering, her hair astream, and she flailed her arms and legs, holding to the paddle's tip he thrust at her and then the gunwale as he dug hard for shore. They reached land in less than a minute, and by that time he too was wet, standing knee-deep in the water, lifting her to the large rock and uncoiling the painter and fastening it to the exposed roots of a stunted pine and clambering up. Her clothes were soaked, and she had never been so cold in her life and George did jumping jacks and made her do jumping jacks also to get the circulation going and when that did not work he told her to take off her clothes.

"B-but you?" she asked.

"What about me?"

"Aren't you, are you c-c-cold?"

He handed her a towel from the picnic hamper and then unscrewed a flask and told her to take a large swallow; she did. She gagged and coughed and drank again; the brandy warmed her and she closed her eyes while George was rubbing at her hair, her neck and shoulders, then her breasts. He did not kiss her, however, not yet; he continued to work down her body and dried her thighs beneath her upraised skirt, her knees, her calves and then her ankles and toes. In years to come she asked him if he had planned it all this way and tipped the canoe on purpose; "Plain dumb luck" he said. But he was smiling as he said it, and she asked him if he'd done this before, done it often, tipping his dates into water and making them take off their clothes. "What a good idea," he said. "Why didn't I think of it before?"

"It isn't funny," Alice said. "It never was funny. I could have drowned."

"In three feet of water?"

"I *felt* like I was drowning."

"No. Not till I kissed you," he said.

They kissed. The brandy and the sunshine and the second towel he dried her with were working all together, and the shock of the cold water and the startled leaping deer; she rested her head on his neck. She liked the way it fit there, just above the collarbone, and she started to laugh about the accident and then she started to cry. He held her, his arms strong. He rubbed at her shoulders and neck. The canoe bobbed placidly behind them, and across the lake she heard a motorboat, and he spread the blanket out on a patch of grass and pulled her down to the ground and they began kissing in earnest and he took off his pants. She would remember it, always, the way he spread her legs and closed her eyelids with his fingertips and kissed the nipples of her breasts and how she held his erection and helped to guide him in. She would remember the pine trees and grass and how the blood was coursing through her, warming her, and how the flesh of his face distended, a little, because he was working above her and his mouth was open and his cheeks hung down. He was saying "Oh, oh, oh," and it was over quickly but Alice would remember how he pulled away, ejaculating, and spilled himself over her stomach, the semen pooling there. Then she was cold once more, the shadows lengthening, the seduction finished, and they stood up not facing each other; she gathered her wet clothes and dressed.

❧

On the drive back to Saratoga Springs he said, "Will I see you next weekend?" She was trying not to cry. She had expected he would drop her at the dorm and wave and drive away. "Do you want to?" Alice asked.

"Of course," he said. "Of course I do."

"You don't need to say that," she said. She was wearing the

blanket over her shoulders, and it smelled of dirt and blood and beer.

"I *do* want to see you again."

"I don't always fall in the water, you know. It's not, I mean, a habit . . ."

"Don't be angry. Are you angry?"

She considered his question. "Yes. No."

He had the heater on full blast, and by now her skirt was dry. "Next weekend's Memorial Day," he said. "I bet there's a parade."

"And?"

"Do you want to go?"

"What? Marching? No thank you," she said.

He pulled into a parking lot where there was a burned-out abandoned storefront and turned off the engine; cooling, it ticked. Alice bit her lip. He offered her a beer, a sack of radishes, a waterlogged pretzel; she refused. In the middle distance, a dog barked. While she stared out the window George repeated earnestly he *did* want to see her next weekend, because what had happened was special between them, not something he had planned. He said she was beautiful, Elizabeth Taylor–beautiful, and he had felt that way ever since the first minute he saw her, at their first dance. If he'd hurt her he was sorry and sorry she fell overboard; he had been busy balancing the boat and keeping it from capsizing and making things worse. He talked on and on about the accident, not talking about what *did* matter and what had happened afterward, until she wondered if he too was feeling shy. She said, "I want another cigarette, I could *really* use a smoke." They smoked. Staring out the window at an Esso sign and the ruined boarded-up store she rested her hand on his knee. Then she let it rise to his cock. He flushed, he breathed "Oh, oh," and now Alice had the advantage; she felt him harden in her palm and understood the power she would have with him, would use for years, and said, "All right, OK, let's meet on Memorial Day."

On Memorial Day George did arrive, and this time they met in Congress Park; he drove a Chevrolet. "What happened to the dark blue car?" she asked. "It isn't mine," he said. This time his jacket and shirt seemed brand-new, but he was wearing dungarees and sneakers and no hat; he confessed the cars belonged to his fraternity brothers and he didn't own one himself. "Were you trying to snow me?" she asked. Mr. Atkinson was walking by, and he smiled at Alice, and she smiled and waved back. "Who's that?" asked George. "My teacher," she said. "He's got the hots for you, I bet," said George, and she said, "I bet not."

"Oh?"

"He's got the hots for Charles Darwin," she said. "He wants us to memorize the ports of call of the SS *Beagle* and the names of the ship's doctor and the crew. He wants us to read Sigmund Freud."

Then Alison appeared, and they shook hands all around. Alison was long-legged, blonde and dating a medical student called Bill; the four of them drove across town to Union Avenue and found a parking place and settled in to watch the Memorial Day Parade. There were firemen and men with flags and drums and piccolos and guns. There was an ambulance and a fire engine and policemen riding motorcycles and a horse-drawn cannon from the Civil War. She asked Bill what kind of doctor he wanted to be, and he said, "I'm going overseas. Just as soon as I get certified I'll be in the army. Germany, maybe, Korea; I'll be in the Medical Corps."

The day was muggy and windless and hot. In the press of celebrants George and Alison edged up ahead. She watched her date watching her roommate, the way he leaned forward to Alison's ear and whispered something about horses and the Veterans of Foreign Wars, and how he made Alison laugh. In years to come she told herself she should have *known* that afternoon, she should have understood already how he would be a Casanova, unstoppably unfaithful, and should have left him there with his hair slicked back with Wildroot Cream Oil and his glad wandering eye. She should have married Bill instead, or somebody like him — boring, predictable — and been a doctor's wife. But then George turned back to her and circled her waist with his arm and said, "Remember where we were last Saturday, what we were doing just a week ago?" and she forced herself to smile, and then the smile was real, unforced, because he was her Romeo, her one true love once more.

⊂⊗⊃

They were married two years later, in the spring. By then she knew how much of him was self-invented, self-proclaimed, how little he had told her that was true. It was true he went to camp in Maine and true his parents had divorced but only after his father ran off with a woman from the next apartment, who had two children of her own and had returned to L.A. He was a scholarship student at Williams, he was flat cold stony broke. Why didn't you tell me, she asked him, and George said he was ashamed. Ashamed of what, she asked him, and he said, the way my mother drinks. The way my parents argue with each other and I can't invite them to the wedding, and Alice said it's fine, it isn't a problem, I don't want a formal wedding and in case you haven't noticed my own father's not an expert in the field. I like your father, said George. I *love* him, Alice said, but that doesn't mean he could manage a wedding; let's do it with a justice of the peace.

Aaron approved. "That's just how I married your mother," he said, "that's the apple—or is it acorn, *acorn*!—falling just beside the tree." A county clerk called Arthur Wheelock performed the ceremony in his office, and he insisted on kissing the bride and putting his tongue in her mouth. "He's senile," Alice told her father, "he's completely creepy and disgusting," but George said, "Can you blame him?" and kissed her the same way. He was wearing a white jacket and black bow tie and loafers with no socks. This had become his signature: a conscious contrariety, a stylish opposition to the uniform in style.

Alison had married Bill, and he had gone to Korea and been wounded there on his first tour of duty and lost the use of his legs. Mr. Atkinson was caught in a police raid on a parlor where the men of Saratoga drank and danced together and the entertainers were boys. He resigned from Skidmore College but continued to live with his mother and was doing research, he told Alice when they ran into each other on Broadway, on a book about Darwin and Marx. George worked his way through D and E—*dentist, dancer, engineer*—but still had not decided on the choice of a profession; he would do so, he insisted, when they needed to be serious but not when he was twenty-three, not yet. "Let's take a canoe trip," he said, "let's explore Saranac Lake."

"Yes," she agreed. "Let's do."

They remained in Saratoga, and he worked in a real estate office. It was, he told her, temporary, a way of making friends and influencing people. He had the gift of salesmanship; he liked residential real estate and sizing up prospective buyers and deciding what they'd want. Sometimes she went along for the ride while he was scouting locations and had the keys for country properties; sometimes they made love together in the bedrooms of strange houses in Schuylerville and Malta and once on the porch of a farmhouse he would be showing in ten minutes to a couple from New York. They were giddy together and daring and in the first years of their marriage Alice had been happy all the time. For nothing could be boring now, nothing could be dumb or dull except she wished her mother could have known this man who was her husband and wondered what her mother would have thought.

X

1972

Aaron was sitting on the porch, and the porch was warm. He liked it best in springtime and best of all in May and June, and this was sweet May's merry month and the rocker and blankets were warm. Nurse Betty in her uniform made a white shape at his elbow, an acrid looming presence, and he could not hear her at all. Nevertheless she was talking; she was moving her lips and hips and gesticulating happily and it behooved him to smile. He smiled. The motion of the rocking chair was predictable, familiar, and he cradled his teacup and rocked. His left eye was no use today and his right eye not what it should be, and therefore the forsythia seemed a yellow streaming band of light, the blue of the sky a bright blur. Yet waiting for a car to come was — the word for it was — *tedious*, the driveway glinting at his feet, the traffic and laughter beyond.

Beyond the porch the driveway with its gravel ribbon led to the wrapped present of the road. The road had been a cart track and then a wide packed lane and then a paved road with a paint stripe down the middle, and he had traveled them all. His daughter Alice would arrive; she was coming to pay him a visit, and therefore he prepared himself and tried to stay awake. He could remember and would tell her how in 1935 when she was three he bought a Model A from Mr. Ford's car dealership and sported up and down the lanes, repairing the tires or the gas line when it leaked or clogged, which was in those days often, and always in his checkered scarf and brown cloth cap. She had been his sunshine girl, his princess, and he remembered how she would leap from the running board into his arms. "Here, *here*," he'd tell her and hold out his arms, and she would take a breath and close her eyes and jump.

Nurse Betty fluffed up a pillow and placed it at his head. She was saying "Roosevelt," and he pictured Franklin Roosevelt, the pince-nez and cigarette holder, the armchair and top hat and bright flash of teeth. He, Aaron, had lost his right arm. To be precise, he told her, he hadn't lost it as in *misplaced,* he had lost the *use* of it, and all such loss was relative: he could see his forearm encased in the black cardigan, and if she pricked it it would bleed. He had had what they call an infarction and also a series of strokes. If she stroked it it would bleed. President Roosevelt's loss had been worse, but all across the nation people failed to understand the extent of his paralysis, and they believed he would walk in due time. In the course of events Franklin Roosevelt died, and then they had the haberdasher and then the goatish one, John Kennedy, and all across America the public had been ignorant; they did not know, for example, about old Woodrow Wilson and the nature and importance of his stroke. By contrast the last President, the one who came from Texas, lifted his shirt for reporters so they could photograph and everyone inspect his operation's scar. Is there no dignity, he asked her, is there no privacy left?

"A beautiful morning," Nurse Betty declared.

"Yes."

"Makes you *glad* to be alive!"

He smiled.

"Roosevelt," she said again, or something very like it, and Aaron remembered the Roosevelt Baths, how he would sample the waters, and afterward he and a fellow from Mortgage and Loans—who? Jimmy Wallison, Peter Austine?—would take a room together and lie in the sulfurous egg-smelling baths, the hot beaded water and pore-cleansing steam, and discuss the Yankees and the pennant race and then they both would enjoy a massage and, later, a cigar. There was one masseur he liked—who? Jimmy Wallison, Peter Austine?—and he could picture the man's rolled-back sleeves, the meticulous tiepin and apron and well-muscled arms and wintergreen and talcum powder and, always, a two-dollar tip. Oh it was wonderful once in this town: the baths, the Spa, the racing touts, the Gideon Putnam for breakfast, the bacon and sausage and poached eggs he loved. He had been wandering, he recognized, and in the light of the forsythia was wondering how best to rock here in peace if not quiet while waiting for his daughter and his grandson to arrive.

"Well, *here* they are," Nurse Betty told him, and he smiled at her: his faithful attendant, his good-hearted girl. When a person has turned ninety-two, the quality of light and the feel of a pillow behind you, the memory of eggs and sausages piled on a plate: these *matter*; he wanted to tell her, these cannot be ignored. They used to call it Murderers' Row, not Tinkers to Evers to Chance who were fielders but Ruth and Lou Gehrig and everyone else, and he himself had objected—Aaron remembered this clearly—to calling them "Murderers" even in jest: a bat is not a gun. A glove is not an axe. The white pinstripes, the cap, the cleats—all these bespoke a uniform, and it was true that the house Ruth built was an engine of capital driving the Bronx, and it was true also they called them the Bombers, but all such military language was, he maintained, irrelevant; it was cold beer, it was Cracker Jacks and the bleacher community buoyed by hope. These *matter*; he told her, these can't be ignored.

He had not been religious. He had no use for temple and had not attended *shul*. There was, however, proof of God—not the white-haired white-bearded old man in the clouds but a principle of divinity, the idea that made him pious—and it's the way the willow and the chestnut tree exist together, side by side, yet never once in nature will you find a chestnut on a willow tree. Or willow leaves on chestnut branches, turn by turn. Such a distinction is nature's device and a complexity of pattern only God Himself could have created, the divine presence everywhere, boy.

He announced this to his grandson who was leaping up the porch. From the running board of his old Model A to—what car was Alice driving now, a Mercury, a Lincoln?—running up the driveway's slope was a small step for mankind, was it not, for at present they walked on the moon. David was a happy child, David was here for a visit, and behind him with her stately gait advanced his daughter Alice with a handbag at her wrist. In such a light, in the dazzle of his one good eye, she reminded him of his dead wife, her mother Elizabeth née Dancey when she herself was forty and resplendent in her beauty and, he grieved to remember it, grief.

Truth be told, he told the nurse (who was not listening, was making the boy welcome and handing him a peppermint), he could not remember the cause of the sorrow but only its lineaments: tears, the black dress, the cheekbones and the almond eyes and full lips set against him, her face on the pillow but turned to the wall and the dark splay of hair on the sheets. He had been so proud of her, so—Aaron confessed it—*vain,* so pleased that this beautiful woman accepted his ring and his name. She was twenty years younger than he. She was a daughter of the Danceys and that meant something in this town, it meant respectability and land, it meant a pleased awareness on his part—and, on the part of others, alarm—that she condescended to marry a Jew. Not condescended, no, *agreed, decided, chose* to accept his proposal and to tell him yes. For this he had been grateful, although in time he came to learn that hidden in his wife's romantic history (but had he suspected it, asked himself why?) lay something not quite so respectable, neither spotless nor unstained, and Elizabeth had tricked him—no, not tricked so much as deluded, *misled*—into believing what she was was spotless, stainless, acquiescent willingly in this their married life.

⤜∾⤛

"Good morning, Daddy," said Alice.

"Morning?"

"It's eleven o'clock," she said. "Ready to roll?"

He smiled. "Where are we going this morning?"

"The store. David needs new shoes, his feet are getting—"

"Shoes?"

"Yes. For running in," she said.

"He's ready," said Nurse Betty. "He's been sitting here an hour now."

He raised himself up from the chair. It was not difficult, really, not painful but slow, and together with his cane and coat they made a processional down not the stairs but the gray adjacent painted ramp, while the nurse remained behind (collecting the blanket, the pillow, the teacup) and what he wanted to discuss with her (the bombing, the tunnels, the Ho Chi Minh Trail) faded from him briefly and he felt himself descending as his grandson skipped and juddered and his daughter took his arm. Now what do you make of it (bombings and rice crops and temples destroyed), he had been planning to inquire, to solicit an opinion, and instead they shopped for shoes for this cavorting grandson and Alice's third child of three. His daughter was aggrieved. She was—nowadays they would call it—*depressed*. She had inherited not only her mother's dark beauty but nature, and there was the goatish George and his fondness for women and gin. He, Aaron, was not fooled by this; he knew his son-in-law, the fellow's shiftless habits, and knew his daughter suffered them and turned her face to the wall.

There had been enough blame to go round. There had been, on his own part, if not ignorance, willed innocence, and he repeated the words to himself: *ignorance, innocence,* which? What might have been a blessing for Elizabeth became instead a curse; what could have made them happy made them sad. Her history—he pondered this—her *his*story could have been glad. Yet there had been devotion once, unstinting attention on his part, and there had been his strong right hand before he lost the use of it, before he misplaced his palm on her cheek, and when he discovered the Vagabonds' gift in the office of Trusts and Bequests.

The writer Karl Marx was a fool. He had meant well, perhaps, and put his finger on the problem of the bourgeoisie, but what he failed to understand is how we like to mow our lawns and mow them all the more attentively if mortgaged; it's the triumph of capitalism, really, a man tends what he owns. *Das Kapital* dismisses what the common man works hard to have: a roof and lawn and garden of his own. Sigmund Freud was not much better; Herr Sigmund failed to understand that all is not always ego or id, a man goes to the office and, because it is his business, opens the Dancey file, reads it and discovers his wife had a baby out of what in those years people would call *wedlock*, and that that baby is provided for, as well as her heirs and assignees, and all other issue till time out of mind.

"Careful," she urged him.

He got in the car.

"Bye-bye," called Nurse Betty.

Now David was jumping around in the seat and Alice was starting the motor once more and in a cloud of spraying gravel together
off they went. He himself had gone to Sarasota, fleeing south for
seven years in wintertime, not following his darling but the starling
in such flight. This too was language, Aaron understood, mere language: the comfort of rhyme. In truth he had no darling but his
daughter any longer and did not know if starlings left; the black
crow remained in the bleak winter trees, and no doubt also the
raven remained—but he never had been able to distinguish between them, the raven or starling or crow. In truth he had enjoyed
the train—the sleeper car, the dining car, the long migration down
the coast—and then the little circus town, the Ringling Brothers'
mansion, the bright flamingos everywhere, and heat. From
Saratoga to Sarasota, the best of both possible worlds. He had
deeded his daughter the cottage, and then he had flown (well, motored; well, taken the sleeping car) south.

"What kind of shoes?" Aaron asked.

"Keds. White ones," Alice said.

"Oh, *Mom.*"

"He doesn't want them," Alice said. "He wants them with arrows and colors."

"Ah. Arrows and colors!" He nodded. And therefore he thought
about arrows, the straight fledged shaft, a headdress of feathers
and shells. He thought about the way bright feathered creatures
disappear and then return; one day in November you notice they're
gone and one day in May they arrive. He thought about David,
Joanna and Claire and how they too were ignorant—the owners of
substantial equity in an enterprise not far from here, that company
first called Edison Electric and now General Electric, the shares in
1926 engaged in what might be called a productive mitosis, split-
ting four for one, then four for one again in 1930, then three in
1954, then last year two for one, so fifteen shares in 1916 would
be—he still could do arithmetic, he still had a head for comput-
ing!—*one thousand four hundred and forty shares.* And in the way such

thoughts of late had led him down their circling path, Aaron remembered his beautiful bride: the night of their wedding, the nights after that. There had been, he remembered, primroses in the window box; there was a bottle of wine. There had been the possibility of—no other word for it!—*bliss.*

⸙

That first time Elizabeth rose from the floor, he should have supported and not knocked her down; he should have offered Gilead's balm and not the clenched back of his hand. Was it because of this, he asked himself, that the hand proved useless now; did he raise his hand to smite her and in turn turn powerless, and could this therefore be adduced as proof of a pattern, the workings of God? If the chestnut and the willow tree stand side by side by the edge of the road, why does the chicken cross it, and what's the other side? He had been, he acknowledged, unbending; he should have been less so and let her explain. His wife had never lied to him, and only her silence, not speech, had misled; he did, he regretted this now.

Sometimes eight people would live in the home, or sometimes seven, or only six, but then new old ones would arrive and assume the vacant place; that's one thing you can take for granted, Aaron knew, it's part of God's pattern, the young will grow old. In due course. In the course of time. You can't imagine it, my boy, but it will happen anyhow and it will happen to you. He should have remained on the porch.

"Are you hungry?" Alice asked.

He shook his head.

"Did you have breakfast?"

Again he shook.

"We're going for lunch afterward," she said. "Grilled cheese for David. And, Daddy, whatever you want."

What he wanted was to rest. What he wanted was, he told her, to lay his burden down. Franklin Roosevelt was dead, and then the haberdasher and the goatish one they killed so young, while Aaron Freedman lived. He had outlasted, if not usefulness, his time's allotted span. If there were such a thing as justice or, not justice, *balance* in the world the man who'd raised his right arm smiting would be laid long since to rest and his bride would rise up from the floor, unbloodied, beautiful, and smile and take her grandson's hand and buy him a pair of blue Keds.

Then Aaron remembered old Wallison's joke, or possibly Peter Austine's. A pair of Jews are courting and they plan to marry. They each have been married before; she's a widow, he a widower, and now that they are older and wiser they decide to spell things out. "My dear," says the bridegroom, "before we get married, I believe I should ask your opinion: how often you wish to have sex?"

She blushes. "I'm very grateful you ask. I think *infrequently.*"

He considers her answer. And, after a minute, inquires, "Is that one word or two?"

It was ironic, was it not, a proof of God as humorist, that he should be alive today and lovely Elizabeth dead. Aaron turned on the seat to his daughter; she signaled and drove left. But he wanted to explain to her—there was so much to tell her, and she was failing to listen; no, that was inaccurate, failing to hear—what parking in the parking lot (a slow processional now down the row, a hunt for a space where she pulled in and braked, a little rocking motion of the chassis settling on its metal springs, and then the handbrake and canceled ignition, the key, the door, the key again) he felt himself obliged this noontime to declare.

Because without such explanation he was nobody, an old man in a shopping center, a receptacle for other people's leavings, waste, and with it he was somebody: the retired executive vice president of what had once been called the Adirondacks Savings Bank. He did not know its present name. He did not care to know. It would be changed again, of course, would merge and divide like a cancer, a not-so-productive mitosis, and there was no reason to be bothered by the nomenclature because by the time he, Aaron, learned and entered it into his statements, his checkbook, the name of the bank would have changed . . .

"Well, here we are," she said. "Hungry?"

No, what mattered in this merry month was lastingness, renewal, *another time, another place,* and therefore he described to his daughter the light on the lake that late September afternoon in — where was it? Bolton Landing? Huletts Landing? — the long day's paddling done and the canoe made fast to the dock, the way her mother seemed a farm girl again, girlish and lithe in her red flannel shirt, at ease with knots, at ease with the lake-weed and small scuttling creatures that rendered him uneasy, at home in the blazon and flare of the trees. So *she* was the one who gathered the kindling and built the fire and gutted the trout, *she* the one who knelt uncomplainingly to tend it on uneven ground, while he busied himself with his papers and pipe.

And on that day in — what would it have been, 1931? — the week before he lost his job and she told him they would have a child, he marveled as so often before at how she chose to suffer *him* ("Aaron," joked Jimmy Wallison, "you have a good head for figures!" and winked and nodded at Elizabeth), how she with all her silent skill yet acquiesced in this his loud ineptitude. And he had been encouraged to play the city dweller while she resumed her childhood chores ("Do you know the one," asked winking Jimmy, "about the traveling salesman and the farmer's redheaded daughter?"), so perhaps it was his own fault finally that he himself had permitted the joke, had joined in the laughter and derision, *derisiveness,* yes, that was it; he had been derisive and wanted to apologize and to make amends. I had a temper, he wanted to tell her, I lost it often at inefficient tellers or grocery clerks or traffic policemen. I saw the way things ought to work and if they failed to work that way then this — or so I told myself — was a failure in others, not me: the sudden flush, the heat in the head, the red encumbrance in one eye, all these were familiar, *familiars,* but I had kept them from your mother, maintaining her inviolate and on a pedestal; she was not subject to such inquiry or enraged correction until that birthday dinner the year my wife turned forty and the night I returned from the bank.

And have I told you how on that particular and fateful Friday morning I bought her a sweater, a pink cardigan I knew she'd like, a perfume she was partial to? Or so I hoped and had been assured

by the salesgirl at Lonergan's, the one with penciled eyebrow lines
and bee-stung lips like Clara Bow's, which was the fashion then, I
think, or perhaps it had been earlier, because who can date precisely or be bothered to remember if the fashion then was bee-
stung lips or the flaming red of Rita Hayworth or, possibly, Jane
Russell. At any rate the girl assured me your mother would be gratified, would wear this particular perfume with pride, and so I made
the purchases at lunchtime and returned to the office and was
searching, I remember, for a file of the Dantley Family Trust and
came upon Dancey adjacent, and nothing could have been or
seemed more natural than to peruse it also, feeling that small flare
of satisfaction engendered by the luck I'd had, the excellent fortune
of marriage, until *hey presto*, everything changed.

"OK, let's go," said Alice.

"Not high-tops," said David. "Anything but high-tops, Mom."

"Alley-oop," said Aaron, and they stood.

Except he was not standing, had fallen to the kitchen floor, had
bloodied his cheek on the wineglass she dropped, and now strong
hands were lifting him; "Are you all right?" his daughter asked, repeated, and he could not answer "No," because when Elizabeth
died—not on that particular evening, of course, but six months
later, her face to the wall, having endured what the doctor declared
was an inoperable cancer, fast-growing, undetectable or at least by
them in those years undetected, but *this* explained her loss of balance, *this* explained her listlessness—a part of him departed also,
not having cursed the not-God in his heaven, since if He existed it
was in the willow, the pattern of leaves, but resolute in his refusal
nonetheless to affirm; why *should* he, Aaron attempted to say, who
had received not a blessing but curse, who had made of a legacy
fury and dust, who leapt from the running board into her arms and
would remain there thereafter (in Sarasota, in the nursing home in
Saratoga, in the rocking chair, the parking lot where Alice tried
and failed to make him stand, to make him breathe) guilt-tram-
meled, responsible, dead.

XI

1976

Alice was searing the bacon and doing so on purpose; she liked it best burned to a crisp. She kept a coffee can for drippings, and a pound of bacon yielded half an inch of fat; she was very careful with the cast-iron skillet, pouring off the liquid, because she had a friend, Marie, whose left forearm and leg had been burned when she toppled a pan from the stove, reaching for it heedlessly, and the hot grease geysered down and scarred Marie for life. Behind her, at the kitchen table, the children fussed and chattered, and in some part of her consciousness Alice was protecting them, standing between her daughters and son and the cauldron of delight they were about to eat. She herself was drinking coffee, watching the light on the maple outside and how the leaves were yellowing and had begun to fall. When there was enough to pour, she poured off bubbling fat.

"How soon?" asked Claire.

"How *soon*?" David asked.

"There's orange juice," Joanna said. "I squeezed it, Mom."

"How many pieces?" David asked.

"Three," Claire told him. "I get four."

"Not *fair*, it isn't *fair*!"

"Here, darling." Alice offered a first piece of bacon from the newspaper she'd drained it on; Claire was supposed to be buttering toast and Joanna producing the jam. Her eight-year-old—his sense of equity confirmed, the share-and-share-alike arithmetic of bacon strips established to his satisfaction—smacked his lips loudly and chewed. *The last shall be first,* Alice thought. She loved these weekend mornings—the three children gathered at the table, jostling, bickering over the size of their portions but not really meaning it, not awake enough quite yet to declare their separate agendas or go their separate ways. They were starting to do so, of course; they would be leaving soon. Her pretty ones, her daughters, and this boy who looked so much like George she was astonished, sometimes: the way he sat and spread his hands and tossed the hair out of his eyes. They were growing up so quickly she couldn't bear it, sometimes, how time both crawled and flew.

David licked his fingers. Alice drank. She was spoiling him, she knew, and would correct his manners later, but a child should be allowed to eat one piece of bacon with his fingers this one breakfast of the week. The coffee was lukewarm and sweet. In the distance a siren rose, fell. In a minute she would deal with eggs: eight brown eggs cracked and beaten, with salt and pepper added and milk already in the mixing bowl, and while the pound of bacon leached into the newsprint, darkening, she drained the fat again but left a little in the frying pan for flavor and added butter and, as soon as the butter had melted, poured in the bowlful of eggs. Then she adjusted the heat.

"What time is it?" asked David.

"The bacon's done, these eggs look hunky-dory. Ten-fifteen."

"Ten-seventeen," said Claire. The girls wore pajama bottoms and a pair of matching sweatshirts that said YALE.

"Ten-twenty," said Joanna. "Time to eat."

"I'm *starving*," David said.

It was their ritual on Sundays; no matter how late Joanna had been out the night before, no matter with whom, she always came down to the kitchen by ten and sleepily permitted her mother to kiss her and took out a dozen oranges and cut them in half by the sink. Next she set up the juicer and commenced to squeeze. Claire would descend to the kitchen also; it was her job to set the table, laying out glasses and napkins and toast. She would watch her sister carefully, waiting for the juice to spurt or a section of cut fruit to fall to the floor. They each had roles; they all played parts, and these were designated early on and could not be changed. It was the family pattern: Joanna exuberant, feckless, slicing oranges in two and squeezing them, and Claire her younger sister with the orthodonture and the list of grievances, closed in on herself like a fist.

"What did you do last night?" Alice asked. "Where did you two go?"

"We went to the movies," Joanna announced.

"Oh?"

"*Picnic.* A rerun. Did you ever see it, Mom?"

She smiled. "That William Holden. Wasn't he a heartbreaker, though?"

"And Kim Novak. Va-va-voom."

"Va-va-voom," repeated Claire. She rubbed at what she persisted in calling a zit. "Is it like *mucha muchacha*?"

"Sort of. Only different." Joanna started humming "Moonglow"; she raised and kissed her spoon.

"Can I have more orange juice?"

"More orange juice *please*," Alice said to her son. He held out his glass and she poured. "You sound just like your father. May I *please*."

⸎

George was not with them, however; George had gone away. He was, he said, on a business trip and when she asked him what sort of business got conducted on Saturday morning he said it was a party in the Adirondacks, up by Long Lake where the fishing was good; she would be welcome to join him and meet his business friends. These were contacts, professional contacts, and conversation on the lake was twice as important as talk in the office and when he got back from the Lodge at Long Lake he promised he'd bring back fresh bass or a pike. Why don't you join me, darling, why not come along.

She didn't even bother to refuse. He had known her answer, that she would say no. He was banking on the certainty she wouldn't leave the children and was doing what she could to keep the family together, to carry on as though they *could* just carry on and time neither crawled nor flew. It was her habit to stay home and his to go to parties, her desire to be peaceful and his to raise the roof. So George had packed his duffel bag and flask and fishing gear, saying, next year I'll take David; then he got in the car and tapped the horn twice, lightly, and drove off. The children waved. That had been yesterday morning, and tomorrow night with his business done he would be back home again, reeking of gin and tobacco and the fish-stink all over his body and daring her to make an issue of it, daring her to question him about the weekend party and who else had been at the Lodge.

Alice added coffee to her white porcelain cup. It steamed. In fact she did not miss him now, not with the children chattering and the smell of bacon in the room and the prospect, afterward, of the crossword puzzle and the *New York Times*. In fact he never had been part of Sunday breakfast, had never shared their eggs and toast, and she minded this part of the weekend much less than the rest, minded the mornings much less than the nights, and with the sunlight dappling the sugar maple behind her and the four of them sitting together she permitted herself the small pleasure of coffee and, later on, a cigarette. She parceled out the scrambled eggs and, smiling at them, raised her cup; she was their mother and it was a bright autumn day and soon they would be leaving home but not just yet, not now.

"So what's on the schedule this morning?" she asked.

"Homework," said Joanna. "There's a Spanish test."

"Tomorrow?"

"*Verdad. Mañana,*" said Claire—a pedant already, and better at Spanish.

"*Compuesta, no hay mujer fea,*" Joanna pronounced. " 'Made up, no woman is ugly.' That's what Mr. Hernandez told us. And he said it would be on the test."

"I doubt it," said Alice. "I can't believe he meant any such thing. Was he joking?"

"No."

"Not Mr. Hernandez," said Claire, and for a moment the two girls smiled at each other, sharing knowledge, keeping secrets, and she wished she could speak to this Mr. Hernandez and tell him to behave himself or he'd be out on his ear. Her elder daughter was a knockout, a *mucha muchacha,* and her Spanish teacher better keep his witty sayings and his Latin Lover attitudes and plump beringed hands to himself.

"I heard another one," Joanna said. "*A lo lejos, aun la barbuda es hermosa.*"

"What?"

"What's *that* mean?" David asked. He had finished his portion of bacon and was staring at his mother's plate; he was waiting to see if she'd offer him more before he began on his eggs. He liked to finish one flavor completely; he did everything in sequence and didn't like, she knew, to mix the tastes.

"*Lo lejos*—is it *los* or *las*? Or just plain *lo*?" Joanna asked.

"'In the distance,'" Claire translated for her brother, "'even the bearded one is attractive. Pretty.' That's what it means."

"It's stupid," he said. "Girls don't have beards."

"*He* doesn't care," said Joanna. She raised her arms and clapped her hands like castanets and sang, "Olé, *mucha muchacha.*"

Alice tried not to look shocked. Instead she swallowed a spoonful of plum jam and asked her son what time his tennis lesson had been scheduled for this afternoon and where they were playing tomorrow and when the game was. "Match," he said, "it's called a match," and she felt, again, excluded by the three of them—the condescension of it all, the way her children *handled* her—even this eight-year-old, even her little boy-man of the house. "Well—game, set, match," she said, and turned back to the window and stared at the tree. The plum jam tasted tart, not sweet, made from greengage plums and with ginger mixed in; yes, that was it, the tang of ginger, the taste on her puckering tongue. There were a blue jay and a cardinal—a *pair* of cardinals, she saw—and she watched them preen.

⁘

The telephone rang. Joanna answered. By the set of her shoulders and lilt in her voice, the breathy breathless "I'll call you later," it was clear to everyone that who was calling was a boy and not one she wanted to talk to in public, or not at least the public her family had become. Claire winked at David; he laughed. Whatever had been going on, whoever was calling her daughter, he was someone that the others knew and had been expecting to call. Joanna turned away from them, offering her back. The girl's skin was flawless, her hair in the sunlight aflame. Deliberately, savoring it, Alice chewed her own final portion of bacon, deciding just this once to keep it for herself. For if she chose to *she* could shut *them* out; she too could keep a secret and not let them know her worries or her hopes and plans . . .

No sooner did Joanna hang up than the telephone rang once again. Again her daughter answered and she felt excluded: the person who served them their eggs. *The first shall be last,* Alice thought. For in truth she could be bitter about the way her husband taught flirtatiousness, how he showed the children daily, nightly, what a man without scruples could manage—what a smile and a dropped voice accomplished in the dance of courtship and how to behave on the phone. George always was a ladies' man, had never denied or disguised it, and at least she'd known what she was getting into when she got into his bed. At least he was clear about that.

"Just a minute, please," Joanna said, and then, "Mom, it's for you." She handed over the phone. The cord could barely stretch across the tabletop, and Alice considered changing her place or going to the hallway extension but leaned across the table instead, putting her elbow down by the plum jam and feeling a twinge in her wrist. "Hello?"

"Mrs. Saperstone," a stranger inquired, and she said, "Yes."

"Is your husband a George Saperstone?"

She nodded.

"And does he drive a blue Mustang convertible? 1969?"

"Correct. Who is this, please?"

"It's Sergeant Alwyn out of Keene."

"Keene?"

"Keene, New York. It's the police. We're in the Adirondacks, ma'am, and your husband's had an accident."

"What happened?" she asked. "Just what exactly happened?"

"I'm sorry to have to be telling you this."

"How is he? I'm sitting down. When?"

"It's not good news," he said. "I'm sorry to be the one to inform you, but he died late last night. Or this morning, maybe, early. He had an accident and we only just discovered him; we had our first weather last night. Our first real snow, I mean."

The children were silent, watching. There was a wind in her ears. The telephone receiver was a loud high wind in her right ear, and all she could manage was "Yes?"

"There was a passenger," the sergeant said. "She's deceased too, I'm afraid."

A vision of hot bubbling fat, the skillet clattering down off the stove and bacon searing her dear friend Marie, a vision of George in the car with some woman from the business meeting and skidding off the ice-slick road—all this assaulted her, the shock of it, and somehow also the not-shock, the certainty when she'd reached for the phone that what she was going to hear would be bad. "A Miss Skellings," said the Sergeant. "Regina Skellings, yes?"

"I don't, know, no her," said Alice.

"Mom?" said David. "What *is* it?"

She glared at him, shaking her head.

"The vehicle is totaled, ma'am. Were they at, what, a party?"

"I don't, no, *know*," she said.

And then the policeman was talking, saying he was sorry, saying there would be an autopsy and the coroner believed death had been instantaneous but it was Sunday morning and would take time to tell; it hadn't been a snowstorm, really, mostly freezing rain and ice. It was early in the season and they hadn't plowed or salted and her husband didn't have snow tires on his car but they were two hours north of Saratoga and here in the mountains an October ice storm isn't all that unexpected and would she be willing to drive up to Keene or was somebody able to drive her and would she want an officer from the Saratoga station to come over to the house? He went on and on about procedure and the need for formal identification of the body and the fact the car was totaled and it was a one-car accident but he ran into a tree; did he have any history of heart disease or seizures or was he diabetic or might he have suffered a stroke?

Alice shut her eyes. She cupped her left hand at her ear. Sergeant Alwyn faded in and out while static intervened and the blue jay chased the cardinal. She couldn't tell him, when he asked, where her husband was staying precisely or the location of the Lodge; she didn't know the names of other people in the fishing party or how many of them had been on the trip. And even though the policeman kept saying "I understand," she knew he didn't understand, or didn't choose or want to, and would keep on asking questions—not quite addressing but not avoiding either the issue of Miss Skellings's presence, the empty flask, and what they were doing at two, maybe three in the morning together on a mountain road, a second fatality there in the car until what she needed to tell him, and did, was "I'm sorry, I can't talk any longer," and reached across the tabletop and hung up the phone.

"Mom?"

"What is it?" asked Joanna.

"What happened?"

"Your father is dead."

"What?"

"I told you. In a car crash."

"Where?"

"In the Adirondacks."

And then in fact she couldn't talk and dropped her head to her plate. In the instant that followed she knew she should rise, should take her children in her arms and start consoling, planning, start the process of accommodation and deal with the fact of his death. But the shock and not-shock contended in her fiercely and she was trying not to vomit, trying not to faint or fall, and it took time before she raised her head and stared at David, Joanna and Claire. "What will we do?" she asked them. "What will we ever *do*?"

Claire gathered a handful of dishes. She carried them across the room and placed them in the sink. She did this in silence; Joanna too was silent and David's bright face had turned white. It was, their mother understood, a pivot point, an absolute dividing line: everything that happened now would happen *after* George was dead and everything that happened earlier would have been *before*.

And while the children stared at her she found herself remembering the way George honked, twice, lightly, tapping his hand on the horn rim and waving and how she had never imagined it would be the final time, the last time she'd see him alive. She imagined the dark mountain road and the snow and ice and trees and freezing rain. She pictured how he took the curve, the way he picked his right foot up and hit the brake but late, too hard, the mirror and dashboard and radio, the granite shelf and tree and plunging car and crumpled hood and shattered glass and then she imagined the woman beside him: a blonde, a redhead, a brunette, a terrified creature with long hair or short and wearing a pea coat or fur coat or nothing at all, her skirt hiked up above her knees or face averted, screaming, gloved or ungloved hand on his . . .

"Mom? Are you all right, Mom?"

"*Mother,*" said Claire.

She shook her head. She saw them, her pretty ones all in a row, and saw the can of bacon fat and knew it had congealed. David was standing now, close at her side. "Oh dear," she said, "oh dear, oh dear," and opened her arms to enfold him and knocked her coffee cup down off the table. It broke. "He wasn't alone," Alice said.

"What?"

"There was somebody with him. In the car. And she's dead too."

"Who?"

"I don't know. A person called Skellings. Regina Skellings. A business friend."

"He said he'd take me *next* year," David said.

"Well," said Joanna, "he won't."

Then David lifted his white strained face and Alice could see he was crying and cradled him, her baby boy, and his big sister said, "I'm sorry, I didn't mean it *that* way, I didn't mean . . ."

"It was snowing. It was icy there."

"You can say that again," said Joanna. "The fucking Adirondacks."

"Fucking business trip," said Claire.

"Those fucking Adirondacks," repeated David, greatly daring. "That fucking business trip."

Now Alice was raising objections, objecting to the way they swore, was ready to correct them who had never used that word before, or at any rate not in her presence, but what was he doing out there on the roads, why hadn't he stayed in the Lodge or the hotel or motel or wherever he was fucking her—this Regina, this Miss Skellings—and come back not sorry but safe? She bent to the cup at her feet. First she collected the porcelain shards, then soaked her napkin in the coffee that was pooling at the table leg, then tore off sections of white paper towel from the towel rack by the pantry sink and the framed picture of the horse David had made her for Christmas—he was good at it, he had an eye and liked to draw horses in corrals, or cantering, or lined up at the starter's gate—and rubbed the linoleum clean with the towel, seeing a spiderweb under her chair and cleaning that up also.

The rest of the morning they stayed in the house, close to each other, unwilling to leave. Her children cried and cried. She was trying to control herself and to not be furious; she rocked back and forth on her stool. That afternoon she would travel to Keene and view his broken body, and the next morning return. There would be weeks and months and years of dealing with the accident, her husband's death, of mastering the fact of it and mustering an attitude. She would learn when to smile and nod and when to turn from sympathy, the proffered lip or outstretched hand; she would teach herself what to answer when asked, and how to deflect the next question . . .

"Oh, Mummy," said Joanna. "Are they sure it's him?"

"They have his wallet. Yes."

She stared out the window, unseeing. She bit at her thumbnail; it tore. She bit at her cuticle, sighing. The old procedures would resume, *sweet George, wild George, our impossible George,* and as though she read it all already in the coffee grounds or darkly through the window glass Alice saw what would ensue from this: the policemen and the lawyers and the newspaper reporter and insurance agent with her husband's life insurance, its surprising yield. She saw herself a widow, her dead parents' only daughter, and the ranks of those who offered her their words of comfort or their wordless presence thick, then thin again, the wound first fresh, then dull, then healed, *dear George, poor George, that terrible George,* the line of suitors come to call, the children growing up, away, and then with children of their own . . .

"We'd better pack," she said. "I'd better get ready to go."

"Where?"

"Keene. Does anybody want, what, something else to eat? Drink?"

Claire said, "Oh, Mother. No."

Part Five

2003

"I have something to tell you," says Jim.

"What?"

"I think you know it already. I think you know what I'm going to say."

Claire looks across at him. "What?"

"Don't act so surprised," he says. He is standing by the Bose. He has inserted a CD but not as yet pushed *Play*. "I believe you've guessed it already."

"No. No, I haven't."

"It's been going on," he says, "long enough for you to have noticed. Of course you have."

"OK, I'll guess," she says. "Animal, vegetable, mineral?"

"What?"

"Twenty questions. You're making me play twenty questions. I gave that up some time ago."

"That's exactly it." He glares at her. "It's just exactly what I mean. The way there's nothing's *fun* for you. There's no excitement anymore."

She feels a weariness—immense, premonitory; she does in fact know what he's planning to say. "All right."

"All right, what?"

"Let me guess. You're having an affair," she says. "You love another woman."

"No."

"Well, not love exactly, maybe not yet. You're sleeping with your secretary?"

"No. And I can't help myself."

"That cute receptionist?"

He shakes his head.

"Oh Christ, Jim. Don't be doing this. Don't make me play

twenty questions. My mother died and I'm just back from the airport and I'm very tired and don't have the time for this . . ."

"It's beyond me," says her husband. "I can't help it."

"What?"

"What I'm trying to explain to you." He remains by the three-
tiered container of CDs; he has lost weight, she notices, and has
his arms crossed and blue sleeves rolled back precisely to the
elbow, and his forearms bulge. He makes a half-turn to the Bose
as though to start the music, then stops himself. "It isn't a woman."

"What?"

"You heard me, Claire. It isn't a woman I love."

"A man, then."

"Yes."

"Another man?"

Nodding, he smiles a tight smile. Again she feels exhausted; the
ottoman is at her side and, giddily, she sits.

"You knew," he says. "You couldn't not know."

"Have I met him? Have we met?"

"What's that got to do with it? No."

"Does he have daughters too? Is he married, your new . . . ?"

"Cut me some slack here, all right?" says Jim. "Not *everybody's*
married."

"Is he?"

"No."

Now Claire is trying not to hit him, not to run across the living
room and scratch his face or spit. "How long?"

"Excuse me?"

"How long has this been going on?"

"It's about, well, feeling *honest*. Feeling like I'm me again, the
real, the *actual* me, I mean, after all these years of faking it."

"Faking it?"

"I don't mean that. I mean," he says, "I'm just extremely tired of
impersonating somebody called Handleman, some CEO of Alpha-
Beta who's supposed to be one of the guys." He spreads his hands.
"I don't feel *authentic* is what it comes down to . . ."

"Oh, Jim, you're a cliché."

"Whatever." He colors. "I'm leaving."

"Leaving?"

"Ann Arbor. Tomorrow; it's Valentine's Day. Not for forever, obviously, but I do need some air."

Claire shuts her eyes. "Alone?"

"No. Robin's taking me. He's got a place in Florida."

"Where?"

"Does it matter? Longboat Key."

Then he describes his discovery, his conviction that he's found himself or at least can begin to start finding himself before this chance is lost; he's been waiting till she came back home to tell her he would leave. It isn't so much about sex, he declares, it's like I've been wearing the wrong suit of clothes, pretending they fit and were tailored exactly, but what I was was faking it and now I require the truth. Is that what they mean, Claire asks him, by coming out of the closet; you've been trying on my clothes? You've been borrowing my skirt? But Jim is impervious, patient; he speaks with what she recognizes as the old boyish excitement, the old self-regarding enthusiasm, telling her he'd always known or at least suspected he had been born to be somebody else, and is tired of pretending, tired of fighting against it; this is his opportunity, a chance he *has* to take. It isn't a good time, says Claire, and he says that's true enough but there never *will* be a good enough time, never a time that is better than others, and he's beginning to think of himself and wants her to think of him—this will happen, he is certain—as a kind of caterpillar who became a butterfly; oh he knows it does sound silly but the caterpillar and the butterfly are really the same creature and it's only a question of which shape comes when and now his instinct tells him, is telling him unstoppably he has to take advantage of this chance for transformation and head south.

He goes on and on in this fashion, wheedling, cajoling her, asking permission, saying their marriage has been wonderful, the family is wonderful, but he has to be true to his nature and his nature is insisting loud and clear that he must change his life. He's certain she knew there was trouble between them—well, not so much between the two of them as between him, Jim, and the straight world he's saying good-bye to; he's sure she'll understand. They will drive to Longboat Key tomorrow, he and Robin, in Robin's car; he'll leave the Wrangler here, of course, and of course he'll call home every night to tell her how the trip is going until she grows accustomed to the notion that he, Jim, is driving his own chosen road. This is my true identity, he says, the empowered self I'm growing into and have always been.

"Always?"

"You got it," he says.

At length there is silence between them. He turns and taps the Bose and plays Ravel. He has selected *Bolero,* with its insistent melody, its endless repetition, and she does not want him to repeat himself or say again how Robin is the man he wants, the man who offers freedom and who understands as she does not that he, Jim, is a wanderer, not a person to be locked up in the office or kept like a caged animal at home. I didn't keep you, she wants to remind him, I didn't build that escapist fantasy you yourself arranged downstairs. She asks him about his new lover instead, and he says Robin is a lawyer with a practice out of Bloomfield Hills. They met last September at Weber's, at a boosters' breakfast for the football team; Robin had attended Michigan and enjoys the sport and gives money to it and what they have in common is a gift for the moment, for being in the moment. The horns of *Bolero* flare blaringly in unison, and Claire remembers a movie called *10* where there was a beautiful blonde called—what was her name?—Bo Derek, and Dudley Moore who desired her, who was crazy with desire and when he asked her why she played *Bolero* she said it was for fucking, and Dudley Moore looked shocked. It's the music I like best to fuck to, whispers this blonde movie star in a cabana by the beach, and now the image of her husband and his new friend Robin is flickering across the screen of her shut eyelids and will not dissipate, *ridiculous,* and Claire can hear herself laugh.

"What's so funny?"

"Nothing."

"What?"

"I was thinking about you and Robin," she says. "Do the girls know?"

"No."

"When will you tell them?"

"We'll tell them together," says Jim. "Or anyway that's what I was hoping. Or we can wait a while to tell them." For a moment he does seem unsure of himself. "Whatever you decide."

"Robin," she says. "It's a girl's name too. Except this is Cock Robin, right?"

"Don't be shitty about this," he says. "I did try to be a good husband."

"Not hard enough," she says. The girls are at rehearsal. "Not hard enough by half."

"It's not my *fault*, Claire. And not yours. It's nobody's problem, in fact. Like the way giraffes are taller, say, than elephants and elephants are built differently from zebras and zebras are different from cows."

"Is that what Mr. Wonderful, Mr. Cock Robin has taught you?"

He shakes his head.

"Have you practiced this particular speech?"

"No."

"No? Well, what about the one about the leopard's stripes? Or is it spots?" She hears herself playing for time. "Why can't the leopard change his spots? How long has this been going on? Oh, *Jim* . . ."

"We'll make it a trial run, OK?"

"What do you want to tell Becky and Hannah?"

"I told them I'm taking a business trip. To a, you know, convention . . ."

"Why?"

"Because I do need to be certain. Because I'll call them over the weekend. Or talk to them when I get back."

She will not cry. She goes out of the living room into the den, her perfectly proportioned den, the room where she is situated but the feng shui of the space feels wrong, with nothing in its proper place, and she makes her way upstairs. Jim is watching her, of course, and gauging her reaction, but she will not let him see her cry and walks the thirteen stairs to the landing and turns left and shuts but does not slam the door and does not lock him out. It happens all the time, Claire tells herself, it happens so often I shouldn't be shocked. She lies down on the bed, their bed, and stares at the ceiling and reminds herself that next Monday is her turn to host Quilting Club since Martha and Julie will be out of town—and so it's just the six of them, except Ann Halpern is coming back tomorrow from that cruise to the Galápagos she insists on calling an expedition, and has been talking now for months about Charles Darwin and his theory of natural selection and the sea turtles and the yellow finches until all the women are dying to tell her, Ann, just please shut up, so they will be seven at teatime next meeting—and forces herself to consider the quilt, to picture the section of star-bursts and moons, and decides she'll bake a lemon cake for Quilting Club next Monday as if nothing has happened and nothing will happen and then she falls asleep.

In the morning Jim does leave. He takes a suitcase and a duffel bag she has not helped him pack; he readies breakfast for Becky and Hannah and she cannot bear the prospect of going down and joining them while they bustle in the kitchen and chatter together; she asks herself what she could say that wasn't said the day before and has no answer, no idea; instead she stays upstairs. At seven-forty, as they are heading out the door and late already, hurrying, Becky arrives at the foot of the stairs and shouts: "Are you all right, Mom?" Claire responds, not loudly, "I've got a headache, I'm getting one of my headaches. I'll see you after school."

This satisfies her daughters. They go, and then she hears her husband on the stairwell and the landing and standing at the bedroom door. He knocks.

"Yes?"

"I'm leaving. I wanted to wait till the girls left for school. But Robin will be here by eight . . ."

"How prompt of him. How reliable."

"Don't be that way," he says.

"What way? What way am I being?"

"Dismissive."

"Funny," she says to the opening door. "It doesn't feel that way to me. It feels like I'm being dismissed."

"What happened in Saratoga?"

"I like your shirt," she tells him. "It's so very, very *Florida.*"

"Why don't you tell me?"

"No."

"Why not?"

"Because," says Claire, "it's none of your business. Not any longer. Not now."

"All right," he says. "I'll call you."

"When?"

"Tonight. Tomorrow. From the road."

"Wherever you are."

"Wherever we get to," he says.

"Fine. Fine."

"A good-bye kiss?" he asks her.

"No."

"I hate to be going away like this."

"Like what?"

"With you so angry. So wound up."

She will not let him lecture her; she does not need, she tells him, his touchy-feely feel-good sweetness when he's the one who's pulling out, who's heading south with his sunblock and his panama hat and bathing suit and boyfriend; she doesn't have to put up with this shit. Exactly why, Claire wants to know, should he be trying to make her believe the whole thing is *her* fault, *her* problem? She needs to pee; her mouth feels stale; her hip still hurts from how she slept and he's standing there all bright-eyed and preparing to escape and saying no hard feelings; it isn't fair, she wants to say, it isn't *right.*

But Jim is unstoppable, enameled in his new identity and schoolboy-eager to be on the road; when the horn sounds in the driveway he takes the stairs two at a time. She goes to the window and watches. There's a bright red car, its trunk lid sprung, and her husband throws his suitcase and his duffel bag into the trunk, then slams it and opens the passenger door. He does not look up at her or lingeringly gaze at the house they bought and remodeled together; he kisses the man at the wheel—a quick kiss, a peck on the cheek—and then the driver reverses and the car is gone.

That night he calls. When he asks her how the day has been Claire can find no answer; she cannot remember a thing worth reporting; she has stripped the beds and washed the sheets and vacuumed the living room and, because while she had been away this week nobody went shopping, driven to Hiller's Market—provisioning the house once more, buying paper towels and lightbulbs and orange juice and toilet paper and coffee and milk: every single item the three of them have used and not replaced. She bought sushi from the sushi bar and bags of salad and two jars of calamata olives and cereal and eggs and fat-free milk and diet root beer for the girls, tracking up and down the aisles until the cart was full and paying with a credit card and loading and unloading the Jeep as though nothing has been changed. "How do you feel?" he asks her, and she says, "Just great, how are *you* feeling?" and he says, a little tired from the trip. We went straight south through Ohio and crossed the river at Cincinnati and then drove through Kentucky and into Tennessee and now we're somewhere dull past Knoxville. It's been a long day's driving: Route 75 the whole way, he says, I'm tired, kiss the girls.

⟨∞⟩

That night she tries to sleep. She cannot fall asleep, however, and blames the espresso and blames Jim and lies awake for hours with nothing in her head but rage, but grief, a set of pictures of her mother and her sister and brother and husband together on some farther shore she cannot swim to, will not reach, and all of them playing Frisbee and laughing and having a terrific time while she flails at the saltwater and fails to make headway or join them. Then they fold up the blankets and beach towels and pack up the picnic things and disappear. In the morning she's exhausted at the prospect of the day ahead but the girls go blithely off to school orchestra practice, inattentive, dismissive, and she turns on the Weather Channel and watches while the meteorologist explains where there's an upper air disturbance, where it's fine across the country this morning and where the snowfall is heavy and where the rainfall is welcome or there is increasing risk of drought. She is glad the girls have failed to notice or, if they noticed, made no fuss about it, and she wonders what this means about the way they relate to their parents and if Jim had been in fact correct when he said this separation was a long time coming, already in the cards and not—to the girls—a surprise.

This morning Claire turns her attention to the stack of mail accumulated in her absence, but there is nothing really, some magazines, some bills, a check, a series of announcements of concerts she won't go to and sales she's missed and movies she won't see. She tunes in to NPR for Click and Clack, the yak-it-up brothers from Boston who make fun of each other and joke with the person who calls in a problem and then give advice—it's *good* advice, she's certain—as to what's wrong with a car. She trusts these men with their Italian name and rapid fraternal patter and their silliness and way at last of getting down to business and solving problems just by hearing what the trouble is and offering a diagnosis; for a wild instant she thinks she should call and ask them what to do about two men in a red sports car driving south. What make is it, they'd ask her, and she'd confess she doesn't know; what year is the car, they'd ask her, and she won't know that either; what's wrong with it, they'd ask her, and she'd say *everything.*

Bone-deep exhaustion is upon her, and on the chaise longue she sleeps dreamlessly till two, and then the girls return, there's dinner, and then again Jim calls. He isn't feeling well, he says, his legs hurt from the driving or not so much the driving as the cramped position in the passenger seat, the forced inaction of the trip, you've no idea how long the distance feels and he has a new respect for General Sherman's march through Georgia; war may be hell, Jim jokes, but so's a peacetime foray straight down Route 75. Why are you driving, she asks him, and he says we didn't know how long we'd stay and Robin has this thing about planes. Where are you, she inquires, what's the town you're staying in and he says, red clay country, cracker country, somewhere just south of the Florida line, I miss you, kiss the girls.

The following morning is Sunday and harder, since the girls are home, and though they sleep till noon and wake up noisily, playing their loud music and lounging around in the kitchen in leggings and sweatshirts they insist on calling "sweats" the house feels empty, altered, and Claire isn't sure she can carry it off. She starts the day by listening to *Weekend Edition,* the news about Iraq and the military buildup there and news about the inquiry into the space shuttle disaster, and pitting herself against the puzzle master from the *New York Times.* Then for an hour she vacuums the house and thinks about her brother and how in Saratoga Springs he promised to vacuum the cottage himself . . .

Now Becky and Hannah are drinking their juice, finishing their English muffins and Velveeta—she can't understand how they stand it, *Velveeta,* a cheese spread with the consistency of peanut butter, a tastelessness they appear to enjoy—and discussing what matinee to go to together, and she wants to tell her daughters how strange it is that "matinee" means "afternoon" because really it ought to mean "morning" when, once more, the telephone rings.

"Hello?"

"Hello? Is this Claire Handleman?"

"It is."

"It's Robin."

She swallows air. Her throat constricts.

"He asked me to call you."

"Robin who?"

"He *told* me to."

She will not yield. "Who told you to?"

"Jimmy. Jim. Your husband."

The girls stand, stretch; they smile at her. Then they walk out of the room.

"Why are you calling?" she asks.

"That's the point. It's the reason I'm calling, Mrs. Handleman. He can't."

"Can't?"

"Isn't *able* to."

Only now does Claire notice the strain in his voice, the taut-strung anxiety he's been trying to control. "What? What is it?"

"They don't know. They think maybe a heart attack. Or a stroke, a minor stroke."

"Who's they? Where *are* you?"

"Florida. In Bradenton. The hospital. He'll be all right, they think, but he did ask me to call you."

"They *think* he'll be all right?"

"It's serious," says Robin. "Jimmy was complaining all last night. He was having leg pains, pains in both his legs and chest, and finally this morning when he had trouble breathing and we were driving past a hospital and it wasn't getting better I thought, and he agreed with this, maybe we ought to go in." His voice rises—high-pitched, querulous, as though this too could somehow be her fault. "To the Emergency Room, I mean, here at Manatee Memorial, and he's resting comfortably but it hasn't been a cakewalk . . ."

"Bradenton? Where's Bradenton?"

"Near where I live. Longboat Key."

"Hold on. Hold on a minute, will you?"

"Yes. OK."

She shuts the door. Upstairs her daughters are heedless, laughing, and Claire does not want them to hear. She can remember sitting in the kitchen with Joanna and David when they were young and when their mother learned by phone their father had been killed. The phone had rung, and they'd been eating bacon, and she never could eat bacon again or smell it without feeling sick to her stomach and wanting to be sick. But *this* isn't like that, not like it at all; this is *not* a policeman or car crash, and she tells herself Jim will be fine. Jim is her husband and she is a grown-up and he will be fine; there's no reason now to panic, she tells herself, and fetches a pencil and pad. Still, panic is the word for what she's trying not to feel and terror for what she suppresses; Robin gives her his telephone number and she writes it down carefully, twice. He's been deciding, he tells her, if the hospital at Sarasota — Sarasota Memorial Health Care — would be better for a heart attack, if that's what they decide it's been, but so far the tests are negative and what that means in terms of the prognosis is positive, it's a relief, but they've been monitoring the patient all morning as a precaution and the Emergency Room doctors in Bradenton are excellent and he lives thirty minutes away. It's funny, isn't it, says Robin, all that exercise, all that fresh fish he insists upon eating and this is what he gets.

Claire sits. He *hates* fresh fish, she says. The shared attempt at humor, or at least lightheartedness, establishes a bond between them, or at least some sort of connection; they care for the same man. It's ironic, isn't it, he says, we drove the whole way here together and he hasn't yet seen my apartment. Jim will get better, I'm certain, Claire says, he's always been strong as a horse. I'll stay in touch, says Robin, I'll let you know as soon as there's news, he does want to talk to you and says to kiss the girls.

❧

She calls Northwest Airlines, in case. There's a flight to Sarasota that is overbooked but one to Tampa she could make, and one the next morning, at 9:15; she reserves a seat, in case. Then she remembers that Meme and Arthur Lowenthal have a condominium in Longboat Key, and she calls Meme Lowenthal to ask about the area; it's terrific, Meme tells her, you can see the Gulf and Tampa Bay from our balcony and there are golf courses everywhere, why do you ask? She says, Jim's down there, he's on a business trip but he isn't feeling well, and Meme says — not pausing, with the openhanded generosity of the insouciant rich — of course you must use our apartment, it's completely empty and you're completely welcome if you feel you ought to go. It might be an emergency, says Claire, and Meme says well even if it isn't you should hop that plane and join him, dear, you can't imagine the pleasure of watching all those pelicans from up above, the way they dive, and sometimes in the afternoons there's dolphins a few feet offshore. I can give you names of restaurants in Sarasota; there are three of them we like a lot and one you mustn't miss. Also, the Ringling Brothers Circus Museum and Mansion; it's a hoot. Do you know anything, asks Claire, about Manatee Memorial, the hospital in Bradenton, and Meme tells her no. But Arthur would, I'll ask him, he's got colleagues down there, I imagine, he's got colleagues everywhere; I'll get back to you, she promises, and give our love to Jim.

In this manner Claire passes the time. The girls go off to Briarwood; there's a sale on running shoes and they require new ones, they tell her, there's no support in the shoes they've been wearing; the treads are entirely gone. Hannah demonstrates this by lifting the heel of her sneaker, and indeed the heel has been shredded away, so Claire gives them money for the bus and money for two pairs of shoes and they promise to be back by five. She wipes down the powder room sink. Outside, light snowflakes fall. She makes her bed and starts a wash and tries to decide if she ought to fly south and if Jim would be relieved or angry that she came. Then she waters the houseplants room by room and checks the kitchen and the pantry shelves, but there is nothing out of place and nothing to buy that requires a trip to the market and no television show to watch or article to read. She tries to focus on what happened just this week in Saratoga—*Saratoga, Sarasota*— her sister and brother and mother's old house, her argument with David and hopes he understands it isn't, wasn't serious, that in her heart of hearts she has apologized already and will do so on the phone today and promises herself she'll call her brother and sister in Wellfleet later on. She occupies herself with place-names— *Saratoga, Sarasota*—and turns on the Weather Channel but there is nothing to notice, warm weather down in Florida until the telephone rings.

This time it is her husband. "Claire?"

"How *are* you, Jim?"

"I'm fine. Well, feeling better. And it's nothing to worry about."

"What happened?"

"Not a heart attack. They've ruled that out."

"That's good. That's excellent."

"They're discharging me," he says. "I'm going to Robin's apartment."

"OK."

"This place isn't exactly what I'd pick for vacation. Not a cake-walk . . ."

"No." That had been Robin's word, a *cakewalk*, and Claire tells herself she doesn't mind; they are entitled to shared language, a word the two men use together. "Cakewalk?" she repeats.

"It's crazy, isn't it, we drive the whole way down here and I haven't even made it out to Longboat Key. It's Sunday already . . ."

"You will."

"It's like the promised land or something."

"Except you aren't Moses," she says.

He clears his throat. "They want me to report back tomorrow on an outpatient basis. How *are* you? How are the girls?"

She tries to say something that matters, tries to reassure him that everything will be all right, and what he must do is take care of himself and not worry about her or Becky or Hannah or anybody but be very very careful; she'll fly to Tampa if he wants or wait in Ann Arbor until he returns. She has not of course forgotten the things he said or how he departed on Valentine's Day, but maybe this is a signal, some sort of second chance or—what do they call it?—warning shot across the bows. You've been working too hard, she says to her husband, you've overdone it probably and hears with gratitude his murmuring assent. He says something that she can't quite hear about fried food, hush puppies, too much good old southern cooking and how it was probably just in-digestion, and through the fade-in, fade-out of his pay phone in the hallway Claire discerns, or thinks she does, that Jim is feeling impatient—but not so much with her, with *them* as with Manatee

Memorial and the Emergency Room doctors who expect him back tomorrow for a second look-see and second round of tests. How's Robin holding up, she dares to ask, and her husband says, oh Robin's the gold standard, he's being completely a brick. Meme Lowenthal, Claire says, owns a condo out on Longboat Key that overlooks the Gulf; she offered it in case you want or need to stay and he says yes, except I'm staying at Robin's, remember? I didn't mean, she starts to say, and he says I know what you mean. Claire controls herself; her husband is not feeling well and so she tells the telephone, all I'm saying is there's an apartment and he says I don't need the Lowenthals' help.

❧

What happens next she knows on the instant she will not forget and will remember forever: Jim coughs; he gasps, he rattles in her ear as though there were a thunderstorm, a wave of water in the line she knows cannot be static and then the phone goes dead. She stares at the receiver: "Jim, *Jim*," she repeats to the plastic. She waits for him to call again and when her husband doesn't call Claire presses Star 69.

It reconnects her to nothing, however; the line does not respond. She calls the number at Robin's apartment, the one she'd copied earlier, but there is only a machine and she leaves a message saying *This is Claire, I'm very worried, I don't know what's happening. Please call.* She will learn what happened later, from the hospital authorities; she will be told he had been speaking to her in the hallway by the pickup door where he was waiting for Robin, and even though it was a hospital and they had an emergency team on the scene in thirty seconds there was nothing to be done. Jim dropped the telephone receiver and collapsed on the hallway floor. The long drive to Florida would seem, his doctors said, to have occasioned an occlusion in his arteries but when they perform a postmortem they will find nothing in his legs, no secondary emboli or blood clots that would suggest a passage upward to the lungs. They cannot be certain or determine absolutely if this was an accident waiting to happen or something the trip triggered and if a regime of medication could have helped. What he was suffering from, they informed her, was a pair of massive pulmonary embolisms, and they killed him instantly and he could not be revived.

Claire doubts this; she's tempted to sue. She's sure the doctors were incompetent; Jim was complaining of leg pains and chest pains and had driven more than a thousand miles and why not diagnose or at least consider the possibility of an embolism and give him blood thinners at once? She imagines herself on the witness stand in Bradenton, asking for punitive damages and being cross-examined and persuading a jury that millions of dollars will teach those Emergency Room physicians a lesson; she raises her right hand and promises to tell the truth, the whole truth and nothing but the truth, so help her God.

But soon the image fades, goes flat, and she knows she will not file a suit or pursue a case for damages in Florida. She has been left, irrevocably, utterly, and nothing she can say or do will change the way he left. Let Robin handle this, she thinks, let him be the responsible party and explain how Jim just happened to be driving by, on the way to Longboat Key and not in his Ann Arbor home. Outside, the dark grows visible; light snow beyond the pane. Robin calls and tells her what he does and doesn't understand about the way her husband died; they commiserate together and complain about the doctors, the behavior of the hospital. I can't believe it, Robin says, I can't *believe* it, Claire. She pours herself a glass of wine and drinks it gulpingly; she pours a second glass and asks herself how could it be—some God of bad coincidence, some melodramatic puppeteer!—that Jim should have collapsed while talking to her on the phone and saying he felt fine.

She drinks. Jim left her, chose to leave her, and just the way their father did he died on the road with a stranger; on a Sunday morning these two men—married and unfaithful, both—were killed because of cars. They both have been extinguished by a just and vengeful God. As soon as she formulates this phrase, however, Claire is ashamed of herself, astonished she could *think* it even, and finishes the second glass of wine. The inventor of the automobile has a great deal to answer for, and if Henry Ford were still alive she'd give him a piece of her mind. She is not used to drinking, or at least to drinking by herself, and she watches her reflection in the window of the house—a widow, a mother of young daughters, a woman with no surviving parents in the middle of Ann Arbor—until she starts to cry. What has she done, what has she ever done to be so left alone, so utterly bereft while the girls are buying sneakers somewhere out in Briarwood and their father died?

It isn't a question she answers, or can; she tells herself she has a reservation on a flight tomorrow morning, early, and if she wants to take it—does she want to take it?—she should pack. She packs. She calls Meme Lowenthal and says Jim died, my husband died, I'm taking you up on that offer if the offer stands. Meme is horrified, aghast; she says of course, of course, I'll call the caretaker and tell him you're staying, how else can we possibly help? The afternoon wears on, wears down, and by the time the girls return Claire has created a semblance of order: she will, she knows, retrieve their father and fly his body back.

XIII

2003

From the Tampa airport Claire makes her way to Longboat Key; once more she has rented a Hertz. The sky is a bright blue. There is a causeway and a toll-bridge spanning windswept water, with traffic streaming south. Trucks barrel past her, swaying. She searches for *Fresh Air* or something familiar on NPR, but all she hears is talk about God and men chattering in Spanish. St. Petersburg has apartment buildings clustered to the highway's edge, and she imagines old people inside, staring out their plate-glass windows at palm trees and the bay. Claire holds to the wheel with both hands. She passes a baseball stadium and high-rise complexes with advertisements for Immediate Occupancy, then follows the exit for Route 41; there are billboards for tires and blown-up photographs of lawyers, malpractice specialists, and signs that make her welcome to the Sunshine State.

She does not feel welcome, however. She is traveling through Florida to bring her husband home. All around her she sees seabirds and uninviting strips of shore and there are gas stations and video and convenience stores and banks. In Bradenton the road winds past Manatee Memorial, where Jim had been a patient, where he was treated and released and collapsed inside the pickup door. She slows but does not stop. There is a store called Piggly Wiggly and something called the Chop-Shop and signs for furniture and funeral homes and insurance companies; then the traffic reduces, dispersing, and she comes upon a causeway with cars parked by the water and people on deck chairs or fishing. The radio is telling her that manatees are dying along the Inland Waterway in unprecedented numbers and environmentalists are pressing for a ban on motorboats and Aqua-skis; the sea cow will be endangered if the present trend continues and Florida cannot afford to lose its population of manatees, its weed-eaters in the Inland Waterway.

"But seriously, folks," says the announcer, "they're worth their weight in weeds, if it wasn't for the holy sea cow we'd have golf courses instead of canals. It would be Algae Avenue all down this part of the world. But *seriously*, folks," he repeats, "another name for manatee is dugong and its scientific name is—get this—Order Sirenia! I asked our Mr. Wizard and he says it got its moniker, get this, because—if you happen to be nearsighted or had an extra tot of rum—the sea cow resembles a mermaid, a foxy *siren* lady to sailors far from home." The announcer makes a joke about the manatee as a "man-tease" and then the music resumes.

She reaches a town called Holmes Beach. There are signs to Anna Maria Island and signs to Longboat Key; at the intersection Claire turns left. Although she has the right-of-way and is driving carefully, she almost has an accident; she jams on the brakes not a yard away from a white Cadillac that neither slows nor stops. The other car is enormous, a 1960s Eldorado with fins, with ornamental wire wheel rims and a mounted tire casing painted red. When she brakes she sees an ancient lady at the wheel, wearing a Yankee baseball cap, and a dog at the rear window snarling, paws scrabbling at the pane. The driver does not acknowledge her but continues down the center of the road. Shaken, Claire pulls into the parking lot of a grocery store called Publix and turns off the engine and waits.

A school bus rumbles by. A man in a wheelchair wheels past. She tries to calm her breathing and, after some minutes, succeeds; she starts the rental car again and makes her way across the bridge to Longboat Key. Meme Lowenthal has faxed her a set of instructions, and the apartment is not hard to find, a gated complex by the bay, with a golf course and a swimming pool and men standing at attention in the guardhouse. Claire gives her name and they direct her to the manager's office, where she is made welcome and provided with a parking sticker and a set of keys.

The manager is bald, and brown, with prominent gold-filled teeth; he smiles ingratiatingly and offers her the code for the elevator and a description of the facilities and services in the complex. "Will that be all?" he asks.

Claire nods. "You're kind," she says. "You're very kind."

"*De nada.*" The manager consults his checklist. "Does Madame wish assistance with the bags?"

She tells him no, she has packed a single overnight bag and asks herself if she should tip him, if he expects to be paid for his courtesy and decides probably not. For an instant, acutely, she misses Jim; he would have understood, her husband would have handled this but now she has to do so alone, her stomach aflutter at how to proceed. The manager opens the door and points her to her parking space and then to Building 3.

❧

The lobby has a marble floor and floor-to-ceiling gilt-framed mirrors. Claire sees herself: a thin, drawn woman in a pantsuit, with a black scarf over her shoulders and a pearl choker and wintry northern pallor in her cheeks. She studies her reflection, and all assurance ebbs, drains. The elevator arrives. She enters the code and nothing happens; she tries it again and again nothing happens; then she checks the code and realizes she has reversed a digit—it's 734, not 743—and the doors slide open soundlessly. With the conviction she is acting, enacting someone else's part she rises to the seventh floor and the Lowenthals' apartment; as soon as she has entered—an expansive water view, a wall-to-wall yellow carpet and long-fluked ceiling fans—she calls Jim's lover, Robin. He answers immediately.

"I'm here," she says, "in Longboat Key," and he says, "Well, imagine that, a local call," and Claire repeats, "I'm here." "How was the trip?" he asks, and she tells him, "Fine." She consults her watch: 3:52. The Lowenthals' bookshelf has cases of shells—glass-mounted ornamental mollusks arranged in the shape of a rainbow. There are abalone shells and sand dollars mounted in ascending order, from the size of a thumbnail to the size of a palm. There are sea horses and starfish and whelks. Robin says he'll come for her at five o'clock and take her to a bar for drinks and they can watch the sunset and figure out what's what. "How will you get in?" she asks, and he says, "Don't worry. Tell the guards."

She worries nevertheless. She feels uncertain, ill-prepared; she knows she must visit with Robin but cannot imagine the things he will say or what she has come here to ask. She feels herself a prisoner inside this glassed-in high-rise tower, staring at the blue-green gulf, with nobody who knows her knowing where she traveled to, except for Meme Lowenthal; she telephones the girls. They are still in school, but she leaves her number on the machine and then says—brightly, absurdly—"Well, that's that, I guess. We'll be back as soon as possible: tomorrow, maybe. Or day after tomorrow. Love."

For an hour Claire prowls the apartment: unpacking her bag in the guest room bureau, arranging her toiletries by the shower stall, pouring herself a glass of Perrier and changing outfits twice. Aimlessly she leafs through old copies of *The New Yorker* and *Vogue*. She has never been to Florida, this separate world of Longboat Key, and nothing in it comforts her or makes her feel at home. A buzzer sounds loudly, repeatedly, and the intercom starts flashing. "We have a visitor. Robin," announces the guard.

"Robin?"

"He says you're expecting him."

"Yes. Send him up."

Then she realizes she will have to take the elevator down, since Robin does not know the code, and gathers her handbag and raincoat and double-locks the apartment door carefully and descends. Arriving, she enters the lobby just as a middle-aged gentleman climbs up the stairs; she asks, "Are you looking for someone?" and he tells her, "Claire."

"I didn't know what you'd look like."

"I knew you by your photograph," he says. He is tall and thin and wearing what she recognizes as a blond toupee. He has a scar on his cheek. His clothes are, she supposes, appropriate to Florida: yellow slacks with a black belt, and a silk shirt emblazoned with white calla lilies.

"Well," she says, "I'm glad to meet you."

"Under the circumstances."

"Yes." Unaccountably, she's flustered, unsure of her manners or how to behave. "Do you want to come upstairs?"

"Let's go." He smells—it's the cologne Jim used—of Paco Rabanne. "You brought your raincoat, didn't you, you want to get out of here, right?"

"Yes, I suppose so. I don't *need* this coat."

"I need," he announces, "a drink."

"Me too." In a single week, she tells herself, she has lost her mother and her husband and flown east and back to Michigan and just this morning traveled south, and it shouldn't be surprising if she feels adrift.

"Who *are* these people? Who owns this apartment, I mean?"

"Friends from Ann Arbor. Do you know them: Meme and Arthur Lowenthal?"

He shakes his head. "Strange, isn't it—so much security. All these apartments being guarded so they can stay safely empty. All those people in the guardhouse and nobody at home . . ."

Her throat constricts. "It's quiet here."

"I think about it often: homeless people everywhere and all this unused air-conditioned space. It's not as if there *are* any homeless, of course, not on Longboat Key."

"The air-conditioning." Claire sneezes, twice. "I guess I'm just not used to it. The plane, the car, the apartment upstairs . . ."

He is polite; he opens the glass door for her, and the door of the little red coupe. She remembers watching Jim lean over and kiss this person on the cheek—when was it? just four days ago— putting his suitcase in the trunk and slamming the trunk-lid and then the two men disappearing south. "Oh Mary," Robin says, "it's so strange to be meeting like this." She starts to remind him her name is not Mary, then understands he knows her name and "Oh Mary" is just an expression; she buckles her seat belt and thinks, *This is the seat my husband was sitting in, this was the belt at his chest.*

❦

There are speed bumps and palm trees and ironwork gates. There are golf courses and ponds. "McMansions," Robin says. He points to stucco homes by the water, with tall capped chimneys and bright copper roofs. "Drug money mostly. It has to be that."

"What brought you here?"

"The boys of Sarasota." He smiles. She wonders, is he joking? "The circus museum. The climate. What else?"

"I've never been to this part of the world."

"What I've been wanting to tell you," he says, "is there's no way of knowing if it could have been avoided. The catastrophe. I've been asking myself—all day, all night, every hour since the aneurysm happened—if there was *something* that could have been done. If Jimmy was or wasn't carrying some sort of bomb inside, if it was an accident or a condition bound to explode." His voice trails off; he signals a right turn and rotates the wheel with both hands. "Could have been in any way, I mean to say, handled— *treated*—better . . ."

"By you?" she asks. "Or the doctors?"

"By all of us. Jimmy was feeling, he told me, impatient; he was itching to get out of there, positively *mad* to leave. He didn't get as far as *you* have, he never even made it here to Longboat Key. And they say it could have happened anywhere, they say—"

"Can we," Claire interrupts him, "wait? I'm just not ready for this conversation yet."

Again there are speed bumps. "OK." The road is narrow, newly paved, with chain-link fence on either side. Robin negotiates a parking lot—dirt, with a sign announcing: "Customers Only. All Others Towed." He parks by a Dumpster, then points to the beach. "Welcome," he tells her. "The Starfish. Best February sunset and Bloody Marys in town."

"I didn't mean," she says, "I *never* want to talk about it. Only that I do need time."

"A little vodka, right. I'm sorry. I shouldn't have rushed."

She cannot tell if this is kindness on his part, or a form of condescension. He opens her door with a flourish, mock-gallant, and strides wordlessly ahead into a wooden trellised area, then down a gangway festooned with starfish into a dark bar decorated with fishermen's knotted rope nets. Lobster pots and a rowboat hang suspended from the ceiling, and the inside wall has a pair of stuffed blue marlins and an oil painting of mermaids draped across rocks. A waitress in a miniskirt approaches, and Robin kisses her on both cheeks and says "Hiya, darling," then turns to Claire and says, "This is Gretchen, isn't she beautiful, isn't she perfect? Too bad she's not my type."

Gretchen smiles; she has heard this before. "Inside or outside?" she asks.

There are three or four men at the bar. Otherwise, the Starfish is empty and Robin points outside. "We're here for the sunset, not company, darling, we need to banish old man winter from our Michigan visitor's cheeks."

"You're from Michigan?" The waitress smiles confidingly at Claire. "A lot of folks come down this way from Michigan."

"Can you blame us?" Robin says. "It's *snowing* there."

Claire's eyes adjust; the bar, she understands, is dark only by contrast to the bright beach and the water beyond. They go out into a sitting area and take their places by the railing, at a table with a parasol and weathered wooden chairs. "What are you drinking?" Robin asks, and she orders Chardonnay. "For me, the usual," Robin says, and Gretchen tells him, "Gotcha." There are no other customers outside on the wooden deck, and almost immediately the girl returns through swinging doors carrying a tray with wine, a bowl of peanuts and pretzels and an outsize Bloody Mary. "Chin-chin," offers Robin. "Your health."

"And yours," says Claire. They click glasses. Seabirds she cannot recognize fly past, and gulls beneath her ruffle, preening, facing what she calculates is north. The sun is warm. "All right," she says, "I'm ready. I'm ready to discuss it."

"Have a pretzel."

"Thank you, no. Why don't you say what you're trying to *say*."

The scar on his cheek is shiny; it makes an *S* beneath his chin and stops at the base of his throat. "How long were you married?" he asks.

"Nineteen years. It would have been twenty this coming October. Does that make a difference? Why?"

"Don't be angry with me. I want us to be friends."

"You're a lawyer, aren't you?"

He nods. Now watching the water, Claire feels three things, and she feels them in rapid succession—so rapid she can't tell which impulse to follow, which desire to obey. First, she wants to throw her drink at him, to wreck his gay complacency and awful floral shirt. Second, she wants to condole with this man who loved the man she lived with, or used to, and loved. Third, she feels somehow flirtatious—or not so much flirtatious as eager to engage in conversation: *I've never been friendly with lawyers, I don't have any lawyers as friends.* It is, she tells herself, the glass of wine; it is the exhaustion of travel and strain of new surroundings and if I sit here just a minute it will pass. The only thing I need to do is wait for this to pass.

"There's dolphins," Robin says.

"What?"

"Out there to your left." His fingernails have been bitten; he points. "Two of them, watch."

And sure enough a dolphin leaps, its black bulk curling suspended above the line of surf. A second dolphin does the same, and then they both submerge. "Oh *Mary,*" Robin breathes, and now she wants to cry.

"They're beautiful."

Clouds come from nowhere visible and, of a sudden, the sun is a haze—a windswept, orange glaze of light; she shivers and empties her glass. Yet sitting here above the tide, with only a few rocks and footprints and seagulls in her line of sight, Claire feels impelled to talk to him, confide in him—improbably, not that he wants to know or will care—and tell what did and did not happen in the house in Saratoga, the news of her new legacy and how her brother and sister behaved. It's not so much the strangeness of their meeting here— two adults adrift in the Starfish, two grown-ups with nowhere to be or to go—as how her brother looked at her and how her sister refused to, the old repudiation and family game of dismissiveness: *who is this person and what do we share but a name?*

"Have you ever noticed," Robin asks, "the way 'immortality' and 'immorality' are spelled the same, or just about, and that's because it suits the priests and nuns to a *t,* if you get my meaning, to add the *t* to 'immorality' and make it last forever? Behind the sacristy, in the confessional, wherever. You two weren't Catholic, of course, you never attended parochial school, but for me it was an issue way back when."

"Oh?"

"Because there's a problem, isn't there," he continues, "about the souls that die without ever having been alive, and haven't had the time to sin, the chance to be immoral if you follow what I'm saying, if you see what I'm trying to say . . ."

Now in the westering beam of the sun before she can restrain herself her eyes well up and overflow and her cheeks are wet. Robin offers the glass bowl of peanuts; she takes a handful, mute. She wants to tell him, wants to *yell* at him, his lover would have been alive if they hadn't gone south in the little red car, if they hadn't been overgrown children together and careless of everything, everyone, *her.* She's crying, not loudly, making no noise but spilling tears nevertheless; she pulls out her handkerchief, pats at her cheeks but they will not dry.

⌘

"Your husband"—Robin clears his throat—"was a wonderful man."

She looks at him. "Oh?"

"I don't suppose I need to tell *you* that."

"No."

"He was trying hard to *find* himself."

"He told me that," says Claire.

"He was such a success, so, you know, *competent.* But he was trying something new."

"Like fucking you," she says. "Like dying down here at the back of beyond. Is that what you're trying to say?"

But Robin is equable, unperturbed. "He said you had a mouth on you."

"I'm sorry," Claire offers. "It's all so, so *strange.*"

"For me too, lady," Robin says. "In case you don't know. It isn't what I'd planned on, not—"

"Another round?" asks Gretchen the waitress, and her companion nods.

In the silence that follows she pictures it: tomorrow they will go together to the funeral parlor in Bradenton, the place where Jim lies waiting, and though Claire cannot remember its name she knows she drove past it, arriving—the awning red, the building white stucco, with pillars—and there will be a man to greet them, solemn in his suit and tie. She and Robin will enter the office and sit in the two proffered chairs and handle the paperwork, deal with the fees, and although these postmortem regulations and interstate procedures are new to her the funeral director will of course be familiar with them, practiced at the transportation of a corpse by hearse or train or in this instance plane to what he calls the dear departed's place of rest, the waiting plot, and choose the oak casket the man recommends, and sign four forms in triplicate, of which she keeps the pink second sheets, wanting only to be done with this, wanting only to be home again and not in this strange place but with her girls. How is it possible, she asks herself, that in one week she's done this twice, that two times in a single week she will have visited a funeral home—one in New York, one in Florida—and never had done so before? Claire shuts her eyes. She opens them and the sun is extravagant: orange and crimson and purple above the horizon line, sinking, and Robin is watching her, staring, incurious, saying, "Welcome back."

"Excuse me?"

He points to her replenished glass, his new Bloody Mary. "Back from wherever you've been . . ."

"I understand," Claire manages, "it can't be easy for you either."

"In answer to your question, I am a lawyer, yes. I—we—could nail them if you want."

"Who?"

"Manatee Memorial. For medical malpractice; they'd settle in a heartbeat, I can promise."

"Heartbeat?"

"I didn't mean that." He shakes his head. "It might in fact take time, a year or two of offers, demands, counteroffers—some pretrial maneuvering under Florida civil procedures. We'd have to establish how he was admitted and treated and why and on whose recognizance he was released. But they'd choose to face a jury about as much as you or I would choose to face a firing squad; trust me on this one, OK?"

"OK," she says. "Except I'm not certain I'm ready to sue."

"Of course not. Neither am I."

What is he proposing; what does he want? "I need to take Jim home," she says. "I need to put his body on the plane."

"Of course. Of course you do."

And as though they have formed an alliance they sit, while the water withdraws and a breeze comes up and the sky darkens down, while another couple arrives on the deck and takes the table next to them and Gretchen appears once more smilingly; they raise and click their glasses and, at the same instant, drink. He speaks now without interruption about her husband's final days, the sense he'd had that Jimmy was in more than *one* way on the road, was being a pilgrim, a *traveler,* and although he knows it does sound hokey that was how Jimmy described it: this voyage of discovery they'd embarked on together—except, alas, too late. I despise the word *existential,* says Robin, but that's the word I want to use; it was *existential,* really, that's what I'm trying to say. In the mild evening air and holding her third glass of wine Claire finds herself, if not in agreement, at least at newfound ease with this aging boy-man at her side. He uses the language her husband had used: *the journey, not arrival, matters; the caterpillar and the butterfly; the dream of an enabling self.* Oh spare me, spare me please, she thinks, but this time without rancor as he rambles on about the solace he has taken in the knowledge the dead man had been happy, searching, was being a beginner at the end. Therefore (and because, if she is honest, she has no alternative; she can't just walk away or insult him again) Claire does remember the questions to ask: *where have I come from and where am I going and what am I doing while here? Tomorrow we collect a corpse, but what do we do with it then?*

"Friends?" he inquires. He raises his glass.

"We have something in common, don't we?"

"At least not enemies," he says. "All right?"

"All right."

"I'll drink to that."

They drink. Then Robin puts his hand upon her hand, surprising her, fingering the wedding ring; his touch is warm, annealing, and he lifts her wrist and together they point: three dolphins in the foam. Claire watches their shapes in the distance retreat. And now she is crying again.

Part Six

XIV

1996

Alice was sitting in the library and the library was cold. Outside, a robin pecked at suet and a squirrel worried at the canister of birdseed, trying to spill it and failing to do so and falling back down to the ground. It was January 10. She knew this from the calendar she'd Xed the day before. The illustration for the month showed frigates in a harbor: tall-masted ships with sails being raised and sailors hauling ropes. In the calendar the sky was blue and cloudless and the warehouses and chandleries that fronted on the harbor were steep-roofed and built out of brick. With her red pen, carefully, beginning at the top left-hand corner and drawing a line to the square's bottom right, then repeating this procedure from the bottom left-hand corner and with a fine line rising to the apex of the right-hand edge, she eradicated January 9. As her father used to say, "Another day, another dolor"; it was eleven o'clock.

The light was weak. It illumined the framed photograph of her daughters being bridesmaids: Joanna ten years old, Claire six, and both of them wearing purple atrocities the bride had insisted on, smiling and holding bouquets. The colors in the photograph had faded over time; the purple looked half-pink. On the same wall—adjacent to her daughters but slightly lower and in black and white—hung a photograph of Aaron standing by his Model A, one foot on the running board, goggles in hand and so proud of himself you could *see* it: nobody had to say *Cheese*. She could not remember the name of the bride, or where the wedding had been held or why the girls were bridesmaids; she did remember the fuss Claire was making, complaining her saddle shoes pinched. "Oh, Mummy," she wailed, "do I *have* to?" and Alice told her, "Yes."

David was not in the picture, however; David was too young. Or possibly he had been involved in it also, off at the edge of the portrait, carrying the ring and being a part of the wedding

215

processional but there was a cobweb, a filigree of fine white web-bing at the lower left-hand corner of the gold-leafed frame she needed to stand up and wipe. That intricate webbing—the veins and cross-hatched glistening—engaged her for a moment, and Alice examined the mirroring glass to make certain it wasn't a trick. What she was looking at, she knew, was what her eye would look like if she studied it instead: milky, fine-veined, blank. The clock on the mantel was ticking, its metronomic repetition loud: tok-*tik*, tok-*tik*, tok-*tik* . . .

She would be hungry soon. She needed something to eat. She tried to remember, and could not, what she had eaten for break-fast, or whether indeed there *was* breakfast that morning, or if it soon would be served. There was the paper to read. There was the jigsaw puzzle by Renoir to finish—an outdoor celebration, Parisians dancing under lights; she had managed the café and part of the paving they danced on, but she was having trouble with the upper right-hand quadrant and those hats, those impossible hats. Instead she imagined a hard roll with butter, a boiled egg and Swiss cheese. She swallowed her orange juice, smacking her lips, and then she tasted it: breakfast in bed, and the waiter saying, "Thank you sir," when George signed for the tip. He had a way with the waiters, of course, and certainly the waitresses, and everybody George encountered in every single restaurant thought he was the cat's pajamas, the cat who ate the cream.

Except why would a cat wear pajamas; what sort of expression was that? And wasn't it *licked* the cream, *swallowed* the cream; what sort of cat could be *eating* the cream and where was her breakfast and how soon was lunchtime and could she be bothered to go to the kitchen and eat? Oh, it was a mystery, and she shivered and covered herself with the brown mohair shawl and peered out the window at snow. For all the years her father traveled down to Florida she humored him, though she had never understood it, really, never saw the point of going south. *Who once flew south,* Alice said to the window, and thought about her father in his rocker on the porch. When he went to Sarasota, Aaron claimed, he did so partly for the weather and partly in order to visit his friends; when the first snow arrives it's a pleasure, and then it stays around and is less of a pleasure: you'll see.

But she had been too busy then, too much involved with the children—their music and tennis and horseback riding lessons, the *hours* she spent every day in the car—to pay attention to winter. In the dark of January 10, with all those ships being readied to sail (the harbormaster in his top hat, the merchant checking off supplies), she could not now concern herself with the bitter weather or whether the robin had suet; *Roberta,* Roberta Harrison, that was the name of the bride. She had married a Boothby, one of that pack of Boothby boys from Schuylerville, and unless she misremembered he died in Vietnam. They had barely had a honeymoon before Paul Boothby left to fight—so *that* was why the wedding had been planned in such a hurry, *that* explained the purple atrocities Claire and Joanna were wearing; he must have known beforehand he'd be on a tour of duty, and at least she wasn't pregnant when her husband died. . . .

❧

In the kitchen she could hear them; Hansel and Gretel: *tik*-tok. The Molly Maids were cleaning up, and they did so two mornings each week. They weren't, of course, Hansel and Gretel but the girl did have a ponytail precisely the color of Gretel's in that illustration Alice had been looking at in the book of fairy tales, the Brothers Grimm or was it Hans Christian Andersen, and wore if not a dirndl at least a dress that doubled as a cleaning smock, hiked up and tied beneath her breasts and wearing black tights like a dancer. "*Good* morning, Mrs. Saperstone. How are we doing today?" And then the girl inquired if there was anything special to do, any particular project or just the usual once-over in the bathrooms and kitchen and dusting the porcelain cats like you like.

The girl was not alone, of course; she came with a companion. She had brought a boy along, although not the same partner as last week's—this Hansel was gangly and black-haired, the last had been stocky and brown. "Two for the price of one," she said, "we'll do you twice as fast."

"*Do* me?"

"Mm-hm," said the Molly Maid. "Right."

Alice attempted to explain that speed was not the point today; she herself was in no rush. Rapidity takes second place in the pantheon of cleaning virtues, slow but steady wins the race. But the boy had plugged in and was using the Electrolux already and while Gretel mopped the bathroom and dusted the mantel's collection of cats he roared across the living room and hallway and was no doubt dreaming of the next house where the owners were not home and they could go upstairs and strip off their clothes, not the sheets. . . .

She herself could understand. She too had been that way when young, so *urgent,* so *avid,* while she and George were courting, when he had been a real estate agent and they would try out the beds. They had nearly been caught once, remember, when that couple from Manhattan arrived ten minutes early and walked around the house and didn't buy it anyhow but found them on the porch. In the first years of their marriage she and her husband were happy together; they had made each other happy, and now that she was sixty-four she wouldn't deny it or choose to forget: we *all* have been Hansel and Gretel and going for walks in the woods. And taking a picnic and gorging ourselves on each other not food and spreading out the tablecloth to keep the grass stains off. Taking radishes and brandy and potato chips and beer and tipping the canoe on purpose except not for a swim.

At least they were company, Alice decided; at least she'd invite them for lunch. She considered the Renoir. She lifted a piece of the puzzle — part of a jigsawed face, an ear and cheek — but did not have the patience for it, not this morning anyhow, and dropped the thing back in the box. In the fairy tale, the lost children are brother and sister and never would act like those two in the kitchen: laughing and looking for beds. And *which* was the girl who ate porridge, and *what* was that man's name who spun gold from straw and *why* was she thinking of fairy tales now when she had visitors, her Molly Maids all in a row. *Who once flew south,* she repeated, and stood, and made her way into the kitchen, where the young people worked.

"Do fix yourselves some tuna fish."

The girl had a beauty mark high on her cheek. She had been scrubbing the sink. She was wiping down the stove.

"And why not take a pickle, too, and a glass of orange juice, I think it's in the fridge."

"That's OK, Mrs. Saperstone."

"No, really. I insist."

"We're not supposed to . . ."

"Nonsense. I'll say I invited you. Both!"

Gretel looked at Hansel. He raised his shoulders shruggingly but did not shake his head.

"Well, that's settled, isn't it," Alice declared. "You two will join me for lunch."

❧

They did. They were acquiescent, uncomplaining, and they opened the can of tuna fish and found the container of fresh squeezed orange juice not from concentrate and Gretel prepared three sandwiches with mayonnaise and mustard and do you want some lettuce, this iceberg will last in the icebox a week. I wonder why they call it that—not *icebox,* of course, there used to be ice blocks and sawdust, but *iceberg,* is it the color of the lettuce, that particular off-putting yellowish white, or how much has been hidden by the frozen outer leaf? And then the children sat to eat and Alice heard herself explaining how she used to fix half a dozen sandwiches each time she fixed their lunch and this was the bare minimum because David alone could eat three. What an appetite he had! What a pleasure it had been to cook for Thanksgiving, to watch them all tuck in at table—that *was* the expression, wasn't it, *tuck?*—with peas and yams and mashed potatoes, because Joanna preferred mashed potatoes, and cider and stuffing and chestnuts and two kinds of cranberry sauce. It was anticipation and the aftermath of feasting she herself had feasted on, the prospect and the memory but not the food itself . . .

Except why do they call it, Alice wondered, Chicken of the Sea? There's no relationship at all between a tuna and a chicken; they don't resemble each other in the slightest or taste the same way, do they, Hansel, even if you slather it with mayonnaise and that runny mustard for lunch. Carefully, she levered tuna fish onto the fork tines and pushed at the bread with her spoon. Letting the morsel expand in her mouth and tasting it, she chewed. Consequently we sit here, she told them, eating icebergs and chickens and white toasted Pepperidge Farm bread that has no pepper in it and doesn't come from a farm. Oh I know you, she wanted to tell them, I know that you'd rather be eating alone or rolling around on the bed. But for thirty dollars an hour, my dear, you'll just have to suffer my company, because nothing *needs* to be cleaned.

"Cold enough for you this morning?" she asked, and Gretel answered, "Yup."

And then—as happened to her often still, though she never could predict what would cause it—her hard scant breath came easily and her eyesight cleared. She was her clear-eyed self again and, chewing, Alice frowned. *Here* were the kitchen counters, *here* the dishes to be done and the unswept floor. In the vanity mirror where hats and scarves hung she saw herself without illusion: trying to interest dullards, trying to keep them at table when they should be gone. They were wasting her money, her time. She was neither so old nor solitary that she needed to suffer these children and spend the best part of a morning on nonsense—the puzzle and the calendar, the Brothers Grimm, this elegiac maundering . . .

It had been a long night. She had not slept at all. Or if she slept it was briefly, and badly, and on the wrong side of the bed. She straightened her shoulders, adjusting her shawl, and chastised herself for the habit of chatter, the pointless garrulity of politesse. For she had had her dream again, the dream that woke her shouting of her father in her car. "Your name, girl?" she inquired, and Gretel wiped her lips and told her "Jean."

"And his?" she tilted her head at the boy across the tabletop and Jean answered, "Toby."

"Tobias?"

He nodded, his whole mouth engorged.

"Well, Jean and Tobias, I'm grateful. I do like company at meal-times, but now I have to get dressed. You can let yourselves out when you've finished the kitchen?"

They stood. To make sure they would leave, she remained. The girl did the dishes, the boy used the vacuum and swept; "Thanks a bunch for lunch," he said. She wasn't sure she had heard him correctly, or if he was making a joke: *a bunch for lunch* indeed! There was tuna fish oil on his shirt. It had happened long ago but Alice could remember as though it happened yesterday: the angle of her father's head, the way it wobbled wide-eyed on the stalk of his thin twisted neck, the thing he had done with his tongue. She could remember Aaron falling—*unfolding*—in the parking lot and how he was deadweight already when she lifted him, when they listened for his breath and tried to take his pulse.

"Bye now, Mrs. Saperstone."

"Good-bye."

"See you next Thursday," the girl declared brightly. They left. Down the path to the car with the Molly Maid sign the two pro-ceeded single file, wearing coats and boots and scarves and caps, she going first where the bread crumbs were strewn and getting in on the driver's seat side, he stowing the Electrolux and the box of rags and cleaning supplies in the trunk. Alice watched. The way young Hansel held himself reminded her of her own son; she rested her head on the pane. When David came in from karate, so dutiful and sweat-stained, so weary with taking his falls and working over boards and bricks, he had had the same composure and power in reserve. That he had been a part of her—a suckling pendant, a lip-pursed mouth—seemed, at such moments, aston-ishing; how *could* this strapping athlete have ever been flesh of her flesh?

Once the children were gone she relinquished the kitchen; she would in fact get dressed. She counted her steps: twelve, thirteen. Her ankles had swollen, her lower legs ached, but she managed the top of the stairs. There were apartment buildings with no thirteenth floor; the numbers went from twelve to fourteen because nobody wanted to live in between—*triskaidekaphobia*, that was the word, a fear of the number thirteen.

In the old days when the house was full there had been the friction of proximity, the loud squabbling racket of children about to take flight. How *could* they all have been so near and now so far away? How *could* this place they once called home fail to retain them now? She loved her offspring very much and missed them on a daily basis—hour by hour and minute by minute, David and J-J and Claire da Loon—but in a way that was comforting, nearly; she was with them wherever they went. Her family was with her, though distant; this caged and shallow-breathing animal her spirit had been tethered to could fly to Berkeley or Wellfleet or Ann Arbor without so much as a by-your-leave, and when and whenever she chose.

She did not choose. She had lived in this house all her life. She had been a child and then young woman and bride and mother here because her father who had bought it from the Dancey family gave it to her in turn. She and George went south on their honeymoon—two weeks of crayfish and martinis, two weeks of lovemaking and music—and by the time they returned from New Orleans her father had moved out. For the consideration of a dollar, and as a wedding present, he had transferred the deed. "It's your house," Aaron told her. "It's where you were born and should stay."

It did not escape Alice's notice that hers was the single name on the deed and the property was registered in her own name only; when she asked him, Aaron said he'd done it for tax purposes and if at some point in the future she wanted a transfer of title—to have the document read *Saperstone et Ux* instead—why, that would be just fine. He smiled at her, indulgent; the place was too much for him to maintain, and she'd have a family soon . . .

Her father disapproved of George but was unfailingly polite to him and did not breathe a word of reproach. There had been much to reproach. There were the business ventures that failed, the investments that couldn't go wrong and then did, the telephone calls after midnight and late afternoons at the track. There were the business trips to Chicago and Los Angeles and Kansas City where she knew—as Aaron must have known also, of course—that her husband was meeting or finding a woman; there were the lipstick smears on handkerchiefs, the gift boxes of scarves that arrived in the mail, and then at last the fishing trip with friends near the village of Keene . . .

In the silence she heard herself breathe. Alice waited; the noise would subside. It was the old familiar feeling: air and not-air passing through the membrane of her body and her throat constricting and enlarging both at once. It felt as though her body's boundaries had been extended, expanded; she was here and not-here, and the *here* and *not-here* were the same place finally. This was true of time as well as place; she was part of the present as well as the past and the future that, receding, would become the past, and the *now* and *not-now* were the same.

"I'm beside myself," she said aloud, and George said, "Yes, I noticed. You're in your favorite position . . ."

"What's that mean?" Alice asked him. "Whatever's *that* supposed to mean?"

"Being beside yourself, darling. It's your favorite position." And then he turned away.

She could have responded, of course; she could have said *his* favorite position was supine, or prone, a spineless lying-down and waiting for the world to pay attention, and if not, to pass him by. Room service was *his* favorite: lounging, wearing a terry-cloth monogrammed robe, the waiters saying "Thank you, sir" when George signed for the tip. Or being the life of the party at parties, telling the same joke again and again and hovering over the drinks. Oh, it was a misery, but in her bedroom she could breathe once more and took off and folded the shawl. When he died she had been young enough to have a series of gentlemen callers, the lawyers and doctors she tried on for size, but the truth of it was, Alice understood now, she'd used up her patience with men. One marriage was enough. One marriage was more than enough. She had had no patience left for all their needy posturings, their hunger for approval and their ridiculous antics in bed and their childish assertiveness: *me me me me me!* When she thought of her husband these mornings it was no longer with anger but a kind of bemused irritation; he had been—what was the word?—*incorrigible;* he was less of a grown-up than child and could not be corrected or changed.

So Alice tried *not* to think about him; he had been her one true love, her white knight on a Mustang charger, but he was also a difficult child and what Aaron called a "luftmensch," a man built out of air. He was the prodigal son, coming home and begging for forgiveness and beating himself on the chest: *me me!* The prodigal son is the one who leaves home and squanders everything; then he returns and all is forgiven, because he gets down on his knees and confesses: *Father, I have sinned.* If she had let George know, she knew, that there were stock market shares they could sell, that would have been the end of it; the trust fund would have emptied out like the bottles of Tanqueray gin.

She would have told him, she supposed, when Joanna went to college because they would have needed the money, but by the time Joanna went to college she had had his life insurance and *that,* at least, was actual cash, not luftmenschlike but substantial because George had valued himself very highly and his life insurance had sent the three children to school. It was peculiar, wasn't it; his get-rich schemes went belly-up, but when he died there was money, and more than enough to go round. She herself had wanted nothing; she had not touched the General Electric shares but left them for the children, when the time came, to inherit and, when the time came, to spend . . .

Inheritance: it troubled her that David took after his father, and not only in the way he moved and looked. They both attended Williams; they both were athletes and charmers—but she had tried to make certain that there all resemblance would end. The acorn, Aaron used to say, will never fall far from the tree. David *was* his father's son, of course, but George did not live long enough to set a bad example or corrupt him utterly; bad habits have to be learned. In some sense it was fortunate her husband died so young, in the flush of his prime, because he would have been impossible at sixty—pinching the waitress and dyeing his hair and slobbering into his gin . . .

The phone rang: shrill, prolonged. When it failed to stop she retrieved it and the man on the line was Joe Beakes. He said hello, she said hello, and they talked about the weather and he said he'd had a cold, the flu, but was feeling tip-top now and asked about her health. She told him, never better, and he said, that's good, that's excellent, and finally came to the point.

"You haven't forgotten?" he asked her, and she said, "Of course not, no."

"Are you up to driving over here?"

"What time is it?"

"One, well, nearly one o'clock. Our meeting's scheduled for two."

He was being gallant; he said, I'm happy to come pick you up, while she played for time, for clues, and then he said the documents are ready for your signature and the call snapped into focus. Alice was bright-eyed, clearheaded again, and told her old suitor, coquettish, that she'd be delighted to go out with him afterward to Mrs. London's or, if he preferred it, somewhere they could share a drink; let's celebrate, she said. Like old times, said Joe Beakes. We'll witness the documents here in the office and need to have the last will and testament notarized, but afterward by all means let me invite you for tea or a drink; he made his joke about billable hours and how for every hour they shared he'd reduce her tab by 10 percent, *she* was doing *him* a favor, not the other way around. He very much looked forward to her arrival at two.

She said, "Hunky-dory, I'll be there on time," and readied herself for an outing, a trip to Congress Park. Alice washed her face and brushed her teeth and brushed her hair and selected her clothing with care. She tried on and rejected the black Ann Taylor and the brown Eileen Fisher and the black cashmere skirt and matching sweater with embroidered pockets and then told herself not to dither and chose the outfit from Talbots Joanna had sent her for Christmas: jaunty yet suitable, maroon, and something the lawyer would not yet have seen. Foundation, rouge, lipstick, mascara; she attended to it all. In this town they called her a lady and a lady she would be.

For the time it took Alice to finish her face her breathing stayed regular, easy, and she reflected with some satisfaction that she still could manage the niceties of makeup and the business of settling her last will and testament, her—*peculiar* word—affairs. She had never slept with Joseph Beakes, had not had an affair with him, but he remained courtly and attentive and to a degree flirtatious; it was a pleasant prospect to ready herself for a visit, to drive to his office and deal with her—*peculiar* word—estate.

So back down the stairs and from Grandmother's house and over the hills she would go. There was money to leave for the children, the money she didn't give George. There was money to leave Kerry Noble, who had scoliosis of the back and had been forced to take early retirement and could barely make ends meet. There were bequests for charities: Planned Parenthood and the Neighborhood Senior Citizens Project and the Good Old Days. There was money for that woman Betty Livingston who took such good care of her father and for three or four others she couldn't at this moment name, but her lawyer had written them down. And it was a happy prospect, Alice reassured herself, a pleasant surprise she would have for the children—David and J-J and Claire da Loon—and she wondered, idly, if they would be surprised. She consulted her watch and the clock in the kitchen: *tok-tik.* The clocks agreed: 1:36.

Aaron died at ninety-two. She herself was a slip of a thing by comparison, younger than springtime and gayer than whatever it was the next line had rhymed with in that song from *South Pacific*—summer? laughter? Her father collapsed in the fullness of time and lasted to a ripe old age but she herself was not a candidate for a heart transplant, said Dr. Rosenthal when she had her appointment last week. You're short of breath, a little, and we need to watch your blood sugar and maybe schedule an EKG and stress test, but you're doing fine.

His expression belied this, however; his face was grave, not gay. He had ordered additional blood work and said we might consider angioplasty—not a bypass, not a full-fledged operation, nothing quite so radical—but this little balloon that can clear out your system; it's a low-risk procedure and we might give it a try. The funny thing is, Alice told him, the single most important thing is something you can do nothing about: have old parents, have good genes. So she either would last for a very long time or die like her mother, and soon. Dr. Rosenthal inquired if she knew which particular variety of cancer her mother had contracted, and how long it took and how old she had been when she died. "Forty," Alice said. Younger than springtime, a slip of a thing, and the truth was—though of course she did not tell this to the doctor—she couldn't remember her mother at all. The sound of her voice, yes, but not what she *said* and not what Elizabeth smelled like or wore.

Therefore she tried to remember, and did, the way the house looked those long winters ago when she fashioned snow angels all by herself, using carrots and coal and potatoes for the snow-lady's face. Eight years old is much too young to be a child without a mother and with a father who had turned sixty already and was about to retire and needed to be asked or else he would forget to shave. It was too young to live alone all day in this cottage she had filled with children, her children—David and J-J and Claire da Loon—and now was empty again. I have two daughters and a son except they live elsewhere today. I have three granddaughters also except they have flown south.

She slipped on her black fur-trimmed coat. She drew on her fur cap, her gloves. Then she let herself out of the kitchen and locked the house behind her and walked down the path in the Molly Maids' tracks and went to the garage and pressed the clicker for the automatic door. It opened. The wind—on January 10, at one forty-five in the afternoon, in Saratoga Springs, New York, in the Eastern Time zone of the United States, on the continent of North America, and in the world and in the universe but not God's palm, he's not a mailman, girls—was raw. She stood for a minute in weak winter sunlight before settling into the car. Her ankles were swollen and sore. This house had been her mother's house and she would tell Joe Beakes she wanted it to be her son's if David was willing to keep it; she very much hoped he would. She would not, of course, insist. It does not behoove—strange word, peculiar word, *behoove*—a lady to insist.

The light in the garage stayed on for its allotted span and then the light went out. She closed her eyes an instant, breathing, steadying her breathing, and saw her mother when younger than springtime and slipping into and out of the doorway, her doorway, a slip of a thing with a man by her side, and the man by her side had a limp.

XV
1916

"A beautiful night . . ."

"Oh!"

"I'm sorry. I startled you."

She shook her head.

"Indeed, I took you by surprise . . ."

"But, Mr. . . ."

"Barclay. Peter Barclay."

"Yes."

"And now"—half-earnest, half-playful, he doffed his brown cap—"you yourself have the advantage."

"Of?"

"Knowledge, Madame. Miss? For I am not so fortunate."

"Fortunate?"

"As to be in possession of *your* name, I mean."

"Dancey. Elizabeth Dancey."

"Miss Dancey. Elizabeth Dancey. A pleasure."

"Mr. Barclay." Minding her manners, she gave him her hand. He pressed and politely released it. "Have you traveled here before?"

"No, never," said Barclay. "I hope to return."

"It *is*, yes, a beautiful evening," she said. "The stars are out."

"The constellations. That one is Orion the Hunter," he guessed. He did not know, as did the girl, that Orion rose only in winter and would not adorn this night's sky. "I watched you while singing."

"Oh?"

"While I was performing. You said you did desire air, but unless I am mistaken you remained within earshot to listen . . ."

"I did."

"And did you approve what you heard?"

Consciously, she changed the subject. "Do you entertain company often?"

"Only when asked. Or inspired."

"It seems they ask you often." Above his cap the full moon rose; his strange form grew familiar and the sound of frogs resumed.

"I was, Miss Dancey, unrehearsed. I missed a whole chorus of 'Barbry Allen.'"

Elizabeth smiled. "But what you sang was sweetly sung."

"You think so?"

"Yes."

"By that time I could no longer see you," he ventured, "and I lost the heart for it."

"Mr. Barclay, you flatter me."

"No."

She turned from him. He followed. But now the maiden raised her hand, as though wavering, uncertain, and he judged the time had not yet come for physical proximity. Instead she asked his purpose here, and Barclay strove to speak. To begin with, he dilated on his long association with his employer Firestone, though emphasizing their companionship and not the relation itself—rendering his own role the more central by omission (neglecting to mention, for instance, the fact of employment and who reported to whom). Instead he found himself describing their shared previous adventures in the wilderness or sparsely settled regions by comparison with which this farmland seemed a town, a metropolis abuzz and teeming with the enticements of romance (here he looked at her significantly, but she did not flinch). Next he discoursed on the wanderings of the companionable members of that famed quartet Thomas Edison, John Burroughs, Harvey Firestone and the absent Henry Ford, whom somehow Peter Barclay rendered on this occasion supernumerary since *he* himself made up a fourth, suggesting (albeit implicitly and not, because she might have questioned it, by explicit utterance) that the mogul's absence went by the others unremarked because of *his* compensatory presence who stood by her side in the dark.

In truth he had attended often enough to conversation of the

Vagabonds so in this maiden's hearing he could replicate it readily, embroidering on theme and subject as though their endeavors were his. The girl might perhaps have found him persuasive without such borrowed finery, but time was short, the chance at arm's length only, and he judged it better to better his station in life.

Therefore Barclay arrogated to himself the character of Firestone. He spoke of their shared purposes, the cares of business, of capitalistic venture and the heavy weight of duty, the dozens—nay, hundreds and thousands!—of workingmen dependent for prosperity on Tom Edison's inventiveness, that spark first struck in Menlo Park or what the Sage of Slabsides—so we refer to old Burroughs, he said— has called the future's landscape and the contours of its face. In time to come our factories, assembly plants and turbines and highways crowded with commerce will be not so much remarked upon as commonplace, and the automobile itself will prove not the exception but rule. *Et in Arcadia ego*, he said.

She raised her lovely eyes to his, and Barclay averred it was Latin he spoke, and how we might fashion *e pluribus unum*, the plural conjoined into one. This represented, as she could not know, the sum and substance of his knowledge of the tongue of Catullus and Virgil, but it sufficed to establish his *bona fides*, his standing as *Magister Ludi* or master of the game. We love America, he continued, we honor its rough history and wish to retain it through purchase; we shall collect the relics—worldly yet sacred—of its diminishing, vanishing past. I predict a time when Ford's acquisitive extravagance will seem mere prudent husbandry (again he studied the girl's face; again she did not frown); when all of us are worms and dust the pleasures of this present moment will have been preserved.

"Worms and dust?"

"I speak of the future," he said.

Prettily, she shuddered.

"You know, perhaps, the poem?"

"Which?"

"A couplet I might say to you, a pleasing thought of a fellow called Marvell?"

Fetchingly, she shook her head. She was enjoying this flirtation, this unaccustomed badinage in the deep dark. "Do say it, then."

He did. Firestone quoted it often, and Barclay knew the verse:

> *Had we but world enough and time*
> *This coyness, mistress, were no crime . . .*

"And next," he said, "there are lines I misremember, but another thought worth quoting . . ."

"Which?"

> *The grave's a fine and private place*
> *But none, I think, do there embrace!*

This last surprised her, seemingly; she raised her white hand to her throat. She gazed at him steadily, keen-eyed. And though he might well have persisted with rhyme, some part of her expression warned him that he must move beyond words. There is a point where language proper proves counterproductive of natural ease; to continue down the primrose path of dalliance was to move from the verbal to physical realm, yet to proceed with care.

Again Elizabeth withdrew, in silence absolute. Again her suitor followed till the gleam of the lanterns was swallowed by distance, and the din of chat behind them grew inseparable from night-noise, a buzzing of insects and bustle of wind in the trees. She was, it must be recollected, barely more than half his age; he himself was nearing thirty and she but sweet sixteen. Yet she knew as he did not the path, and what Peter Barclay saw was the girl's re-treating form, the shapely paleness of her back disguised by bush and branch. Here was quarry worth pursuing, albeit skittish and alert.

Therefore he blundered forward, arms outstretched. The snapped twig and the slippery leaf gave him but momentary pause, so sharp was his ambition to be by the maiden's side. He was formulating a new phrase about "Time's winged chariot," and how it was a Model T, not drawn by horses nowadays, and how he hoped she'd ride with him to have the pleasure of it soon, the speed and power both. Made brave by applejack and rhetoric, he forayed after "Phyllis" (call her shepherdess or country wench, call her Audrey or the unplucked rose, it mattered not to Barclay in his rutting forward rush) until the city slicker—though he'd boasted of his sojourn in the wilderness, his habit of adventure— was in short order lost. She was skipping lightly down the hill, or so he guessed, or seemed to see; but in his haste to join with her he turned his foot athwart a log and felt the ankle twist.

"Christ," Barclay cried, and this proved his first utterance of uninflected authenticity. "*Damn!*"

"Sir?" Of a sudden the girl reappeared, though how she heard his cry and came so fast he could not comprehend. "Did you say something?"

"No!" Sitting, he rubbed at his ankle in pain.

"Is it broken, do you think?"

He shook his head.

"Turned? Sprained?"

Above him, she was a vision of innocence, and Barclay cursed his own profanity. "I'm sorry."

"Can you walk?"

"If you would help me to my feet . . ."

She did so, bending down and taking his arm and pulling him upright with what he recognized to be a farm girl's practiced strength; that hand of hers could milk a cow or wring a chicken's neck. Gingerly, he tried his weight; the ankle throbbed but held.

"I'm sorry," Barclay said again; his fair rescuer said, "Hush."

"You must think me a great fool."

"No."

"Clumsy, then."

"A little, yes."

"Is there a place I might lie down?"

Gravely she gazed at him. "Certainly, sir."

"Peter. You must call me Peter."

"Peter," said the girl.

"That's better, then."

"Are you all right?"

"Not really, no."

"The dining tent—it's not so far. Or I could call for men to carry you . . ."

"No."

"They have a stretcher, surely . . ."

He waved off the offer.

"We could return?"

"Not yet. Is there no . . ."

" *'Fine and private place . . .'* "

"You mock me."

"My grandmother's farmhouse," she said.

&

In this manner they proceeded and in this fashion acquaintance matured. Step by halting step and necessarily together they advanced through the dark wood. In time to come he would reflect that what gave him the advantage was the way he yielded it, and in the weighted scale of courtship he rose by falling down. By having demonstrated weakness and permitting her to take the lead he managed what mere braggadocio could not induce: ascendancy, as Peter Barclay came to see, was enabled by descent.

In the event, however, he was not conscious of seduction's tactics; he concentrated only on the pain in his right ankle and the soft encumbrance of her narrow waist. She steadied him, then inquired, "Can you manage?"

"Yes."

"Does it hurt you very much? Am I not being gentle?"

He shook his head, then nodded it. Now *she* was the leader and *he* her young charge, and she cajoled him sweetly, teasingly. "Not far," said Elizabeth, "it isn't far," urging her wounded swain ahead as he himself had urged her on not fifteen minutes since.

She was, it must be repeated, untried; her youth was full of promise undelivered till this night. Had he persisted with glib reference to the primrose path of dalliance she might have grown offended or self-protective, self-aware. Yet as the man's pain subsided so too did his pleasure increase. What first had been unfeigned alarm became feigned helplessness instead, and as she helped him forward he held back. By slow yet certain stages did they make their way together, and as though in preparation for what was soon to come their steps grew consonant; he remarked upon their matching names—*Barclay, Dancey, Dancey, Barclay*—while they approached the house.

A path, a meadow, a hillock and orchard: all these were an enchantment through which the couple moved. Familiar to the man but not the maid this coupled gait and linked approach; familiar to her but not to him the landscape they traversed. He knew as she did not the nature of the prize he sought; she knew as he did not the place where he might find it. And when at length a door appeared it must have seemed to Barclay that his fair guide had magicked it; he by himself would have remained till daylight in the ditch.

That fine and private place, the grave, requires of its occupant the same horizontal posture as the one ordained by bed; now as he stood and walked with her he quickened palpably, rising. A night owl hooted in the middle distance, and small creatures scurried away. She murmured encouragement as they went on, and yet he quizzed her carefully.

"This place belongs to?"

"My grandmother."

"Your mother's mother, so I understood. And she is?"

"At my parents' house. . . ."

"For the evening only?"

"No."

"But liable to soon return?"

Elizabeth made a confining gesture, dropping her hands while his own spirits lifted. "Grandma is an invalid."

"How so?"

"She can no longer climb the stairs. My parents keep this place because she wants them to, and not because she uses it . . ."

"I might lie down."

"Your ankle?"

"Hurts . . ."

"Poor Peter," said the girl.

❦

He would hold the memory dear. The hint of musk, the warmth of flesh, the susurrus of her rustling skirt remained with him through thin and thick and subsequent adventure. Although a magnate's close companion and by custom used to luxury no meeting Peter Barclay planned would outstrip this extravagance; forgotten his indignity; annealed his ankle's pain. She sat him down, undid his shoe, then pressed the blue vein by the bone.

The truth of his experience, in truth, was limited; those parlor maids and bar-girls who furnished Barclay his conquests had been indifferent or businesslike and reciprocating only as the bare stripped animal reciprocates when flat. Often, indeed, he had known himself used at least as much as user; often when offering dollars or drinks he had mused with postcoital sorrow on the lovelessness of what for lack of an alternative the world calls the act of love. That ultimate virginity of mind which masquerades as worldliness had been the rake's lot heretofore, and though he might disguise to her the nature of his circumstance he was neither so foolish nor so much a knave as to keep it hidden from himself: he lost his heart to Miss Dancey the while she lost her maidenhead to him.

Little wonder, then, he wondered and would not share the scene. In the tapestry he wove of conquest this remained the shining thread; this was to be his talisman and golden amulet. Those suitors and antagonists, the French—so Firestone had taught him—call a wound a blessing, and as though blind Cupid's arrow had been fired from its quiver with himself as purposed target Peter Barclay felt *blessé* and bore that wound for life. When he solaced himself thereafter with wife or lewd companion, it was indeed solace he sought. The constraint of his subsequent labors, his marriage, his duties in Brazil, Liberia, and elsewhere—all these enforced a distance, and he permitted enforcement. His masters sent him elsewhere, and Peter Barclay went.

But man can dream, can daydream or awake erect at slumber's end, and for this particular fellow the vision of the girl beneath and beside and above him would not dim. If in later years his ankle twinged it made him more glad than aggrieved. Though he would go ten thousand miles and settle in a continent more dark than the farm's darkness, Elizabeth Dancey remained his bright beacon, his Pharos and welcoming light. When old and nodding over wine he saw her move in the firelit glass; while on his deathbed babbling what he babbled of was her embrace, the dining tent and forest path and the verdant fields . . .

And she? She understood as he did not that what was past was history and not to be repeated; she knew on the instant, or so it would seem, that theirs was a prologue to nothing and drama with no second act. Of the swell who found her in the scented night, and took her hand, and took her arm, and limped with her in conspiratorial shared silence to the empty house, then struck a match and by its flickering uncertain flame discovered the door and the stairwell and bed—of him her seducer she sought nothing more and, were she to have met him in daylight, would have passed modestly by. No gossip she, nor self-propelling arriviste; her motive and comportment stayed as mysterious to her as him and in her lifetime equally not to be repeated. In subsequent behavior she would prove cautious, provident, but from that August dark till dawn she relinquished self-possession and was instead possessed.

In the throes of their shared frenzy is it possible a vision came of what their congress would produce and how their act would ramify, repeat? Did *she* put on such knowledge and come to see with clarity both sequence and its consequence, how cause becomes effect until effect in turn turns causal? Did he predict the motorcar would prove a lethal engine and those who followed after them would die while embracing within it? Or that the man who married her would collapse long decades thereafter in his great old age while standing in a parking mall and dreaming of Elizabeth herself no longer young?

Vagabondage is a tangled skein, and though Peter Barclay was practiced enough he had no skill sufficient to unweave what would ensue: the years in Liberia, exiled, the years she would return as wife to this very cottage and bed. The stay-at-home and wanderer are united too in this: her cries, her sighs are silence now; his animal exuberance has stilled.

❧

"Good-bye."

"Good-bye, then."

"We break camp this afternoon."

"Yes."

"I *wish* it were not so," he said. "I *do* wish we could stay."

Where this preternatural knowingness had come from she herself could not construe, but she was both clear-eyed and calm. "Of course you do."

"And I'll come back."

"Is that a promise?"

"A promise, yes."

"Will you cross your heart?"

"And hope to die," said Barclay.

"No! Don't hope that; don't make such a wish." Passionate, the girl shivered.

"Well, I promise anyhow to try."

"Yes. Yes, that's good enough."

"You'll wait for me?"

"I'll wait," she said. "I promise."

"Good."

Then there was silence between them. She laid her hand upon his hand, her head upon his shoulder. In this attitude they waited for some moments. At length Miss Dancey roused herself. "Leave me."

"Yes."

She ventured it: "My dearest."

"Yes."

"You can find your way without my help this morning?"

He smiled.

"I need to clean up, rearrange myself. The bed"—becomingly, she colored—"its linens have been soiled."

He frowned.

"I need to set the house to rights."

"Your parents . . ."

"No. There's nothing to tell them. Nothing to say."

"In that case, my dearest . . ."

"Good-bye."

Part Seven

XVI

2003

Joanna and David return to Wellfleet after *West Side Story.* They have spent the day together, and she shows her brother through the house; she gives him the bedroom next to Leah's and walks him through the guest wing—its heat turned off—where sometimes in the summer six people stay the night. "Not too shabby," David says, and though he means this as a compliment the word stays with her: *shabby,* and she sees the Bay View Inn as a stranger might: ramshackle, ill-maintained. Harry and David meet briefly, and when she introduces them Joanna says, "Aren't you two in some sort of business together—Harry and David? Mail order, right?" She laughs at this, *male order, right,* but the men are silent, shaking hands, and she tells herself not to be nervous and not to overdo it; their names may be Harry and David, but that doesn't add up to a joke.

It's Friday night, eleven o'clock, and the performance went well; Leah was just terrific, David says. Where did your daughter learn to dance, where did she get that *accent;* who was it, Chita Rivera or Rita Moreno who played the part on Broadway—she could give them a run for their money. That's sweet of you— Joanna smiles—it's very sweet but let's not exaggerate, and did you notice in the program how she called herself Artemisia? I did, says David, what's that about, and she says Independence, it's called self-definition and how to horrify Mom.

The Cape has been buried in snow. For the whole time she's been away it must have snowed, Joanna thinks; this is an old-fashioned no-nonsense February, the real thing. It looks the way Route 6 first looked when she visited in winter—when she and Mr. Ex-Right Ex-Husband #1 drove out for the weekend and fell in love with the quaint narrow streets and humped ice on the beaches and the dry-hauled fishing boats. In wintertime the sea remains, the sand remains, the pine trees and the sky remain, and the only thing that changes in the landscape is how scrub oak leaves turn brown. She and Mr. Ex-Right made the baby then who danced and sang so well tonight and they bought the house down by the harbor because it was available, the perfect place for vacations and maybe the whole year. It will be a good investment, her husband had assured her, and the worst they could do is break even and rent the place out in July . . .

Joanna understands, of course, that when you're young and happy the world is young and happy too; the landscape is enchanting and a cranberry rake and rowboat are objects to acquire. For the first years she'd adored it here: the clambakes and cluster of freshwater ponds and square dances on the Town Dock. Those first summers they went sailing and gave cocktail parties; they met psychiatrists and actors and selectmen and were sociable all season long. She'd filled the rowboat with flowers and hung cranberry rakes on the porch. When Leah was born it seemed lovely and safe to spend the whole day at the beach—with a red umbrella and a cooler packed with sandwiches and plastic buckets and spades—building castles out of sand. When your love life is good and bank account full the world is your oyster and ready for swallowing whole . . .

And then one day you're thirty and then thirty-five and forty-four, and Mr. Ex-Right Ex-Husband #1 is living in Chicago with a brand-new towheaded family while you're spending your nights with a loser called Harry and wondering what *ever* seemed romantic in these snowdrifts, these empty and echoing streets. You have enough money to manage year-round but not enough to use the house only for the summertime; you rent rooms out to make ends meet and drive to Boston once a month and then maybe three times a year. It's not so much Cape Cod that changed but her relation to it; now when she looks she sees trouble and loss, new roofs that mean the old ones leaked, new windows that signify dry rot and not a happy couple moving in.

David has been watching her. "How long have you lived here—fifteen years?"

She nods.

"So are you, aren't you planning to . . ."

"To what?"

"To continue with the B&B?"

"Why not? It's what I do."

"Except you won't have to," he says.

⊷⊷

And this is true, she understands, this is what they mean by Fortune's Wheel. There's that TV show, *Wheel of Fortune,* and the Ferris wheel she sat in at the county fair; things turn but stay the same. They strap you in and start the machine and sometimes you're sitting on top of the world and sometimes at the bottom, but always the chair is the same one you're riding; and what goes up comes down. "I'm rich," Joanna tells the dashboard silently, "well, not rich *rich* but able to *deal...*"

By the town offices in Eastham a van has been pulled over, and she sees it being searched; there are two boys at the side of the road, and a policeman with a flashlight peering in. The van is dark and battered and the boys are wearing sweatshirts, black, and that's all she has the time to see before the red light changes. The patrol car's flashing beacon both comforts and alarms her; there's someone on the job tonight—but what sort of job is being done, what kind of peace being kept?

"And you," she asks her brother. "Will it change the way you spend your time?"

"My time? For me it isn't time but place. It's should I move to Saratoga ..."

"And?"

"And the truth is I really don't know."

There's another storm system coming, the weatherman has warned them on the evening news: a true nor'easter sliding up the coast. Next week could be a doozie, folks, a lollapalooza like '78, and by Monday morning we'll see. It's snow or maybe freezing rain and sleet or just plain rain or maybe a little—make that a *lot,* folks—of each. Mother Nature hasn't finished with us is what this storm is saying; not by a long shot, not yet.

"It's hard to process, isn't it," Joanna says, "to know how much has changed."

He nods. They drive past Consider the Lilies and the flea market and movie theater; it's eleven-fifteen and the arc lights are on, and the plowed sides of the parking lots are head-high and forbidding. This car, for example, says David, you could trade it in. Or keep it for Leah, she'll be driving soon, and get yourself a gussied-up version, a brand-new Legacy Outback wagon, compliments of L.L. Bean. With fancy leather seats—he pats her knee—and a CD player and optional GPS, the whole nine yards.

"You're joking," says Joanna, and he tells her not a bit.

"What's GPS?" she asks him, and he says, "Global Positioning System," it means you know just where you are and how to get to where you're going and you can't get lost. The whole nine yards, he says again, and she says I think that's how much dirt they need to fill a grave.

For a mile there is silence between them, no traffic on the road. The curio shops and lobster shacks and seasonal motels have closed; there are ropes across the unplowed entrance drives and signs saying "Come Back in June."

"What do you think about Harry?" she asks.

"Is this a change of subject?"

"No. Well, yes." A truck appears, its headlights bright, a string of little yellow lights above it at the roofline, and they meet and pass each other and the road grows dark again. Trusty-Rusty roars and clatters over frost heaves; she cracks her window open and hears the high-pitched wind. "I know you've only just met him, only just now had the chance to meet, but I do want your opinion."

"Why?"

"Because I value it." Inside the car, in the dim interior together, it's easier to talk. "So much is changing, David . . ."

"Yes." He clears his throat. "And I'm grateful that you asked, but it's too early, isn't it, for me to *have* an opinion. And it's *your* call, anyhow . . ."

She has watched him watching Harry and knows what David

thinks. "You're telling me, aren't you, I ought to do better. You find him—what would Mom say—vulgar?"

"Touché. I want the very best for you. I want you not to settle, I *hate* to think you're settling . . ."

"*A boy like that,*" Joanna sings, then trails off to silence again. She turns the heater to high. Now they are passing Cumberland Farms and the Liquor Locker and gas stations that signal the entrance to Wellfleet. At the sign for the town center she turns left; they're almost home, she's almost at the Bay View Inn, and Leah will join them after the opening night party.

"She *was* good, wasn't she?"

"Spectacular," he says.

"She's not sixteen. It isn't learner permit time."

"It will be soon enough. Just let her keep the car."

Joanna pulls into her driveway and parks beside his rented Taurus and Harry's bright blue Firebird, and they get out together and shut their doors at precisely the same instant so it sounds as though a single door is being closed. She thinks about those black children in Eastham, hands at their sides, affecting nonchalance, while their van was being searched. She thinks about her daughter and the painted flush on Leah's cheek and the delight she took in curtain calls, the quick reprise of her dance number while the audience whistled and clapped. They were *standing* for her, on their feet, the whole auditorium clapping because Leah stole the show . . .

"A Legacy Outback," she says. "I suppose it's the right thing to buy. With a legacy, I mean."

She and David walk up to the porch. On Holbrook Avenue the Connolly house has lights on in the cupola, but no one else appears awake and there is darkness everywhere—made darker somehow by the snow, its iridescent gleaming. In Wellfleet there are homes called Morning Glory, The Moorings, Nevadun, but she named her house for the view of the bay, and Joanna is proud of the welcoming sign. There are grapes festooning the *B, V,* and *I* so the emblem is spirited, festive, and as soon as it gets warm enough she'll retouch the purple cluster where the paint has chipped.

At the kitchen table Harry is sitting by himself, eating pretzels, drinking beer. He works at the post office counter from Monday to Saturday noontime, and mostly he waits until Saturday night to get drunk. But tonight he has the television on and is watching a show about hookers, thin girls and fat girls in Miami parading up and down the street and getting into cars. It's reality TV, a documentary, with close-ups of the girls, their teeth, and when they go down on their customers the camera goes out of focus but the sound stays on. Then they talk about their pimps and johns and how hot it gets in the Florida summer, and when she and David join him Harry lifts the Remote and clicks *Mute.*

"Hey," he says. "How goes it?"

"Happy Valentine's Day," says Joanna.

"How *goes* it?"

"Terrific," says David.

"Do we need to watch this?" she asks.

"I've been having a party, see, my own private show." Harry has been smoking, drinking, and the air smells rank. "All by my lonesome with pizza and beer and this whore called Chiquita who gets off on whips. What you can get on cable now . . ."

"How dainty," says Joanna.

"And then they do these interviews. They ask the guys which girls they like—fat ones, thin ones, young ones—and what way they like it best . . ."

"Do we *need* to hear this?"

"Speaking of dainty," he tells her. "This kitchen is a mess. I'm a little lubricated, maybe, but this kitchen is a mess." He sweeps his arm out widely, encompassing the beer bottles and the cardboard box of pizza and the *Cape Codder* on the floor and the litter box and empty overturned cat-food tins and cigarette butts and unwashed dishes in the sink.

"*Your* mess," she tells him.

He peers at her, then David. "Right . . ."

"I'm not your housecleaner, mister."

"Who said you were?" he asks the ceiling. "Me?"

Embarrassed by the room's squalor, angry at the stench of it, Joanna retreats to the door by the porch. "I just yesterday quit doing laundry. Towels and sheets. There's no more laundry service here."

"And what's *that* supposed to mean?"

Mungo Park, her cat, is hiding. "It means it's not your house."

Harry repeats this in a high whine, mockingly: "*It means it's not your house.* What else is new . . ." Then he clicks on the sound again, and one of the girls is leaning in the passenger window of a Cadillac convertible and saying, what you want is my little white mouth on your big black cock; it's raining, baby, let me in and I'll do whatever you want.

The driver opens the passenger door. The camera pans to the car's windshield wipers, their slapping back-and-forth, their rhythmic beat, and Joanna crosses over and hits the *Power* button and shuts the TV off.

"Hey," Harry says, "that was my *show*!"

"And as long as we're discussing it there's something else you need to know. I'm out of this business as of March first. Which means you're out of here also."

He stares at her. "Say that again . . ."

"You heard me the first time. March first."

"Wrong. I'm out of here tomorrow, bitch." He pushes back from the table and stands. "Why wait? First thing in the morning I'm history."

"That's it," Joanna says. "Exactly."

"This dump. This shit-hole." He pulls out a handkerchief and rubs his face and drops his bottle of Budweiser to the floor. It tilts, spills, foams.

"Why wait till tomorrow?" David asks. "If that's the way you feel . . ."

"Hey, smart-ass," Harry turns on him, "just because you're her kid brother don't mean you get to tell me"—he breaks off, befuddled, blowing his nose—"don't mean how it's your business. You show up for a goddam day, an *afternoon,* and all of a sudden—"

"Listen," David says. "You wouldn't want to stay. I mean, really."

He has moved to Harry's side—younger, stronger, bigger—and is ready for a fight; Joanna sees this, sees her brother with his arms out, loose, and remembers his karate and thrills for an instant to think she's being protected. Then she thinks of *West Side Story* and how children die in knife-fights and how Harry can be sweet, and says, "Look, Leah's coming back; let's just forget this, both of you, and in the morning you can pack."

"You know what I think about, Valentine's Day, I think about old Al Capone and that massacre of his. That theme party he put together in a garage in, where was it, Chicago? Not roses and hearts and balloons. I mean, I'm just a guy who works at the PO who thinks maybe his landlady will treat him decent if he's nice, and always pays the rent on time—well, don't I, haven't I always?—and your baby brother condescends to visit us from, where is it, Berkeley, and suddenly I'm out on my ear, my ass, not good enough, and what I want to say is don't come begging for it, lady, when he's out of town again . . ."

"I won't," Joanna says.

"Because in the morning I'm off to Aunt Gracie's. I've got a standing offer there." He winks at David leeringly. "A standing lying-down offer, you see. Complete with water view."

"Fine," David says. "I'll help you pack."

"Capone's. Speaking about Al Capone. That restaurant out on Route 6, you know, the Sheraton, well, I bet someone's got a party there, I bet they're celebrating loud and clear, *bang, bang*"—he aims his finger at Joanna—"and got you in their plans for the garage. Capone the bone. It's what we *mean* by entertainment, not some shitty little musical with pom-poms and the high school band and some teenybopper who calls herself Art. You jump out of the cake and go rat-a-tat-tat or you get in the car with me, baby . . ."

"You're drunk," she says. "You're disgusting."

"Fuck off," he tells Joanna. "Both of you. Your daughter too, you stuck-up cunt. Your little Miss—" and that's when David hits him, twice, doing something rapid with his hand and elbow, and kicking Harry's ankles free with a side-sweep of his own left leg, and the man falls to the floor. He falls in a clattering pratfall, a noisy spread-eagled half-comic collapse. "Oh shit, oh *shit,* my nose is broke."

"He'll be all right," David says.

"It broke, it's *bleeding,*" Harry cries.

"All over my freshly mopped floor," says Joanna. "I told you I wouldn't clean up."

Harry builds himself back to his feet. He smooths his hair, he feels his nose, he looks for an instant as though he might fight but watches David watching him and collects his cigarettes and stalks out of the kitchen. "I'm out of here," he announces. "Go fuck yourselves, all right?"

"Good-night," says David.

"Good-bye," says Joanna. "Sleep tight."

She is astonished by how quick this was, how quick this *is*—her brother's physical ferocity, his elbow in her lodger's face—*ex*-lodger, *ex*-lover, she reminds herself—and how in the morning she'll take down the sign and not be a B&B. That was pretty impressive, she says to David, do you do this often, and he smiles and shakes his head. Then for half an hour the two of them do clean the room—washing and mopping and taking out trash. Upstairs they hear Harry muttering, moving about in the hallway and flushing the toilet and slamming his door; did you hurt him very much, she asks, and he says, I promise, no, I mostly hurt his pride. Mungo Park appears and rubs at her ankles purringly. Joanna hugs him, feeds him, lets him out, and while she's standing on the porch she sees the headlights of a car, dipping and bobbing and making its way to her own plowed drive. Leah-Artemisia gets out of the back, laughing and waving good-night to her friends, and skips up the steps to the porch. Her daughter has come home.

❧

In the morning the sun ascends brightly and the harbor glistens; the tide is low, the trees are motionless and there's the sort of windless calm that heralds a clear day. It's Saturday morning and Leah sleeps in, but Harry is wearing his postal clerk uniform and has his bags ready to go: two suitcases, a cardboard box, a plastic Pan Am flight bag and pants and coats on wire hangers and the six-packs of ale and beer and cans of soup and tuna fish that had been his contribution to the pantry.

"Do you want coffee?" she asks.

His eye is swollen, blue and black. He keeps his face averted.

"No hard feelings?" asks Joanna, and he shakes his head. "Does that mean yes?" she presses him. "Or no?"

He is filling the Firebird's trunk, his dignity shored up by silence. His cheek and nose are red.

"You can stay, if you want to, till March first." She watches from the porch. "You're paid till then . . ."

"One more load," he says, "I'm outta here . . ." and brushes past her where she stands. Then he emerges from the kitchen with the radio and blue plastic flight bag and his green parka; these he lays on the backseat. Then he slams the car's trunk shut. His masculine ego is wounded, she knows, and he wants to get away as fast as possible, but she cannot keep from teasing him, a little, sipping her mug of hot coffee and resting her toe on the railing and smiling down from the porch. "Be seeing you," Joanna says, and waves. He gets in the car and drives off.

In time to come when they will meet on Main Street or at the post office window he will maintain his silence, his pretense of apartness, and she will remember him sprawled on the floor, her brother standing above him tight-handed. She will remember other things also: the way that he called her Old Glory, his flag, the way he cleaned out the basement and liked it when she sat on him and the rough soles of his feet. When she had needed company he had been her company, and if he chose to talk to her she would have been happy to answer; "No hard feelings," Joanna would have said.

But Harry is a chapter—she knows this all already—in a story she won't finish and book she prefers to keep closed. He will be the low she sank to when she was invested in sinking, and she will be the woman in the 2003 Legacy Outback with the leather seats and GPS who leaves all this behind . . .

❧

She and her brother take a walk. They walk down to the dock—its fishing boats on railroad ties, the harbormaster's door ajar—and past the shuttered theater and the trailer camp and out Chequessett Neck. They walk past Mayo Beach and the snow-submerged greens of the golf course and the frozen expanse of Herring Creek—a trickle of water, a cluster of gulls, men raking for oysters and quahogs—and up to the high crest of Sunset Hill. It's very cold this morning, but Joanna exults in the chill, wintry air. "How long are you staying, how long can you stay?" she ventures to ask David, and he says, "That storm they're predicting, I'd either best be gone beforehand or just stick around."

"Oh do," she says, "please stick around."

"Until the storm is over, yes, why not?"

"We'll make snow angels," she tells him, and puts her gloved hand out and they walk arm in arm.

David talks about Marconi. "Last night," he says, "remember, when we were passing the sign for the Marconi Station I found myself thinking about him: that fierce Italian staring at the ocean and convinced he could cross it with wireless calls. The telegraph. So this is where it all began, this thing we've made out of modernity that may yet wreck us all. If it doesn't work it's madness—crazy old Guglielmo—and if it does it's called a vision and they salvage the transmitter and call it history."

Men drive past them where they walk, lifting their hands from their steering wheels, and two of them tap lightly on their horns. Joanna waves back; she tightens her scarf and lengthens her stride while her brother continues to talk. That these *mujahideen* and *mullahs* can reach across the ocean is Marconi's dream turned nightmare and David wouldn't mind at all, he says, if we returned to pen and ink and sent letters by Pony Express. Back before the world became a village there was no chance some millionaire ex-playboy Muslim with a kidney problem and a penchant for apocalypse could bring down buildings made of glass and steel ten thousand miles away. Or think of Thomas Edison, our fairy god-father—he laughs—and Ford and Firestone; they did more to change the national landscape than any three men you can name. Lately I've been working on this web site—he gestures at the bay—these new design modalities, but now I find myself thinking about egg tempera instead.

"Egg tempera," she asks. "What's that?"

"The old way of working, I mean. Real bristle brushes. A blow-pipe for paint. The colors that they used to use; you know: veg-etable pigments, the white that comes from pulverized bone, the black that's charcoal—something burned . . ."

"Of the three of us"—she smiles at him—"you're the real romantic."

"Touché."

Near the crest of Sunset Hill they see a red shape flapping like a great wounded bird in the marsh grass and cattails—but the red is unnatural, rising and falling and folding back onto itself. The shape makes no noise she can hear, and Joanna moves closer to see. When she is near enough she sees it is a cluster of balloons—red helium heart-shaped balloons left over from Valentine's Day. They have floated free or been released but now the air has leaked away, and the Mylar party favors rise a foot or two, then fall back to the cattails. Joanna pauses, watching; I wonder how long they've been trapped here, she says. It isn't a sign, says her brother, they haven't been *trapped*, it means there was a party and the party's done.

❦

Leah is in the kitchen, eating a muffin and drinking herb tea. "Welcome back," she says. "Were you, like, out there *walking*?"

"It's beautiful," says David.

"But seriously cold," Joanna says. "They say there's another storm coming."

"You were terrific, Art. I've been telling your mother all morning . . ."

"What did you think of Maria?"

"She was terrific also. Except she couldn't sing. Or dance."

The girl laughs.

"I take that back," he says. "She sang, but out of tune."

"Totally. And Tony?"

"Face it, darling, *you're* the one."

"I always think," Joanna says, "that I can tell the parents by the angle of their vision. The way they're looking only at their own child in a tutu or playing the tuba or being a sailor. But you were *different*, Li-li, you were the one we all stood for and applauded. And not just me and David, *everybody* knew how good you were . . ."

"We missed a chorus of 'America.' Like, totally. Did you notice?"

"No," David says. "You covered just fine."

"We'll get it right tonight," she says. "Maisie and Tom called. They said they want tickets."

"We might make a foursome," says Joanna. "We might just see the show again. Or maybe the matinee tomorrow?"

"What happened to Harry?"

"Gone. He's gone."

"He left early," David says.

The girl is inattentive, unconcerned. She finishes her muffin and stands and yawns and stretches so her sweatshirt rides up and reveals the tattooed dolphin on her hip. Then she turns to her uncle — half-solemn, half-flirtatious, perfectly poised between adult and child — and says, "I'm wizard glad you saw the show. I'm wizard happy you came."

He bows to her. "I'm glad your mom invited me. And very damn pleased to be here."

XVII

2003

He has told Leah the truth. He feels at home with his sister and niece, these members of his family, and tries to be of use. David quizzes the girl for her history test and helps with the pronunciation of her first-year French. When she asks him if he's been to France he tells her he spent time there when he was trying to paint.

"How old were you?" she asks him, and he says, "You've got *years* yet. Twenty-five."

"Were you alone?" she asks him, and David says, "Most of the time."

"Tell me about it, OK?"

Again she seems poised between grown-up and child, and he cannot decide if her interest is real or, as he half-suspects, feigned. Leah stares at him, expectant, and David says he's grateful for her company but will keep the lecture brief. "No," Li-li insists, "I want to *know,*" and he thinks maybe she means it and does begin to talk. At Williams he had majored, he tells her, in art history; he wrote his thesis on the use of furniture—chairs and tables mostly—in portraits by Vermeer and, later on, van Gogh. It had seemed a good idea, a linkage between generations of Dutchmen—the sort of half-assed declension-connection you write about in college—and he loved the Clark Art Institute.

"What's that?" she asks, and he explains: a museum in Williamstown, not the college museum, but near where he lived, and a wonderful place to get lost in. I'll take you there someday, he promises, you and your mom and you'll see what I mean, we'll look around . . .

Leah props her chin on her closed fist and leans forward, wide-eyed, an ingénue auditioning for the role of confidante. Then, after Williams, David says, I moved to the city—Manhattan—and held two gallery jobs. This was, what, 1989. I had some friends in the

263

city and we shared a loft on Grand Street; Soho was on a roll back then and everything was—it's the word we used—copacetic, *cool*. The girl touches her nose ring and smiles up at him, indulgent. He has no way of knowing if they still say "copacetic" or if when she said "wizard glad" she had been making a joke. You call yourself Artemisia, he says, and she was the hell of a painter, but Ms. Gentileschi had a time of it too; it isn't easy, Art.

And when you're in the business—David shifts position on the couch—of trying to sell paintings it occurs to you, sooner or later, that maybe you too ought to paint. You're just as good as—maybe better than—those attitudinizing clowns who show up in the gallery, and it doesn't occur to you, didn't occur to *me* anyway, that I was as half-assed as everyone else and following their lead . . .

So I went, he says, to France. Van Gogh himself had gone to France, and it seemed like an omen. He tells her how he started off in Paris, *everyone* starts off in Paris, or at least they used to, but it was lonely and expensive and dirty and too cold. He didn't drink absinthe or cut off an ear but spent six months going to museums and trying to learn how to paint. Then he met a girl whose family invited him south to their villa for Christmas, and though it didn't work with her he did fall in love with Provence.

"Provence?" she asks, and David says *provincia*, the wedge of France that's on the sea and in the winter relatively empty and, by comparison, cheap. Then he reminds himself that Leah's fifteen and has barely left the Cape, and he's been talking about Williamstown and Paris and New York and Provence as though she too had traveled; he says again, I'll take you there, I promise, sometime soon. He talks about the *mas* he rented near the village of Valbonne, the brilliant sky and olive trees, the museums he would visit and the drawing class he took from an American in Grasse.

"The trouble is, the trouble *was*, I thought I had some talent. And they made it look so—well, not easy, *possible*. Cezanne's house with his brushes—or at least *somebody's* brushes—and apples on display, all that pottery in Vallauris, the Picassos in Antibes. And they did seem so, so *casual:* those artists of the southern light—

Bonnard, van Gogh himself in St. Remy, Gauguin. I learned I wasn't good enough, is what it all came down to . . ."

James Belton was his teacher's name, and he smoked a pipe while painting; he said tobacco is good for the paint. He had a mane of flowing white hair and a flamboyant impatience with the world of the bourgeoisie; he made long complicated pronouncements about sculptural mass and the reticulated line, the plane of the drawing and the shit storm that was capitalism. He said, money is the *death* of true expressiveness, expression, because as soon as you have something to protect you can't be truly free to paint—to draw that hydra-headed dog, for instance, or deal in figure-ground . . .

Yet Belton was the well-heeled son, as David came to understand, of a doting father on Wall Street who funded his expatriate life and paid for the gallery shows. His own compositions were blockish, thickly mottled, and one night over too many bottles of wine he said, "I've pissed it away, I pissed away my talent; boy, don't let it happen to you."

"Mom says you do karate . . ."

"Used to."

"She says you were a black belt once."

"Not quite." He shakes his head. "I gave it up at brown."

Abrupt, inquisitive, Leah asks, "Why didn't you love Paris?"

"I told you; it was cold, wet, dark . . ."

"I have an Edith Piaf CD. 'The Little Sparrow,' is that what they called her?"

He nods.

"Why?"

"She was about this big around"—he makes a circle with his fingers—"and they say she could warble all night. But as long as we're speaking of names," David says, "that cat of yours? Mungo Park?"

She nods.

"Why did you two call him that?"

"Mungo Park was an explorer."

"Right. But he was a Scotsman, and always getting lost, and he died in Africa . . ."

"It's his *name*," says Li-li, and the French lesson is over, and she laughs.

❦

When Claire calls to tell them what happened to Jim, it is Wednesday afternoon. She has been to Florida and flown back with the body, she says, and that's why she hasn't been home. I can't believe it, says Joanna, and Claire repeats she can't believe it either, two deaths in the same week. It's been a shock, she confesses, a total shock, the reality hasn't sunk in; she got to Ann Arbor on Thursday, and the next day he left on a business trip and by Sunday Jim was dead. What can we do, how can we help, asks David, and their sister says she's been coping but will need them later on. The two of them offer what comfort they can, and she thanks them and tells them she'll call.

David helps Joanna, shopping. They drive to Provincetown or the Stop & Shop in Orleans and range the aisles—he pushing the cart, she checking her list—like a couple starting out together on shared domestic life. She tells him which cleaning supplies she prefers, what variety of bread to buy, and they discuss the quality of cheese and fish for sale. He extends the term of rental for his car. David understands he's marking time, deferring decisions as to what comes next, but there's no urgency, he tells Joanna when she asks, and digs out the path to the porch.

His sister has a whole network of friends; she seems to know all the people in Wellfleet and greet them each by name. She introduces him as "My kid brother," and he makes the acquaintance of doctors and fishermen, cooks and carpenters and divorcées, the man who owns the boatyard and the tellers at the bank. While they drink coffee at The Lighthouse or he drives her to The Bare Necessities David sees how seamlessly she fits into the fabric of the town. They loiter in the parking lot or at the restaurant counter and talk about the weather or the prospect of war in Iraq and whether or not we are fighting for oil; they talk about the dead whale and bottle-nosed dolphin that washed up on Tuesday afternoon and where their children and grandchildren are. They talk about the building boom, how it seems unstoppable here on the Cape, and if and when it will stop.

David tries to paint. He buys art supplies in Provincetown and visits the few galleries that remain open in winter; he studies what they show. Joanna says, "Use Harry's room," and he sets up an easel and fashions a draftsman's table from a plank door and old sawhorses he salvages from the garage. Although he had made light of it, talking to his teenage niece, he feels the old desire: to capture the visible world in a line and fix what's transient, fleeting . . .

To start with, he works in pastel. He sketches the landscape he sees from the window: the locust trees, the back of a restaurant down by the pier, the far glimpse of shoreline and beach. He spends an hour at it a day, then two, then four until Joanna says, "What are you *doing* and when can I *see* it," and he says, "It isn't any good. Not yet." The color-field feels saccharine, or leached away; he doesn't want, he tells himself, to be doing Christmas cards or ads for the chamber of commerce, and when he tries to work in oil the canvas defeats him, resistant. What he's after and has not attained is a way of rendering, the representation of a scene that moves beyond technique . . .

Therefore he draws. He uses charcoal and pencil and ink and fills a sketch pad with the stuff of memory: a rocking chair, a kitchen sink, a paddock with horses and man in straw hat, the jade plant by Adrienne's hot tub. He works rapidly and without consulting models or old photographs, and his wrist and hand begin to feel more flexible. He has always had the gift of imitation, of accurate proportion, and it is no challenge to sketch apples or acorns or ladies reclining; he gets perspective right. What's hard for him is attitude, a way of looking at the world that renders it original and not derivative. This is much more difficult, he knows, than accurate shading and volume or those pastels he had been working on in Berkeley: the water and the offshore rocks he complained about back in Bolinas, a false equivalence between sound waves and waves.

From a photograph his sister owns, David draws their grandfather: a pair of eyes, a fringe of hair. He draws a carving knife and fork and the turkey from Pederson's farm. He draws their mother on the table with a sheet pulled up beneath her chin and her thin nose and sunken cheeks and the mortician's apparatus: needles and a jar of adult tinting cream. He draws—it takes up the whole of a page—his left hand. He draws his own penis, a series of buttocks, then breasts. At the end of two hard weeks of work he looks at what he accomplished, and it fails to please him but does not embarrass him either. When Joanna asks again, he says, "All right, fine, come on up," and jokes about inviting her into the room; it was never off-limits before.

"I suppose that's true," she says, "except it should have been, maybe. These are very good."

He closes the sketch pad. "Not yet."

The will is still in probate and is being registered; it's a formality, the lawyer assures them on the phone, and likely to be finished by month's end. The filing does take time. Meanwhile, they follow Beakes's advice and liquidate the trust, dividing it in three equal parts—"Like Gaul," says David, "like Caesar's France"—and selling off the stock. When the transaction is complete and the money has been transferred to the Cape Cod Five Cents Savings Bank, they celebrate with the best dinner they can buy. They purchase caviar and oysters and lobsters and champagne; Leah joins them for the celebration, and when they have eaten the shellfish she extracts the remaining scraps of flesh and gristle for the cat. At ten o'clock she goes upstairs and David and Joanna settle in the living room and share a second bottle of champagne.

"I bet they thought there's some mistake," she tells her brother, smiling. "I bet when they saw that deposit they double-checked for fraud."

"Fraud?"

"Or maybe just—what was that Monopoly card?—'Bank Error in Your Favor.' 'Get Out of Jail Free.'"

"Something like that," David says.

They click their glasses and drink. *"Salud y amor y pesetas,"* Joanna pronounces, and he says I was remembering you in the kitchen, that day we got the phone call, when you were practicing Spanish with Claire; what was the word, *"compuesta?"*

She nods. " 'Made up, no woman is ugly.' What an amazing sexist he was . . ."

"Who? Your Spanish teacher?"

"Right, Mr. *'Mucha Muchacha'* Hernandez."

"Did you ever forgive him?"

"Who?"

"Dad."

She shakes her head.

"He left us high and dry," says David. "Didn't he?"

"Mom never got over it, really. And I don't think I have, either."

"It was promise, not delivery. It was always what would happen next . . ."

"No hay mujer fea," Joanna repeats, and they drink.

"I've lived my life by that proposition," he says, a little ruefully, and his sister laughs. I think I always knew, he says, there would be *something* coming; Mom was always saying, wasn't she, *expect the unexpected.* Some part of him, David continues, had known for *years* that she was being secretive, as was her mother before her, lord knows, a woman of whom we know nothing; is there a gene for secrecy, he wonders, some DNA routing for silence? He settles his weight in the couch. "I thought that kind of behavior was for Protestants, I thought it was the WASP but not the Jewish way of being buttoned up . . ."

"Are you glad you didn't marry? Or had—God help you—kids?"

"You don't mean that, the last part."

"No."

"Mostly I'm surprised," he says. "And that I'm, somehow, thirty-five. Mostly it seems accidental."

She drinks.

"I've been thinking about it," he says.

"What? Marriage? Children?"

"Family."

They talk about how Jim collapsed and wish they knew how to help Claire. They talk about their mother's secret or, David says, not so much a secret as a trust fund they'd not known about, although it develops their mother had known and—for reasons of her own, perhaps, a waiting till the time was ripe—had simply failed to disclose. He has never cared much about money. He wanted to buy what he wanted to buy and travel when and where he wished, but his tastes are not expensive and he made enough from pickup work to pay the rent. He asks Joanna if she'd been surprised, and she says, "You bet."

"I don't think *I* was, really, I think maybe it's why I never really felt I *had* to work—you understand, run the corporate race, climb the corporate ladder—I think I knew we had some sort of safety net. Something to catch me when I fall. Fell . . ."

"It's late," his sister says.

"You go on up. You need some sleep."

"And you do too . . ."

He smiles. "I'll sit here just a little longer."

"OK." She stands and bends to where he sits and kisses the top of his head: "Don't let the bedbugs bite."

"I haven't heard that in, in, how long . . . ?"

"Years. *Centuries.* Night, night."

Joanna climbs the stairs. He thinks of their mother: the telephone ringing, the dishes to wash, and then he shuts his eyes:

> *David is ten or eleven years old. He is sitting with his mother in the theater in New York. Alice takes him every summer; it is her chance, she tells him, to be alone for a weekend—well, not alone, she's always happy for his company—and to get out of Saratoga at the height of tourist season, since in Manhattan you don't notice or it's always tourist season, which amounts to the same thing. She makes him come to Shakespeare, and in order to sweeten the pill—that's what she calls it, "sweeten the pill"—a musical of his own choosing, whatever he feels like, she says.*
>
> *This afternoon they're watching* Henry IV, Part I. *He remembers the fat man, John Falstaff, and how he holds his belt and rolls his belly and how the audience laughs. Alice is wearing her pink silk suit,*

and he himself has on a tie and blazer, and the usher who leads them to their seats and offers them a Playbill *says, "What a little gentleman." There is a drumroll and fanfaronade. A fanfaronade, says his mother, is a fancy word for "fanfare" and he wonders if she means "fanfare" or "-fair" and what it would mean to be foul. Fair or foul is where a fly ball lands, or a grounder on the third-base line, and it's how you describe the weather but not a fanfaronade.*

Why should he remember this, he asks himself, why sitting in his sister's house a quarter of a century later should he find himself inside a hot dark theater and using his Playbill *as fan? What do "fanfare" and "fanfaronade" have to do with the death of his mother—and was he ten or eleven years old and therefore how long had his father been dead and, pondering irrelevance, the byways and blocked paths of neurons firing in his head recites, of a sudden, a line from the play he has not remembered in years:*

"I can call spirits from the vasty deep," Glendower says, and witty Harry Percy counters, "Why, so can I, or so can any man, but will they come when you do call for them?"

The great Welsh magician grows angry. He huffs and puffs and promises to blow the whole English house down. Then Hotspur and he come to grudging agreement and make a grudging alliance, and it doesn't matter anyhow because Prince Hal destroys them all and grows up to be Henry V. Then David and his mother eat at a restaurant called L'Escargot, a French restaurant near the theater, and she tells him slow but steady wins the race. You'll learn to like garlic, she says. I myself like snails in garlic butter very much, but they take some getting used to. It's an acquired habit, darling, don't feel you have to rush.

Which has been his slow but steady; what race is it he runs? He understands that when he left he did so with a vengeance, not taking any prisoners and burning all the bridges and dropping out of touch. When you travel you take yourself with you, just like the snail its shell. David remembers a time in Provence when he and his friends—Yves, Jacques, Colette and a woman whose name he cannot remember, Eliane, Helene?—were preparing snails, and how Jacques explained you have to leave them in a bowl of meal, cornmeal or oatmeal for two days so they befoul themselves re-placing what they have already eaten with the grains and then you must wash them very carefully and clean them of each trace of slime and then, *voilà,* the garlic and butter and a good fresh crusty bread is suitable for eating anywhere. "Anywhere," said David, it's "anywhere" not "anywheres," and Jacques who did not like to be corrected shrugged his shoulders, saying, *En tout cas. Néanmoins.*

So he had learned the proper way to clean a snail and, later, cockles and mussels and periwinkles, and he carried his snail plates and serving implements—the small pronged fork, the dou-ble-bladed gripping spoon—from house to house for years. White wine and escargots have lured full many a maid to his side, and he is grateful for the sweet processional of those who shared his table, then bed. But no companion in his life has made him forget his dead mother, and when he thinks of Adrienne or those who came before he thinks of them without regret: the champion Mr. Dance-Away, the expert at departure . . .

This has to stop. He has to start his adult life and not in thrall. He asks himself what he would do in Saratoga Springs and if it would make sense to call their old house home. His mother had hoped so, said Joseph Beakes, but David has his doubts. If she had wanted him to live with her, she would have asked directly; if Alice had wanted to leave him the cottage she would have written it down. Tonight when he was working in the kitchen—prying open the shells of the oysters and slicing the boiled steaming lobsters in half—his mother was a presence in the room. But *palpable?* he asks himself, and the answer is immediate: yes, yes. *Benign?* he asks himself, and knows the answer and does not avoid it: benign.

In the morning he goes for a run. He jogs up Sunset Hill and then down the road to Duck Harbor; a Volvo and an old red truck are parked in the paved parking lot, and David rests and stretches, doing knee bends by the fence. The sun is bright and the wind has ceased and, stretching, breathing, he closes his eyes.

A man and a large black dog emerge from the dunes; the man leans on a walking stick and the dog is tired, clearly, after his romp on the beach. He pants; his fur is matted from the water and wet sand. They make their way toward the pickup truck and, passing, the man smiles and nods at David where he stands. "Long way from home. Want a ride?"

This is a joke, David sees. He shakes his head. "That dog a Newfie?"

"Half and half. His mother was. His dad is anybody's guess."

They talk about the height of the snowdrifts and how late this winter has lasted. The dog scrambles into the cab of the truck and lies down, patient, heaving. When they have exhausted the subject of weather, the man opens the truck door and climbs in and, letting the engine idle, says, "You're not from these parts, are you?"

"No."

"Barclay. Paul Barclay." He reaches through the driver's window and offers his left hand.

"David. David Saperstone."

"Take care of yourself," says Paul Barclay, and throws the truck in gear and rumbles off.

⁂

At the Bay View Inn the mail includes their mother's ashes in a box. Joanna has unwrapped the canister, and it sits on the living room table: dark purple plastic with a seal reading "B&B & C" and a small medallion on a chain. The medallion has raised lettering:

Alice Freedman Saperstone, 1931–2003.

His sister lights a cigarette. "Well, here it is."

"What did Becker call it, 'The Closet of Memories'?" He lifts the canister. "It's very light."

"Yes, isn't it? Powder and bone. Let's scatter it."

He looks at her. "Right now?"

Joanna nods. "Right goddam immediately, brother."

She has been crying, he sees. She fingers the container and, with her left hand, taps the cigarette against a yellow ashtray. "I want Mom in the house," she says. "But not this part of her, OK?"

"Don't you want Leah to join us?"

"No. I need to do this *before* she gets home. With full military honors, but not so she's a part of it; she's been spooked enough already and doesn't need to watch . . ."

In his room he peels off his damp clothes and dresses in the jacket and black tie he'd worn when flying east. Joanna too has changed for the occasion, and when he comes back down again she stands at the foot of the stairs wearing black, a skirt and shawl he has not seen, and with her hair clipped back. She takes his hand. "Thank you for doing this, David."

They get in the Taurus and drive through town and stop at the stop sign for Route 6 and, crossing it, take Gull Pond Road down to the ocean and park at the parking lot's guardrail. Joanna is cradling the urn in its box, and she kicks off her shoes. David does the same. They open the car doors and stand at the crest of the dune, then descend. The wind is high, with ice in its teeth, and spume lifts off the waves.

There are dog tracks and footprints and bird tracks and weeds. Much of the beach is hard-packed sand, not porous as in summer weather, and they move rapidly away from the cleared level of the parking lot to where the dunes are high. There are blown drifts of snow. Gulls have settled at the tide line, preening, staring out. At length Joanna stops beneath the shelter of a massive dune—its top green distant bramble, its striations orange and ochre and brown— and asks him, "Here?" "Here," he says, and pries loose the cap. They fumble a little, shivering, arranging the direction of the ash and bone because the wind makes eddies, blowing, and they each take a handful and toss it away but it falls at their feet nonetheless. Then David scoops out a hole in the dune and they pour their mother in and tamp it down with yellow sand and watch the wind eradicate the imprint of their hands. There are pieces of driftwood and clusters of kelp. Joanna puts the empty urn in the pocket of her parka and they reverse direction and walk back.

XVIII

2003

The spring is slow in coming; deep snow stays on the ground. Then, when the rains come, snow washes away and ice in the harbor breaks up. David continues his visit to Wellfleet and is a welcome companion, but after some weeks he grows restless and by the Ides of March leaves. The days grow warmer, the nights do not freeze. When her daughter turns sixteen Joanna throws a party and is pleasantly surprised; it is not the disaster she feared. Leah's friends are well-dressed, well-behaved—or at least they try to be—and her high school guidance counselor, who doubles as an acting coach, says Artemisia's wonderful, she's got a talent to *die* for. I don't need to tell you this, I'm sure you've known it all along, but your daughter's the real thing. If every year I had *one* student like her, I'd thank my lucky stars.

Increasingly, she does. Her lucky star is in ascendance, and the money helps. Joanna finds a carpenter to cap the chimneys so no more grackles can fall down the flue, and he fixes the leak in the upstairs back bedroom and replaces the back hallway stairs. She hires a painter to spruce up the kitchen, first stripping off the wallpaper and dealing with the plaster where it cracks. He also paints her bedroom and the living room and as soon as it is warm enough will do the outside trim. These improvements have been long deferred, and it makes her happy to deal with the repairs. The manager of the Cape Cod Five Cents Savings Bank now smiles and nods when she comes through the door, and he always has a pleasant word about the weather and how much he likes what she's been doing to the Bay View Inn, that new entrance by the porch . . .

The money changes things. There's no point pretending otherwise; inheritance has changed the way she lives. In Hyannis, at the Subaru dealership, it gratifies her to write out a check for a new L.L. Bean Outback and not to finance it. When she first drove Trusty-Rusty into the lot the salesman barely glanced up

277

from his desk, imagining—or so Joanna imagines—that she was just another bargain hunter on the edge of poverty, just a flustered lady customer, but when she takes the chair in front of him and crosses her legs in their stockings and says, I'm here for the top of your line, Walt—his name is printed on the brass desk plaque—I want the very best you have, he caps his pen and looks at her attentively. Then he discourses on the virtues of the new Subaru suspension system, the ABS and GPS and V6 engine and the surround sound and extended warranty and customer satisfaction while Joanna only half-listens, and then she says, I hear you, Walt, I want that white one there.

She has never been so far in debt as to max out on credit cards or fail to meet her mortgage, but lately things were dicey and the hole was growing deep. Last fall, for example, she should have locked in the fuel-oil price and guaranteed deliveries at that price all winter; now the cost of oil is twice what it was in September, but now it doesn't matter; she can pay. She leafs through catalogues from Crate & Barrel and the Pottery Barn and Williams-Sonoma with the cheerful certainty that whatever she wants she can buy. As David had suggested, she gives Trusty-Rusty to Leah, first replacing the muffler and tires; she also gives her daughter an IBM ThinkPad and cell phone and sponsors an acting-class visit to Manhattan for spring break. *Oklahoma!* has closed, and no one wants to see *Gypsy,* so they settle on *Urinetown* and the musical of *The Producers,* which costs her an arm and a leg. But it's no problem, she tells Leah, she has an arm and a leg left—a whole new supply of arms and legs!—and warbles the Billie Holiday song,

> *Them that's got shall get,*
> *Them that's not shall lose . . .*

Li-li knows the second phrase, and they sing the next lines together:

> *So the Bible says,*
> *And it still is news.*

"What a voice she had," Joanna says, and Li-li drops an octave and pretends to hold a cigarette in one hand and glass of whiskey in the other, singing, "God bless the child, that's got her own, that's got her own . . ."

Because she wants to trim her weight, Joanna continues to smoke. She limits herself to six cigarettes daily, and this seems sufficient; on Independence Day she plans to go cold turkey—but not just yet, not now. Three mornings a week she joins Maisie at The Bare Necessities, and it's a habit she's happy to keep; the friends drink Lemon Zinger tea together and discuss their exercise and diet regimens and neighbors and the grim news of the world. "There's nothing we can do," says Maisie, but anyhow each Saturday noontime the two of them and a dozen other townspeople stand in front of the town offices on Main Street, holding placards that say "NO MORE WAR" and "GIVE PEACE A CHANCE." When the war breaks out they continue to stand in silent protest on Main Street, but the heart has gone out of it, hope's going dim, and with that macho gang in Washington peace never had a chance . . .

Sometimes it is pleasant weather or a light rain falls; sometimes people smile and honk approvingly but more often they roll down their windows and shout. Fat old men wait till she's watching and turn their thumbs down at her or their middle fingers up. A van that has its windows lettered with the sign "PISS ON IRAQ" keeps circling in the parking lot, and sometimes Joanna sees it at the dock or idling past her house. She thinks maybe Harry's inside the white van, or one of his old army buddies, and this doesn't frighten her but nonetheless she's saddened by the bigotry in town. She plants marigolds and tulips in the rowboat, and she remembers "Flower Power" and how people once believed that marigolds might make a difference to the future of the planet; she cleans and repositions the cranberry rake on the porch. In April the forsythia starts, and the first hyacinths bloom.

When Claire calls it surprises her; they have been out of touch. Joanna had written, of course, and called, but her sister had deflected all offers of assistance. Two deaths in a single week, she had commiserated on the phone, are two too many, and if you could use some company I'm happy to come out and help. Claire thanked her and refused; she could manage by herself, or anyhow she had to try, and there was nothing anyhow that needed to be done. The way she said this was, however, so soft-voiced and forlorn that Joanna repeated I'm happy to help. No, Claire said, I mean it, I have to learn to do this by myself. Are the girls all right? Joanna asked, and Claire said, no, not really, in Mom's case they'd been expecting it but everything about Jim's death has been a shock. Was there any warning, asked Joanna, had anything been wrong with him? and Claire said no, nothing at all.

So when her sister calls to say I won't pretend I'm managing, I can't pretend these weeks have been easy and I'm wondering if maybe we could come for the weekend—the three of us, there's a sale out of Detroit with companion tickets to Providence and it would be a great escape for me and the girls—Joanna can't refuse. I have to admit it, Claire admits, I've been terrified to call. But she has planned it already; she'll rent a car at T.F. Green and arrive on Friday morning and be out again by Monday afternoon; she's reserved the tickets and the car but there's no penalty attached if she cancels the tickets by midnight, and she wanted to make certain Joanna wouldn't mind. Don't feel you have to say yes, she says, if this isn't a *good* time. Then her voice breaks, bereft again, and she says it's school break for Becky and Hannah, but she can't bear to send them south and stay home alone. The girls have been wonderful, really, and when she asked them what they wanted they said a visit to Wellfleet, they really really missed their cousin and wanted to catch up. "You don't mind, do you?" Claire repeats, and Joanna tells her, "No."

The three of them do visit; their appearance is a shock. The girls are almost Li-li's age—Becky is fourteen and Hannah fifteen—but she hasn't seen them in two or three years, and this is the time of adolescence. Becky and Hannah are changing, of course; they have grown beefy and pimpled and, there's no other word for it, *Midwestern*. They wear braces and use words like "pop" when they ask for a soda and say "awesome" and giggle together unstoppably; they're like something out of *90210* or *Married with Children* or one of those canned-laughter sitcoms Li-li refuses to watch.

But somehow the cousins get along; three's company, it seems. That too was the name of a sitcom, *Three's Company,* and the girls are so fresh-faced and innocent-looking they might as well be on TV. Leah drives them up to Provincetown and they spend the afternoon ogling men and women on Commercial Street; it isn't tourist season yet, not warm enough for full display, but nonetheless Becky and Hannah are excited and come back burbling about what they've seen — the couple with handcuffs and a greyhound, the ones who shave their skulls or wear chain links and a djellaba, the ones who embrace in the shops.

The three girls play music together, Becky playing the guitar and Hannah banging away at the upright piano Joanna is considering replacing and her daughter performing songs from *West Side Story* or Lucinda Williams or just singing scat. They whisper and cackle together like ladies from the Monday Club who've known each other all their lives and never were apart. It's good for them, Joanna thinks, to know that they have family, *are* family, and to spend time on the porch . . .

The real shock is her sister; Claire has changed. Her hair is going gray, and she has allowed it to, and she's letting it grow out. She wears no makeup and has been gaining weight and there's a tear in the sleeve of her blouse that doesn't appear to concern her; in any other woman these things might not be notable, but given the way she used to behave it's a genuine shift of behavior. On arrival Claire asks for a drink. There's something slurred about the way she speaks, and giddy in the way she moves — a lurching-forwardness that seems so out of character Joanna wonders if her sister's ill or maybe on medication. She doesn't know which, or how to ask, and wonderingly she watches her guest pour herself a second glass of Chardonnay, and then a third and fourth.

On their first evening in Wellfleet, Joanna prepares bay scallops in cream sauce, fresh asparagus, wild rice, and the meal is, she has to admit it, delicious. The cousins talk about how strange it is to be a tableful of women—five of them, and no men in the room—and how much they miss their father. We none of us have fathers, do we, Becky offers musingly, as though there's no distinction between Jim's death and being the child of divorce. It isn't the same, Hannah argues, it isn't the same deal at all.

The girls finish their berries and wander away to listen to music—there's this CD she burned Art insists they must hear—while the adults remain at the table. Joanna has been telling Claire about the problems with the Wellfleet dump—the difficulties of allocated water and septic system monitoring and enforcing Title 5 and how the town officials here are either functional illiterates or flat-out corrupt; she's beginning to think next time around she might make a run for selectman, because *somebody* has to do it, *somebody* has to stand for the principles of conservation and long-term not shortsighted land use, and it might just as well be her; strange as it seems she's got a conscience now, a *consciousness*, or at least the beginnings of a commitment to what she supposes is called civic duty—when she sees Claire has fallen asleep. Her sister is wheezing, breathing stertorously, and her head has dropped back on the chair. Joanna stops talking; Claire startles awake—but for that first glazed wide-eyed instant it's clear she doesn't know whose house she's in, or why . . .

"Are you all right?"

"Not really, no."

"Tell me about it."

She shakes her head.

"Why not? I won't be . . ."

"What?"

"Surprised, I guess. Shocked."

"You'd be surprised." Claire finds this funny, or seems to, and laughs and then goes silent.

"What's wrong?"

"Can we talk about it tomorrow?"

"You must be tired . . ."

Claire nods. "I'd prefer to, you know, wait a little. Get my sea legs . . ." Again, she smiles. "No time like the present, correct? Why put off till tomorrow what you can do the day after?"

Joanna stands. She clears the table, carrying the dishes and the cutlery and place mats and dinner napkins and bowls. Claire empties the bottle of wine for herself and makes no move to help. This too is unlike her, uncharacteristic, and when Joanna returns from the sink she sees her sister is crying.

"Oh, sweetie, what *is* it?"

"Jim. Being here. The way you seem so, so *together.* Did I remember to tell you those scallops were terrific, did I tell you that?" She wipes her eyes rapidly, helpless. "The way I'm not. Not together, I mean." Great tears are rolling down her cheeks, her eyes are red-rimmed, brimming, and she seems a child again.

"You're missing Jim?"

She shakes her head.

"I thought you said . . ."

"What I mean is everything, *everything's* wrong, and I don't want to talk till tomorrow, OK?"

"Or the day after tomorrow—just know you can tell me whatever you want to. Whenever you feel like it . . ."

"I will, I promise." Claire stands unsteadily, lurching. "Only not yet, not tonight."

Over coffee in the morning she does talk. Her reticence has disappeared and instead she's voluble; she's been waiting in the kitchen with the coffee percolating and skim milk in a jug already by the microwave. When Joanna appears Claire kisses her and heats the milk and, once the bell signals completion, pours them each a cup of coffee with Equal and milk as though the house were hers. She says, "I didn't sleep at all, not worth the mentioning, but anyhow this morning I just feel so *rested,* so ready to get on with things and if you're still willing to listen I do want to tell you, I haven't told anyone else."

Joanna nods. Her kitchen has been painted white, and the shelves are yellow, and she has positioned rosemary and pots of basil and oregano on the windowsill. She is wearing her new dressing gown, the scarlet silk from Italy, and the room that was so run-down fairly sparkles in the morning light; she kicks off her slippers and sits.

"This strange thing has been happening," Claire says, "the strangest thing is happening, it feels like everything's changed. And my true north was south. You make certain assumptions—or *I* did, anyhow—and the assumptions turn out to be wrong, one hundred and eighty degrees. It turns out that south was true north. You know about Mom and the money, of course—the way we thought we knew our grandmother, or knew *about* our grandmother, and there'd be no surprises, no family skeletons in that particular closet—and how we were exactly wrong, one hundred and eighty degrees . . ."

The sun is up and the tide is out and the mudflats look pink. Claire manages a half-laugh: "But you don't know about Jim. I haven't talked to anyone about it, not even Becky and Hannah, I just haven't been able to tell them; *they* don't know. And *you* mustn't tell them, of course. But it develops, doesn't it, that our family keeps secrets; we're"—she spreads her hands—"silent as the grave. Or maybe the right word *is* 'closet' for this particular skeleton, this thing I've been trying to hide. Conceal. Well, Jim was leaving, he had left, and who he left me for was somebody called Robin, and Robin is a man."

Joanna peels an apple and then quarters it and offers half to Claire. Her sister's face is loose, slack, worn, but there is something restored in it also: a mobility, an openness. Noisily she chews on her first slice of apple and then continues to talk.

"You live out here near Provincetown and maybe aren't surprised by this; maybe half the people in Ann Arbor are—I can't help it, I still think of them as—*queer*, gay, same-sex partners, whatever it is that we call them today, but this thing about my husband was a shock. *Is* a shock, Joanna, I still can't get my mind around it, can't believe . . . not that he was gay, of course, it doesn't bother me by now, but that I never noticed and didn't have a clue. It makes me so ashamed—not ashamed of him and Robin, I don't mean that at all. But that I never noticed and was paying no attention; he's dead, of course"—she snaps her fingers—"*pop,* he's gone, he was driving south, *they* were driving south together and Jim sat in the passenger seat too long and had a pulmonary embolism, a *massive* one, and now I can't apologize, can't ask him to forgive me and I think maybe what bothers me most is how *final* it is, how completely it's over."

"Over?"

"History. Finished. Done. *Done.*"

"Are you certain?"

Claire nods. She drinks.

"Passata la commèdia. Finita la mùsica."

"What's that supposed to mean?"

"It's something Li-li says. At the end of a performance all the actors are supposed to say, 'The comedy's over. The music is finished.'"

"Well, she's right."

Down by the harbor the flags flutter lightly, and there is a westering breeze. They sit in silent harmony and watch the sunlight play across the stand of locust trees and where the shadows fall.

"It's very peaceful here," says Claire. "I'm very glad I told you and it doesn't sound so terrible."

"No," says Joanna, "it doesn't; what's terrible is Jim is dead, but not that he was gay." The "PISS ON IRAQ" van drives past. "We don't seem to do very well with our men." She smiles at her sister. "Do we?"

"No. Or *by* them, either. And I suppose that's true, was just as true about marriage, for Mom."

"And Grandma, by the sound of it . . ."

"We really do know how to pick them," says Claire.

"So here we are"—Joanna offers her last slice of apple—"the three of us alone again. David never married; you're a widow; I'm divorced . . ."

"The Saperstone children," says Claire.

They drink. "What have you done with your share of the money," she asks, and Claire says, "I put it away for the girls. Jim was the one with the income, of course, and I need to make sure we can handle tuition and don't *want* to sell the house. More coffee?" she inquires, pouring herself a second cup, and Joanna shakes her head and says, "No, one's my limit, thanks."

⁓

At lunchtime, David calls. He's calling from Berkeley, back in the saddle and emptying his apartment and moving out, moving on. The trouble with Berkeley, he tells Joanna: it's three thousand miles from the coast. She laughs. He says I've been thinking about it, been giving it a lot of thought, and what I'm going to do, I think, is move back to the cottage and try it on for size. If you two don't object. Why should we, asks Joanna, and then Claire joins the conversation from the living room extension and says, of course we don't object and it's a good idea. Home is the place— what's that Robert Frost line?—where when you have to come back finally they can't throw you out . . .

I've been thinking about it a *lot*, he repeats. You know that old expression: there's nothing certain except death and taxes? Well, inheritance is the third thing—it's where death and taxes meet. It's the crossroads, the conjunction of the two; it's where that pair of certainties becomes a third because everyone goes through it and it isn't a question of whether but when: death comes when it will come. So it doesn't matter, really, if what we inherit is money or debt, a set of cats or cutlery or a portrait of Grandfather Aaron: what matters is the way we deal with what's been left behind . . .

There is static on the phone. "I *hear* you," says Joanna, and she knows by the creak of the wood on the floor that Claire has taken the rocker and is shifting her weight in the chair. I've been doing some research, he says. I looked them up, the Vagabonds, and they really did exist, they covered a whole lot of ground. It wasn't only *our* year, I mean, 1916; they made a habit of it, those—what would you call them—excursions? and they racketed around the country playing hookey, being tramps.

"Some tramps," says Claire, "with wagon trains and a dozen railroad cars and cooks."

" 'Hallelujah, I'm a bum,' " says David, "right. But notice how they don't call themselves bums, or tramps, or hobos—they were the *Vagabonds*, and thank you very much.

"So I wondered how often it happened—how many trips they took. And it turns out they traveled a lot. The year before they made Grandma's—what would you call it?—*acquaintance*, they went to California and the Pan-Pacific Exposition. That was the start of it all. In 1918—the war was on and plans fell through and they skipped 1917—the four of them went south. Four carpet-baggers in the land of Dixie," David says. "And next year they pretended they were Minutemen wandering around New England and the next year they visited Burroughs and played at being Rip van Winkle, in the country of Washington Irving, and by 1921 they roped the President in."

"Which President?" Claire asks.

"Warren G. Harding," he says. "By that time John Burroughs was finished; he had grown too old to travel and maybe already had died. So instead they included the women, and President Harding and his secretary joined up with the Vagabonds in Maryland. Then they skipped 1922 and by the next year Harding too was dead, and they sojourned—listen to me," David says, "I *sound* like them, describing it; what kind of word is *sojourned?*—up in the U.P."

"Where's that?" Joanna asks.

"The Upper Peninsula," he tells them, "the lumber camps in Michigan, and the mining towns. And by 1924, the final year, they went back to New England and visited with Calvin Coolidge in Vermont. By this time everybody's old and the party's winding down, but he's their second President; not bad for a party of axe-wielding hobos in suits. What I'm trying to get at," he says, "is how they celebrate those virtues they're in the process of wrecking; they honor rural America and then light it up and pave it over and fill it with cars. With a neon sign for customers: 'Ye olde *Dew Drop Inn.*' "

"I'm starting over," says Joanna. "I'm an ex-inkeeper now."

He knows that, David says. He thinks maybe inheritance has changed them all, and what's so strange about this piece of history is it's been there all along. I mean, he says, what's new is that we *know* about it now.

"*Finita la commèdia,*" says Claire.

But David is up on the soapbox again and he speaks about their newfound wealth and altogether unexpected legacy from Henry Ford and Harvey Firestone and Thomas Edison, those anti-Semitic potentates and self-anointed Vagabonds. The ancient books and plays and fairy tales, he says, are *all* about inheritance, how when you come into what they used to call a competence you marry well, regaining thereby your rightful place which some foul duke has stolen. Or you gain through inbred virtue the fortune by society denied, the foul witch felled, the dark plot foiled, because every single one of the contrivances that structure all those stories have to do with maiden ladies, eligible bachelors, Cinderella, Sleeping Beauty, Rumpelstiltskin and the rest: the undeserving rich, deserving poor. And what they have in common is how *young* the people were: the ones who wait till twenty-five in Austen are old maids, the ones who wait until thirty in Dickens are ridiculous, figures of fun.

The sisters laugh. Yet nowadays, David continues, we have to wait till we're forty or fifty to come into inheritance, to get what our own parents leave, and it makes no difference, really, if it's ten million dollars or a rocking chair. The stakes are not the same but the game is constant, isn't it, the rules of the game when there's more than one person apply to the family silver or silver mine alike; he's rambling, he admits it, he's tired and thick-tongued and talking too much, but Marx observes, remember, that a change in quantity brings qualitative change; if Harry and I, Joanna — he pauses — have an argument between us that's a fight between two people, but if we have a hundred thousand men on either side it's called a war. At any rate and in any case the actuarial tables, David repeats, have changed the problem of maturity beyond all recognition, what good does it do to hang around like characters in some timeworn farce until you die of boredom, waiting; we're relatively young, the three of us, and Mom only made it to seventy-two; I'll bet Wellfleet is *full* of sixty-year-old babies waiting for their folks to die and inheritance-ship to come in . . .

"OK," says Joanna. "We hear you."

"Say hello to everyone," he finishes. "Li-li, of course."

"OK."

"The tax bite's coming down, you know. The IRS will hit us up."

"She provided for that," says Joanna. "I checked with Beakes's office; there's been a set-aside."

"We'll call you tomorrow," says Claire.

❧

That afternoon there's a cocktail party out on Bound Brook Island, and the sisters go. The season is beginning, the painters and investment bankers and psychiatrists from New York and Boston are starting to return to the Cape, and Joanna says we won't stay long but you might find it amusing, a few of these people are fun. The whole place belongs to the National Seashore, but some of the houses are grandfathered in, and Bound Brook's just the way it used to be, oh, twenty years ago—thirty, maybe forty years, and long before *I* got here. Grand*mothered* in, says Claire, in our case that's what happened, and they laugh.

The road is barely passable—deep-rutted and soft where the rain failed to drain—and everyone arrives in Range Rovers and Toyota Land Cruisers and Jeeps. Joanna maneuvers her white Subaru through the sand and muck with some distaste, and she finds it remarkable that just two months ago she wouldn't have noticed mud smears on a car or, if she noticed, have cared. She thinks about how much has changed, how strange it is to be the well-dressed sister, the one using makeup and perfume, and she checks herself out in the vanity mirror and offers her lipstick to Claire.

Their hosts are Neil and Mary Patterson, and the house is a series of boxes: cedar siding, wood shingles and glass. They walk up the curved flagstone path. Years ago, Joanna confesses, she had had a thing for Neil and, she admits, a thing *with* him, though all of that is over now and nothing she still dwells upon or thinks about too proudly. Mary was gone on a business trip, she was a buyer for Talbots, and one night in June Neil showed up on the porch of the Bay View Inn with a bottle of tequila and one thing led to another, and it lasted the whole summer of, when was it, '95? You're not shocked, are you, she asks Claire, and Claire says I don't shock so easily now. It's good to have a date for cocktails, isn't it, Joanna says, someone to go to a party with, and she and her sister link arms.

Neil greets them. "The heavenly sisters."

Joanna leans forward and kisses his cheek. "Thanks for inviting us. Having us."

He sports a white goatee and rimless glasses and shaved head; he stares at Claire frankly, assessingly. "I've heard *so* much about you."

"And I about *you.*"

"None of it good, I expect."

"I wouldn't say that," says Joanna.

"It's because what she told me was *bad,*" says Claire, "that I've been wanting to meet you."

He laughs and steps aside. "Welcome to Wellfleet, Joanna's kid sister. What are you drinking?"

"Whatever you pour me."

"All *right!*"

"You two are flirting," Joanna complains. "Isn't it too soon to flirt?"

The view is spectacular: marsh grass, low dunes, a sunset beginning out over the bay. Ten or twelve people are drinking Campari and soda or gin and tonic or glasses of wine and there is a bartender in a white coat; everyone is talking about winter and how long it's been since they were last together on Columbus Day, which was when they closed the house, and how this year the cold weather simply wouldn't quit. "'The winter of our discontent,'" says Neil. "I heard about your mother"—he touches Joanna on the arm—"and wanted to tell you how sorry I am."

"That's sweet of you."

"No, I mean it," says their host.

Mary Patterson is formal, clipped; she says I'm glad you're here, enjoy the view, *that's* crab dip and *that's* guacamole. Then she turns back to a group by the window and does not talk to the sisters again. Paul Barclay and his wife, Eileen, have just returned from Boston and a visit to the hospital; their son was in a car crash and has broken both his legs. "We've got to thank our lucky stars," Eileen says, "he's alive." Her eyes well up, spill over. "Our Johnny will be *fine*!"

The party is not a success. Claire drinks too much and laughs too much and has a gaiety about her that seems almost entirely false. By seven o'clock she has her arm around Ike Phillipson, a man Joanna despises, who has had three marriages and can't keep his hands to himself. He can't keep his opinions to himself, either, which is worse, because he admires Cheney and Bush and says if we had ten Donald Rumsfelds the world would be a better place, and safer for democracy; and everyone around the world will be grateful to us soon. I don't agree, Joanna says, the world may well be terrified but it won't be grateful. Those fucking French, he says. I bet you like those fucking frogs, Joanna, right? you admire them with their taste for fashion and their blow-dry foreign minister and Old World hypocrisy and how they treat their own *A*-rabs like dirt and suck up to Hussein. Pardon my French, he says.

It's pronounced Arabs, not *A*-rabs, says Claire, but she says this smilingly, and Ike refuses to stop. They're playing to the camera, he says, they're playing for contracts and oil. When this war is over we'll stick it to the French. And Baby Doc still lives there, doesn't he, in a villa by the water, and they folded in the Second World War in about ten minutes, didn't they, and were *happy* to collaborate; I *hate* the frogs, he says, I've drunk my last glass of frog wine . . .

Joanna taps her watch. "Our daughters are waiting, remember?"

"I remember, yes," says Claire. "But this is so much *fun*!"

"You're the life of the party," Neil tells her.

"This house is *perfectly* placed. It's got" —she mouths— "feng shui."

"Where did you hide her, Joanna; why did you let her stay away?"

"It wasn't *my* choice," she protests.

"That's true." Claire laughs. "I'm this poky Midwesterner, right? This stick in the Ann Arbor mud, and I've been playing hard to get." She makes a circling gesture with her index finger and jams it on a piece of driftwood sculpture, hard. Then she licks and sucks her finger: "This *stick* in the Michigan mud. . . ."

When they finally leave in the lantern-lit dark Ike follows them outside. "How long are you staying?"

"Till Monday."

"Can I see you tomorrow? What are you doing for dinner?"

"She's eating with me," says Joanna. "We're eating French food together. Those *pommes frites* you call Freedom Fries. Good night."

And then she starts the car and spins her wheels and hopes she's spraying his Docksiders and blazer, but Ike is halfway up the flag-stone path and smiling, hopeful, waving at Claire, who leans out the window and blows him a kiss. Then she settles back in and arranges her skirt and closes the window again. "What an asshole," she says to Joanna. "What a total complete fucking asshole."

"He wasn't after *my* telephone number . . ."

"But Neil is cute," Claire says.

⌘

That night they eat grilled tuna and watercress salad and squash. Joanna brings out the family silver, with the fish forks and the fish knives and the salad forks—with the initial E on one side and, on the other, D—and sets the table with care. When did you learn to cook like this, her sister asks, and she says I only tolerate, these days, things that swim or fly. And ever since Mad Cow Disease, I've given up on red meat.

Li-li and Becky and Hannah go, *Right,* and Li-li says there's this party over at Stacey's house, if we totally promise to be back by midnight can we go? It pleases her to be the elder, the driver, and she seems to enjoy playing guide. And promise not to drink,

Joanna says, and her daughter says, I promise, we'll only do coke, mom, and crack, and maybe some ecstasy too for a chaser. They laugh. The cousins leave. While they are cleaning up the kitchen Claire talks about the summer; she dreads the prospect of living in Ann Arbor once the girls go off to Interlaken, and has Joanna heard of it? that music camp up north? It's good for them, they love it there, but she doesn't have any notion, not the slightest idea what to do. She's thinking she could volunteer at Operation Rescue, or maybe work for Food Gatherers or sign up for the summer school; there must be a course she could take. Why don't you stay with me, Joanna asks, why don't you come back here for July; there's room enough, lord knows, and I could use the company and it would be fun.

Claire stares at her. "You mean that?"

"Yes."

"How was David?"

"Fine, he's fine."

"As a houseguest, I mean. As someone to live with?"

"We're *sisters*," says Joanna. "It's time we try to be sisters again."

"Really?"

"Really and truly," she says. "As long as you promise me not to see Ike."

"I promise," Claire says, smiling. "Cross my heart."

Joanna gathers up the tablecloth and shakes it out on the porch. The nighttime air is mild, May's harbinger, and she wonders if she'll change her mind or regret the invitation and tells herself that *someone* has to supervise her sister and keep Claire out of trouble. She nearly laughs out loud at this—the thought that *she's* the responsible one, the one with both feet on the ground—and finds herself doing a dance step and strutting down the porch stairs to the rowboat where the tulips and the marigolds and dusty miller thrive. She drapes herself in the white tablecloth and does a cheerleader's twirl. Then she thinks about how long ago she used to do that particular twirl and thinks about their mother, how Alice would have wanted this and would be gratified.

Car headlights rake the bay and music drifts down from the

Connolly place: a fiddle, a guitar. The streets of Wellfleet are dark. There's time and chance and change. She and Claire will spend the summer together, and maybe David will return or they'll meet again in Saratoga Springs and help him with the house. They will choose what matters, room by room, and will not argue about it and will sell or give away what no one needs to keep. There is, Joanna tells herself, a kind of body-knowledge that can outlast change, and chance, and time; Mungo Park appears, slides past her, and climbs with feline dignity back up the steps to the porch.